A TALENT FOR SURRENDER

Sadie extended one leg, lifted her foot and placed it directly under Dan's nose. 'Kiss my foot.' Sadie's voice was clear and imperious. Dan leaned forwards and pressed his lips to the top of her boot. He could smell the leather and a hint of something grittier and unpleasant. She pushed him away with her foot, forcing him back on his heels.

It wasn't a violent movement, yet the force behind it took his breath away and shocked him to his core. 'The sole . . . a worthless trainee slave like you is only worthy to kiss the sole of my boot.'

He leaned forwards and rubbed his lips against the dirty leather, kissing it as tenderly and eagerly as he might a pair of cherished lips. The leather felt rough and dirty against his skin. He could feel his cheeks burning.

By the same author:

THE ART OF SURRENDER

A TALENT FOR SURRENDER

Madeline Bastinado

This book is a work of fiction.
In real life, make sure you practise safe, sane and
consensual sex.

First published in 2007 by
Nexus
Thames Wharf Studios
Rainville Rd
London W6 9HA

A catalogue record for this book is available from the
British Library.

www.nexus-books.com

Typeset by TW Typesetting, Plymouth, Devon
Printed in the UK by CPI Bookmarque, Croydon, CR0 4TD

The paper used in this book is a natural, recyclable product made
from wood grown in sustainable forests. The manufacturing
process conforms to the regulations of the country of origin.

ISBN 978 0 352 34135 8

Distributed in the USA by Holtzbrinck Publishers, LLC, 175
Fifth Avenue, New York, NY 10010, USA

For my friend
Martin Tordoff
1953–2007

Always in my heart

One

Jo Lennox sat back in her chair with her feet up on the desk. Her discarded panties lay on the top of the in-tray. Her legs were spread wide and she'd hooked her stiletto heels under the desk's polished mahogany edge. The phone was cradled between her ear and her shoulder.

'Tell me what you're doing now, Costas . . .' Her voice was soft and throaty. Her index finger began to tease her clit. Her nipples ached.

'My mouth is clamped over your cunt. I can taste you. Hot breath gushes out of my nostrils. You can feel my beard stubble scratching your skin.'

'I begin to rock my hips, rubbing my crotch against your face.' The final word rushed out in a hissing gush.

'I match your rhythm. My fingers pull your lips apart. Every little lap of my tongue makes you gasp and moan. My cock is on fire.'

Jo's nipples tingled with excitement, standing out against her pale skin, hard and dark.

'You are so wet and slippery. Your cunt tastes divine. I want so much to make you come. I suck your clit into my mouth and run my tongue over the sensitive tip.'

Her back was arched, her legs rigid. Her crotch burned. 'I'm rubbing myself against your mouth, my hips are pumping,' Jo whispered into the phone.

'My cock is so hard it's painful; I want to touch it, but I manage to control myself. I slide two fingers into you.'

1

'I moan as they slip inside.' Her voice was ragged and breathless.

'I move my fingers in and out. I know you're getting close.'

Jo pressed her feet against the edge of her desk. Her chest heaved. She pictured Costas in his suit and tie, crouching under her desk, his mouth clamped over her aching cunt.

'Your clit is dancing in my mouth. I look up and I can see your nipples, thick and erect, pointing at the ceiling,' Costas whispered.

'Yes ... yes. I'm wound up with excitement. I'm going to come any second.' A tear of sweat ran down between her breasts.

'Your legs are rigid. Your hips are pumping, grinding your hot crotch against my eager face. Can you feel that?'

'I can ... I'm nearly there.' Jo's voice was a hoarse whisper.

'I slide two fingers into your arsehole and suck on your clit.'

'I'm ... coming.' Jo pressed her soles against the edge of the desk. She was panting and gasping. She was quivering all over.

'I can feel you coming. You're gripping my fingers so hard it almost hurts me.'

'Your cock is aching, trapped and painful. You want to fuck me, but you know it's not allowed.' Jo spoke in a rapid, short burst. Her hips pumped, rubbing her clit against her fingers, wringing out every shred of orgasm.

'So I suck your cunt. I eat your orgasm. I can taste it. It's all I want, for you to come in my mouth ...' Costas's voice was hungry and urgent.

Her body was rigid. Lightning bolts of excitement jolted up and down her spine. Jo howled at the ceiling, her back arched and her legs locked.

* * *

2

The corridor smelled of polish overlaid with the faint but unmistakable aroma of school dinners. Dan's chair was slightly too small and his knees jutted almost to his chin. He felt foolish and gangly.

The floor was buffed to a high shine. Dan remembered his schoolboy self taking a run down a very similar corridor and allowing his momentum to carry him on so that he slid around the corner like an ice skater.

The stunt once earned him a trip to the headmaster's office and a week's worth of detention. Maybe that was why it felt so uncomfortable to find himself sitting outside the head's office again. Not nervous exactly, but definitely unsettled.

Not that he expected Jo Lennox to be as scary as his old headmaster; she probably had less nose hair, for a start. From what he'd heard, Ms Lennox was a far less forbidding and distant headteacher than those he'd known as a boy. She was a woman anyway, and the fairer sex had been distinctly thin on the ground in public schools in those days.

A pupil came down the corridor, a backpack dangling listlessly from one shoulder. His shoes were scuffed, his trouser bottoms covered in mud. He plonked himself down beside Dan. He sat there quietly for a minute, elbows on knees and chin on his hands. Dan smiled at him.

'Are you somebody's dad?' The lad's voice was breaking, wobbly and cracked.

'No, I'm just here to see Ms Lennox. Are you somebody's dad?'

The boy shot Dan the kind of look only teenagers are capable of, intended to convey pity, contempt, boredom and a sort of world-weary disenchantment with the adult world.

'Lofty Leighton caught me smoking in the science store cupboard and he hit the roof. He said there were

3

flammable chemicals in there and I could have started a fire.'

'I suppose he's got a point.'

The boy gave Dan the look again. 'Can you smell smoke? Can you hear fire engines?'

The door opened and a tall blonde woman stepped into the corridor. She smiled at Dan. If this was Ms Lennox, she was nothing like his old headmaster. Her hair was long and shiny, the front pulled back and held in a clip behind her head. Her eyes were green and sparkling and her lips were shining with red gloss.

'I hope you don't mind waiting a bit longer, Mr Elliot. I just need to have a few words with Josh here. It shouldn't take long.'

'Of course not.' Dan was surprised his voice sounded normal, because ever since she'd appeared his heart had been beating double time. The undersized chair and his jutting knees made him feel foolish and wrong-footed.

'Come into my office, Josh.' She pushed the door and held it open, her arm outstretched.

Josh sighed, picked up his backpack and loped into her office as if the whole experience was unutterably boring. He passed under Ms Lennox's arm, and Dan realised that she was exceptionally tall for a woman.

In the couple of seconds it took for Josh to enter the room, Dan took the opportunity to sneak a look at her body. Curvy but not fat, with more than a glimpse of cleavage on display. His eyes travelled down her torso and he noticed the womanly curve of her belly, the long slope of her thighs and shapely calves clad in what he was fairly certain were old-fashioned seamed nylon stockings; he could see the telltale shaping at the heel. She wore black suede stilettos that looked like something out of a forties movie.

When his eyes reached her face again Dan realised that she was looking directly at him. She raised one immaculate eyebrow, the tiny gesture managing to convey both disapproval and amusement and he felt instantly guilty. Before he had a chance to apologise, she'd disappeared through the door.

Five minutes later, the door banged open and Josh let himself into the corridor.

'She says she'll be out for you in a minute, OK?' He shrugged his shoulders as if the message he'd been asked to convey was both boring and embarrassing.

'Thanks. How did you get on?'

'She confiscated my fags and told me off. She's not bad really.'

'That's good.'

Josh shrugged again. 'She could hardly give me detention on the last day of term could she? There were only a couple left in the packet anyway, and I've got two hundred in my backpack; my dad gets them duty free. I can make quite a bit selling them in the dorm. Don't tell her that though, will you?' For a moment Josh looked like the frightened child he was, all bravado gone.

'Tell her what?' Dan winked.

Josh smiled and hoisted his backpack onto his shoulder. 'You're not bad either.' He gave Dan a wave and ran down the corridor. As he approached the corner he stuck out his hands to steady himself and executed a perfect slide, disappearing out of sight.

Jo sat at her desk reading through the long letter Dan had sent her. Actually, it was the second letter; she'd got her assistant to reply to the first, saying she didn't think it appropriate to allow him to make a film about her school and she'd assumed that would be the end of it.

A week later she'd received another letter explaining in more detail why he thought Hall Croft would make an ideal subject and assuring her of the purity of his motives. It sounded straightforward enough and she might even have been interested if it hadn't been Dan Elliot making the request. His documentaries always had a hidden agenda.

Jo was sceptical by nature and, given Dan's reputation, she found it hard to take his letter at face value. She hadn't even bothered to reply, but Dan had followed it up with a phone call several days later and had been so charming and courteous that she'd finally agreed to meet him.

From their chat on the phone and their brief exchange outside her office he didn't seem what she had expected. He was handsomer in the flesh; more manly and well groomed. On screen he always came across as slightly dishevelled, as if he'd got ready in a hurry. Another aspect of his façade, she assumed.

She got up and went to the door. Dan turned to look at her as it opened and, for a moment, he looked up into her eyes. Because of his low chair Jo could almost imagine he was kneeling at her feet. His head was tilted back slightly to meet her gaze and the expression in his eyes was of naked adoration. Either that or wishful thinking on her part, but either way her nipples grew hard and sensitive inside her bra and an icy tingle, like Jack Frost's fingertips, slid up her spine.

Dan picked up his laptop bag and got to his feet. His body seemed to uncoil, as if he'd had to fold himself up to fit in the chair, then Jo found herself looking up at him. He was uncommonly tall and slender. He stuck out his hand and she shook it. His grip was firm yet sensitive. She hated it when men felt the need to prove their strength by crushing your fingers when they shook hands.

'Pleased to meet you properly at last, Mr Elliot. You're very tall.'

Dan laughed and Jo noticed that he had even white teeth.

'Yes I am, though I was just thinking the same about you. Not as tall as me, of course, but pretty tall for a woman.'

'Yes. It's a very uncommon experience for me to have to look up at a man. But it's a welcome change, I assure you. A constant vista of bald spots and dandruff does tend to pall after a while.'

'Well, if nothing else, I've been able to provide you with a refreshing change of view.'

'Shall we go through to my office?' Jo held the door open.

Dan whistled as he walked into the room. 'This is impressive. Not at all what I imagined. Very Victorian and imposing. You can imagine Matthew Arnold's study at Rugby looking like this, can't you?'

Jo sat down behind her desk and gestured for Dan to take the chair opposite.

'Yes, it was like this when I took over and it seemed a crime to change it. And, to tell you the truth, I think the old-world formality works in my favour. Kids daren't lie to me in a room like this.'

'I know how they feel. Do you know, when I was waiting for you outside I felt fourteen again? Instantly in the wrong and expecting a caning.'

'I'm sorry, the Education Authority no longer allow me to oblige you on that score.' Jo smiled. 'You went to public school, of course?'

'Of course? Is it that obvious?'

'I think so. There's something about that deliberate, bumbling charm you project on screen. Somehow you have to have had a public-school education to pull it off, because there's actually a lot of confidence and privilege underneath it. Sort of like Hugh Grant. He can afford to look a fool because underneath it all he knows he's quite a catch.'

Dan looked at her silently for a long moment and Jo knew he was weighing her up. She noticed that behind

7

his fashionably slim-line glasses he had bright-blue eyes. The knowing intelligence she saw there belied the calculated boyishness of his appearance.

'You're right. When I'm working I deliberately cultivate awkwardness. If my subjects see me as a little bit innocent, there's no threat and they're much more likely to open up. That's the theory, anyway, but I must admit it's a bit strange sometimes because how I come across on film doesn't represent who I am at all and that can take some getting used to. Do you know what I mean?'

Jo nodded. 'I do. In fact I often have a rather similar thought about myself. I put on a professional persona at work but it's not necessarily who I am. Not entirely who I am, anyway. It can be very unsettling when the way you look doesn't accord with the way you are.'

'Don't tell me you are a Janus too?'

'Janus? I can't place the name.'

'Roman God. The month of January is named after him; he had two faces. I named my production company after him.'

'Of course, I knew it sounded familiar.'

'Actually, I feel as though I'm giving away all my trade secrets. Probably not a good thing when I'm trying to get you to agree to make a film with me.'

'Yes, I must admit, that is my main concern. I mean . . . your films are never about what they say they are, are they? There's always a secret subtext. You don't hoodwink your subjects exactly – after all, they know your reputation before they agree to it – but there is an element of deception, isn't there? You always manage to get them to reveal more than they intend to, or something they hadn't intended to. You can understand my reluctance I'm sure.'

Jo looked at Dan as she spoke. His hair shone in the light and there was a slight shadow of stubble visible on his jawline. She bet he was one of those men who had to shave twice a day otherwise he ran the risk of looking like his namesake Desperate Dan. His eyes were remarkable; the same shade of blue as cornflowers and shining with wit and insight.

'You make it sound manipulative and . . . I don't know . . . rather dishonest?'

'Of course it is. And you know it. You can't tell me that you consciously play the innocent and then expect that act to work on me.' Jo thought she saw a momentary flash of emotion in Dan's eyes, shame possibly or alarm.

'I'm sorry, Ms Lennox. It's become something of a habit but, as you've been direct with me, I owe you the courtesy of responding in kind.'

'Please, call me Jo. Ms Lennox is the persona I put on during the day, my mask if you like. Out of office hours I'm just Jo.'

'Thank you. And you must call me Dan. Let me tell you about the project. Hopefully, that should put your mind at ease.'

'Please.'

'You're right when you say my films usually have a hidden agenda. It's always my intention to get my subjects to reveal more than they intend, because that's what the public wants to see; the real person, not the public face they hide behind.'

'It's interesting that you achieve that by hiding your true self then.'

'Yes, I suppose it is. But I'm full of paradoxes and contradictions, I always have been. And it gets results.'

'I must say, this isn't inspiring me with confidence. You admit you have a secret agenda and still expect me to agree to it . . .'

Dan shook his head. 'I think you misunderstand the intention of the film. You see it's the kids I'm really interested in, not the school as such. I want them to

9

show me their true selves. Teenagers embody the kind of paradox we've been talking about. They show one face to their parents, another to teachers and yet another to their friends; different faces to different groups of friends, in fact. They're in the process of discovering who they are and trying to fit into a world they don't understand. They try on different personas, they keep secrets as a matter of course; that boy Josh who was in here, for example – that's what I'm interested in. The school itself doesn't come into it.'

'That's interesting. Of course, I'd have to get permission from the parents.'

'I understand that. I want to contrast two differing groups of kids; the other group will be from a comprehensive school. Public schools are even more of an anachronism these days than they used to be; completely removed from most people's experience so I didn't want to go for that. Hall Croft is ideal because it's a small private school; the kind of thing more and more parents can afford these days. I want to get them to tell me how they feel about sex, drugs and life in general, then discuss what they say to their parents about those things. I think it has potential.'

Dan's eyes glistened with enthusiasm as he spoke. He was leaning forwards slightly in his chair, legs crossed and hands folded in his lap. Jo noticed that his fingers were long and slender and he had a gold signet ring on his right little finger. Though he was simply dressed in black trousers and sweater, she was fairly certain the sweater was cashmere and she recognised his watch as a Rolex.

'And you're certain nothing in it will reflect badly on the school?'

'Not at all. If you like, we don't even need to identify it. I'll agree to whatever terms you feel necessary.'

'OK . . . I'll have to think about this for a while. If I

10

decide it's feasible I'll have to arrange a meeting of the governors and run it by them. How does that sound?'

'It sounds wonderful, thank you. Would you want me to come to the governors meeting? I'm perfectly happy if you think it would help.'

'Yes, thank you. But, as I say, I need to sleep on it. I'm curious. What made you interested in Hall Croft in the first place? There are plenty of private schools, why mine?'

'Actually, it was my sister's idea. I was talking to her about the project and told her we were trying to find a suitable school. Her kids come here; Emma and Alex Colston. Emma does her GCSEs next year and Alex just sat his A-Levels. He's got a place at Durham in October.'

'I had no idea, but now I know I can see a family resemblance between you and Alex. He's definitely inherited the height gene from your side of the family.'

'Yes, he's going through a terribly gangly phase at the moment. I remember it well. I was growing so fast I felt like a stork; it was hard for my mind to keep up with my ever-lengthening limbs.'

'He's also something of a charmer. I can see where he gets it from now.'

'You flatter me.' Dan waved the compliment away with the back of his hand. 'Anyway, Alex speaks very highly of you.'

'Really? What does he say?'

'Well . . . as a matter of fact he reckons you're pretty sexy for a teacher and I have to admit that now I've met you I agree with him.' Dan leaned forward and looked at her over the top of his glasses. 'Is it true that you always wear stockings, never tights? That's what Alex says anyway, but I'm perfectly willing to believe it might just be wishful thinking on his part. After all, eighteen-year-old boys do tend to have one-track minds.'

11

Jo smiled. Dan was still leaning towards her. His glasses had slid down his nose a little so she could see straight into his eyes. Without the barrier of the lenses, they were even more captivating. The swirling patterns in his irises reminded her of old-fashioned glass marbles. The hairs on the back of her neck were erect and sensitive and, as she opened her mouth to speak, she realised she'd been holding her breath.

'No, I don't. In fact sometimes I'm completely naked.'

He raised one eyebrow like a villain from a Victorian melodrama but the interest and arousal she saw in his eyes was genuine.

'Are you wearing them today?' He mimed twirling a waxed moustache.

'Why? Do you want to borrow them? They might be a bit small for you but I've got some at home that are your size . . .'

Dan laughed out loud. 'Actually, you might be nearer the mark than you think. The film I'm working on at the moment is about sex. I've got involved with a group who call themselves Hellfire 2000. They're . . . well . . . kinky, for want of a better word. They're people who believe in dressing for the occasion – and not just the women.'

'And were you tempted to join in? I can see you in suspenders and high heels.'

'Not yet, but when we start the filming I'm definitely going to give it all a try. Otherwise I'm only going through the motions.'

'Sounds like fun. I hope you enjoy it. And you never know, you may discover your inner pervert.'

'Do you think we all have one of those? Even the vicar and those people who campaign against pornography on TV?'

'Especially them.' Jo put her elbows on the desk and

rested her chin on her steepled fingers. 'I expect you'll find it interesting, if nothing else.'

'I'm open-minded about it anyway and I certainly intend to give it a go.'

'Suck it and see . . .' The way Jo pronounced 'suck' made it sound utterly obscene.

Dan sat there silently, never breaking eye contact. He was smiling slightly and Jo noticed that his lips were dark and unusually full for a man. The sensuality of his mouth gave his angular face a softness and a hint of sin; as if he'd just got out of bed with his legs still wobbly from orgasm. There was no mistaking the confidence and challenge in his eyes, or the arousal that had darkened his cheeks and made his breathing shallow.

'I brought this for you to look at.' He picked up his bag and took out a DVD. 'It gives you an idea of the kind of thing we do.' He stood up and laid the DVD on the corner of her desk. 'Good to meet you at last. And I'll look forward to hearing from you.' He held out his hand for her to shake.

Jo leaned across the desk and took his hand, noticing that the palm was damp and, this time, his grip was less firm. He let himself out, leaving Jo looking at the door.

Maybe she'd hit a raw nerve with her 'suck it and see' remark. Whatever had unsettled him, he'd clearly felt the need to reassert his authority; to change the balance of power back in his favour.

She'd been right; he was an intriguing man. He was as intelligent as he was charming and undeniably sexy. He was funny too and humour in a man went a long way.

But it was his honesty and openness she had found most appealing. Once he'd dropped his on-screen façade she'd found him unpretentious and candid. She'd liked his willingness to try everything Hellfire 2000 had to offer. He was perfectly willing to be vulnerable and

13

didn't see any weakness in it. She picked up the DVD and put it in her bag.

Jo left her office and walked through the building towards the residential wing. The school was housed in an old manor house. It had been built by a noble medieval family, the Halls, from whom it had got its name. The building had been much amended over the years, receiving a new façade, or wing, or interior redesign every time architectural fashion changed.

Neglected for centuries, the house had grown dilapidated until it was bought by a wealthy industrialist in the early 1800s. He'd had the place totally renovated, ransacking it of virtually all its period authenticity.

Jo thought it was a little sad to live and work in a house with such a rich heritage that had been so thoroughly robbed of any signs of its past. It was as if the building had somehow been neutered and forcibly silenced.

The last relics of the original building's majesty were some stone carvings and wood panelling in the Long Gallery which had only escaped destruction because of the Victorian taste for the Gothic.

Jo was walking through it now; the quickest way to reach the residential wing. These days it was little more than a corridor, a route from one part of the building to another. But its flagstone floor and vaulted ceiling always reminded her of a cathedral cloister where monks once walked in silent contemplation. During the school day, of course, there was no silence here. The hubbub of childish voices, the clattering of shoes and the trilling of the children's mobile phones made the space seem crowded and full of life.

She loved the contrast; the way the school was completely transformed in atmosphere and appearance by the pupils' absence. It was only then that Jo felt she could sense some echo of the building's history. Tall windows along the outer wall of the gallery provided a spectacular view of the gardens, which had been sculpted by some unknown ancient gardener in the style of Capability Brown to resemble a natural rolling landscape.

A broad drive led up from the gate to the entrance, flanked by an avenue of poplars. To the left, the garden sloped down to a lake, spanned by an arched stone bridge that always reminded Jo of the picture on a willow-pattern plate. Beside the lake there was a folly, a ruined tower in which, it was said, the house's builders had once paid a hermit to live.

Hall Croft was a special place to live and Jo didn't take it for granted. Not many people could pop into their own chapel if they felt like a bit of solitude, or nip down to their own lake for a dip if they wanted to cool off. Swimming in the lake was off limits to the kids, of course. There was an indoor pool in the sports complex that was usable all year round and strictly supervised. Jo used it herself, swimming fifty lengths before break-fast three days a week. But, during the holidays, she relished the secret pleasure of a swim in the cool green lake amongst the moorhens and ducks.

At the end of the Long Gallery was the main entrance to the house, seldom used these days except on formal occasions. She walked up the staircase. Jo's flat was made up of the entire second floor of the wing. Her living room ran the length of the flat, looking out over the lake. From her bedroom, she could see the chapel and the orchards. The flat was spacious and relaxing. She always felt secluded and peaceful here; cut off from the school and its hectic rhythms. She let herself in.

TWO

She dropped her bag onto the sofa. The windows were open and there was soft jazz playing. Jo could smell garlic and meat cooking. 'Anyone home? Costas? Please tell me it's you. Otherwise I think I've got gourmet burglars.'

Costas appeared around the kitchen door. 'Hello, I'm cooking lamb. I thought we could both do with an end-of-term treat.' Though he'd lived in the UK since his teens, Costas still spoke heavily accented English. He walked over to Jo. 'I hope you don't mind.' He leaned forwards to kiss her.

Jo wrapped her arms around him. She could feel his hard muscles and the bulge at his crotch. His mouth tasted of wine.

'Of course I don't mind. You know I love your cooking.'

He bent his head and kissed her throat. 'Just my cooking?' He lowered his voice. 'Our phone call earlier left me feeling a little excited . . .'

She could feel his hot breath on her skin. 'Well, the afters are usually pretty good as well . . .'

'In that case, I hope you are hungry . . . Let me get you a glass of wine. I'll be a few minutes, the meat needs basting.' Costas turned and walked towards the kitchen.

She sat down on the sofa. The aroma of herbs and lamb coming from the kitchen made Jo feel somehow relaxed and nurtured. Costas was her personal assistant; he hated being called a secretary and Jo had to admit that the title didn't really suit him. Aside from not being the expected gender for the job, the word couldn't begin to encompass his role or how important he was to the running of the school.

Apart from handling all the school's admin, he was a qualified teacher and still found time to take two classes a week, teaching his native language of Greek. The two of them had become lovers fairly soon after Costas had come to work for her. From the very beginning he had been a surprise and a revelation. Going to bed together hadn't been that big a leap when it had finally happened; more an acknowledgement of the bond that had developed between them than a moment of seduction.

It was in the bedroom that Jo had found him most surprising, though, she supposed, it wasn't entirely surprising that the same power dynamic that existed between them in the office should continue behind closed doors. Sexually he preferred to defer to his partner. He was generous, sensual and focused on her pleasure.

He came out of the kitchen with two glasses of wine. He handed her one and sat down beside her. She took a sip. 'Mmmmm, Mavrodaphne. I didn't think you had any left.'

'My cousin, Vasos, sent me over a crate for Easter. How was your meeting with Dan Elliot?'

Jo shrugged. 'He wasn't what I expected at all. Much sharper and more direct than he comes across on screen.'

'I'm not surprised. The bumbling upper-class inno-cent is just an act he puts on to make his victims feel at ease.' Costas sipped his wine. 'So are you thinking of letting him film here?'

'Let's just say I'm not as negative about the project as I was. He's given me a DVD to watch.' She picked it up and showed it to him.

'Do you want to watch it now?'

Jo shook her head. 'I need to wind down. It's been a hectic day.' She took a long swallow of wine.

'Can I help you, perhaps?' Costas put down his glass. He leaned forwards and stroked her upper arm with a fingertip.

'You men are all the same . . .' Jo put down her wine and got to her feet. 'One-track minds. And it goes without saying it's a dirt track.' She unbuttoned her dress. 'No matter what the problem is you see orgasm as the solution.' She undid the last button, slid out of the dress and tossed it aside.

Costas slid onto his knees, an expression of adoration and naked lust in his eyes. Jo was dressed in black French knickers and a matching camisole. Underneath she wore a boned suspender belt. Her stockings were very fine; real nylons with seams.

His dark eyes were shining. His hair was thick, black and glossy. His olive skin and handsome face reminded Jo of Rudolph Valentino playing a gigolo; the kind of man who preyed on women for his own selfish pleasure. The impression was accentuated by the black shirt and trousers he was wearing and, with his dark hair, he looked suitably monochrome. But the stereotype didn't fit him at all, and Jo found the contradiction amusing and somehow erotic.

He knelt in front of her, his hands resting on his knees, patiently waiting for orders.

'You can start by kissing my feet.' Jo could hear the arousal in her own voice. He smiled at her then leaned forwards and laid a hand on either side of her foot, holding it tenderly. He kissed the suede of her shoe. His mouth covered every millimetre of her foot. She could

18

feel his hot breath and the scratch of his stubble through her stocking. He ran his fingers along the length of her stiletto heel.

She knew that the cold cruelty of the heel spoke to something in him that desired subjugation; as if it symbolised her dominion over him. He loved being ordered to take the heel into his mouth and suck on it like a slender metallic cock.

He wanted that now; she was in no doubt. But making him wait was perversely pleasurable for them both. He'd grow more and more hungry for it until the desire to have the heel between his lips was the only thought in his head and his whole body was wound up with hunger and excitement.

Jo was tingling all over. Costas's body was taut and trembling. He began to lick her instep through the stocking, his hot eager tongue snaking hungrily along her skin.

He couldn't help touching the object of his desire, running his fingers up and down the slender heel. Jo was pretty certain that, inside his underwear, his cock was erect and painfully constricted.

Delicious shivers of pleasure slid along her spine like a lover's fingertips. Beneath her camisole her nipples were painfully erect, clearly visible through the silk.

Costas's mouth moved across her foot. He was grunting as he breathed, snuffling like a pig at truffles. He was leaning forwards, and Jo could see two inches of coffee-coloured skin above his waistband where his shirt had ridden up.

He lifted his head and looked up at Jo, his eyes full of pleading and capitulation. 'Please, Jo, may I suck your heel?' His voice was thick with desire.

In answer, Jo took a step back and sat down on the sofa. She crossed her legs at the knee, allowing her foot to dangle in midair. She began to examine

19

her fingernails, feigning disinterest. Costas shuffled forwards. With one hand he pulled at the fabric at the front of his trousers. It was an unconscious gesture – he knew that touching himself was not permitted under any circumstances – but he was obviously so uncomfortable and squashed that he'd needed to ease the discomfort.

Jo saw all this using her peripheral vision as she faked unconcern. They liked to pretend that his need for domination was a matter of supreme indifference to her; something she tolerated but did not encourage.

Costas sat back on his heels and lowered his head to take the heel in his mouth. The heel slid between his lips and he let out an unconscious sigh of contentment and relief.

He sucked on the stiletto as if it was a miniature cock. He was damp around the hairline and perspiration glistened on his forehead. She could see his erect nipples through the fine cotton of his shirt.

Jo's skin felt sensitive and alive. Heat and liquid were spreading between her legs.

Costas put out a hand and grasped her ankle, steadying her foot. He began to suck more rhythmically, sliding the heel in and out of his mouth as if he were an experienced cocksucker delivering a blowjob.

Jo could see the bulge at his crotch. She knew that someone as well endowed as Costas would be constricted painfully by his trousers. From time to time, he'd touch it with the heel of his hand, an unconscious gesture of discomfort and frustration.

Her rigid nipples poked through the silk of her camisole, demanding attention. Blood boomed inside her brain. 'I want you to suck my nipples for me. You know what I like.' When he didn't respond immediately she sharpened her tone. 'Now, Costas.'

He opened his eyes and reluctantly released her heel. Jo pulled her camisole over her head. Her nipples were

20

wrinkled and erect, standing out against her pale skin like raspberries. She opened her legs, spreading them wide. Costas moved forwards, still on his knees. Jo slid her bottom to the edge of the sofa and laid her hands on his shoulders.

Costas lowered his head and took her nipple in his mouth. Jo sighed as his tongue flicked across the sensitive tip. He put one hand on her hip and used the other to stroke her back. His fingertips trailed up and down her spine, eliciting a wave of shivery tingles.

He began to step up the pace, sucking hard on her nipple, nipping it between his teeth and pulling on it. Jo could see the shape of her breast elongate and stretch. She could feel his moist breath on her skin.

She stroked his hair. Her nipples burned with delicious pleasure that seemed to radiate outwards and diffuse throughout her body like a badly needed blood transfusion.

Tension throbbed in her belly. Her crotch ached. Costas reached up and began to finger her other nipple. He rolled it between his fingers, mimicking the treatment his mouth was giving to its twin.

Jo had both hands on Costas's head, holding him firmly in position. Responding to her excitement, he began to bite her nipple, gripping it between his teeth and pulling it away from her breast. She loved the way it looked when he did that, pointed and stretched. His fingers on her other nipple reproduced the sensation, pinching and tugging.

Jo moaned and gasped. The pain was intense and focused yet, somehow, her body transformed it into the most exquisite pleasure. The more it hurt the better it felt. She relished the contradiction, the perversity of asking for pain and enjoying it. It made her feel dirty, corrupt and perverted.

Heat coursed through her bloodstream. Her cunt was tight and painful. She looked down at Costas. He was panting and moaning as he sucked on her nipple, the sound mingling with Jo's own groans of pleasure. She could feel the moisture flowing freely inside her silk knickers.

'Costas . . .' Her voice was a breathy whisper. 'I want you to slide down my knickers and lick my cunt because I need to come now. And, just in case you forget, your cock is off limits. I'm the only one entitled to relief.' She kissed him on the top of the head. 'I'm sure you don't need reminding that the penalty for disobedience will be both severe and unpleasant.'

Costas released her nipples and sat back on his heels, looking up at her.

'Yes, Ma'am. I hadn't forgotten.' He reached out and gripped the waistband of her French knickers. Jo lifted her bottom off the sofa and he slid them carefully down her legs and over her feet. He located the crotch and brought it to his face, inhaling deeply. 'Heaven . . .'

'That reminds me. I'm missing several of my favourite pairs. Have you been stealing them from my laundry basket again?'

Costas hung his head in mock shame. 'I'll bring them back once I've washed them, I promise.'

'If you like the smell so much why don't you go directly to the source?' Jo opened her legs. She used her fingers to spread her lips.

Costas shuffled forwards on his knees. He bent his head and covered her pussy with his mouth.

The first moment of contact was pure and intense. Jo's thigh muscles began to quiver involuntarily and her breathing quickened. Costas's tongue travelled up and down the length of her slit. She felt him circling at her hole, pushing gently into her. It slid upwards, pausing to tease the sensitive opening to her urethra. Sometimes she made him drink piss directly from her cunt. No doubt he was thinking of this as he used the tip of his tongue to stimulate her there.

She gasped as his mouth found her clit. He covered it, spreading his lips and brushing his tongue across the tip. Jo knew it wouldn't take long for her to come. Already heat and pleasure were radiating outwards from her groin and tingles were rocketing up and down her spine.

Costas concentrated on her clit, sucking it hard into his mouth and pinching it between his teeth as his tongue flicked across it. Jo began rocking her hips in response to his moving mouth, establishing a rhythm which he quickly followed. She watched Costas as he licked her. Every so often he would reach down with one hand and pull at the front of his trousers. His frustrated excitement heightened Jo's arousal. She could feel her clit beginning to twitch in his mouth as she neared her peak.

Jo could see her nipples standing out hard and wrinkled. She ground her cunt against Costas's mouth, responding to the rhythm of her need. His breath was hot against her wet pussy. His stubble felt scratchy and rough. The thought brought an image of Dan Elliot into her mind; five o'clock shadow darkening his masculine jawline and, for a moment, she could almost believe it was him and not Costas with his head between her legs.

Would he lick cunt as eagerly, or as well? Would he take the submissive role as willingly and naturally? She closed her eyes and thought of him, on his knees instead of Costas, his lanky body bent over and hunched as he lapped at her clit. She imagined his hair damp and floppy and the light glinting off his glasses. Or perhaps he'd take them off first, fold them carefully and put them away before he got down to work. As Costas's tongue circled her clit she imagined Dan using his long fingers to spread her cunt and lash the swollen bud with his tongue.

Her hips rocked faster and faster. She ground her crotch against Costas's face. The tension in her belly was intense and focused. Costas's right hand moved away from her hip and, moments later, she felt his fingers pressing into her cunt. She arched her back and moaned as they entered her, three bunched fingers.

Would Dan enter her like that as he licked her? Perhaps he'd press an audacious finger against the wrinkled opening of her arsehole and push it inside just as she was about to come. Would he handle his cock, as Costas did, in unconscious excitement?

Jo was tingling all over. Her nipples prickled and throbbed. Her muscles were rigid. Her back was drawn into an arch.

Costas sucked hard on her clit as he circled his fingers against her G-spot. She was moaning and sobbing. She pulled her lips apart, stretching them to create tension on her clit, intensifying the sensation.

He sucked again and she pressed her heels into the carpet and raised her bottom off the edge of the sofa. With one slow deep thrust of her hips, she ground her crotch against his face.

Her clit began to dance in his mouth. Her already quivering body began to shake uncontrollably. The tension in her belly shattered like a dam bursting under the weight of the roiling water behind it.

Pleasure flooded over her, engulfing her and taking her breath away. Her cunt gripped his fingers as she came. His mouth was fastened over her clit, sucking the orgasm out of her. Her body bucked and bowed. Orgasm possessed her, one small peak after another building towards an apex she knew would be spectacular.

Costas sucked hard on her clit, riding it out with her. He was handling his crotch more frequently now, rocking his hips, unconsciously mimicking the action of his fingers inside her.

Jo began to sob. Each small orgasm raised the pitch of her arousal, building towards the big one. The gap between peaks was growing shorter. Her body was rigid and tense. She was gasping for breath, hyperventilating. She felt as though her cunt was vibrating in his mouth as the pressure built. Her muscles contracted over and over again, each throb and flutter bringing her closer to the exquisite moment of release.

Costas sucked at her taut clit, matching the rhythm of her pumping hips. She could hear him breathing heavily, snuffling and grunting, making little throaty, mewling noises of pleasure and excitement. She knew he was getting off on her arousal and growing loss of control. His cock must be agony now, trapped and hard and taut with blood.

The thought of his erection was all it took to bring her to the edge. She tilted her hips, forcing her clit against his mouth one last time. She held her position, body frozen as if she'd been petrified. She was howling. Pleasure coursed through her body like lightning.

She could feel her cunt gripping his fingers. He sucked on her clit. Looking down, she could see Costas's eyes closed as if in prayer. His eyelids seemed to gleam in the light and his dark lashes fluttered as he licked her. He had one hand pressed up against his crotch. His hips rocked manically, rubbing his trapped erection against his fingers.

Her chest was heaving. Her muscles ached. As the peak subsided she became aware of an intense thirst and painful muscles. In an instant, her clit became hypersensitive and she instinctively drew away. She covered her crotch with one hand and cupped Costas's face with the other.

He pushed his wet hair away from his face and shook his head, sending a shower of water droplets flying.

'That felt incredible. I thought you'd never stop coming. You were hurting my fingers.'

'I've had better.' Her voice was an exhausted whisper and she could barely lift her head off the sofa.

Costas laughed. He ran his hands up and down her stocking-clad thighs. 'I love making you come.'

Jo propped herself up on her elbows. 'I could tell, actually. You could hardly leave your cock alone.'

Costas's face coloured. 'I'm sorry. It wasn't deliberate. I just couldn't help it. It's your fault for being so damned horny.'

'So you're blaming me? You need to take responsibility for your own actions. I gave you an order. You disobeyed it. It's quite simple, really.'

'Yes, Ma'am, I'm sorry. I deserve to be punished.' Costas was looking at the floor, his hands by his sides.

'And you will be, I assure you. I haven't decided how yet, but I'm sure you won't forget it in a hurry.'

'Thank you.' Costas stroked her belly.

'I suppose you want permission to come now?'

Costas shrugged, feigning indifference. 'Only if you want me to.' He looked down at his erection. 'I can take it or leave it.'

Jo laughed. 'Go on then, force yourself.' She propped herself up on one elbow and watched as he undid his trousers and pushed them down to his knees. Then he stripped off his shirt.

Using his customary overhand grip, he cupped the helmet and began to slide his foreskin up and down. He let out a long hiss of satisfaction and relief. Jo could see that his scrotum was thickened, his balls contracted and tight. When the tip of his cock came into view, she could see that it was shiny and purple with engorged blood.

He reached between his legs with his free hand and began to finger his balls, kneading them inside their sac. He wanked himself rhythmically. On the down stroke his helmet seemed to rest beneath his palm for a moment before disappearing again under the foreskin.

Costas's eyes were closed, his lips slightly parted. Jo could see his tongue, pink and glistening. His chest was heaving as he pumped his cock. His long nipples stood out hard and dark. Jo lazily reached out a hand and gave the nearest one a pinch, rolling it between thumb and forefinger and was rewarded by a momentary opening of his eyes and a smile.

His eyes snapped closed again and he was lost in his own world; a kingdom, Jo knew, in which cock and pleasure were all that existed. His right hand stroked his balls and his left moved rhythmically.

He was breathing noisily now, hissing and panting between groans. He pulled hard on his balls and turned his other hand and slid his foreskin down hard towards the base of his cock.

An arc of sperm landed on the carpet. Jo watched, captivated, as semen landed on the floor and pooled there. His body was rigid, covered in sweat. Costas turned his face to the ceiling as his cock pumped out volley after volley of creamy spunk.

Sperm was dribbling down his cock and over his fist. His other hand still cupped his balls. He didn't move for ages, long after he'd stopped shooting; he just knelt there, head bent back and chest heaving.

Jo watched as his breathing slowed and his muscles relaxed. He released his cock and opened his eyes. He brought his sperm-covered hand to his mouth and licked it clean. He turned to her and smiled. 'Thank you.'

'I'm glad you enjoyed it.' She reached out and touched his softening cock. 'It's hard to believe it's the same beast. What does it feel like to be attached to such a changeable bit of equipment?'

'Do you know what Socrates said when he became impotent?'

She shook her head.

'He said it's like being unshackled from a maniac.'

27

'Interesting. Perhaps that's why you prefer me to keep yours under control.'

He shrugged. 'It suits me. Let me check on our dinner.' He stood up.

'Good idea.'

He disappeared into the kitchen.

Jo turned and called after him. 'And while you're there you can get something to clean the spunk off the carpet.'

His head appeared around the kitchen door. 'I bet you're going to punish me for it, too, aren't you?'

'You'd be disappointed if I didn't . . .'

Three

Dan walked up the path followed by his film crew. The house, a 1930s suburban semi, could have been in any town in any corner of England; a gravelled drive, a well-tended garden and a Range Rover parked outside. But this particular home, on the outskirts of Highgate, was host to a meeting of the Hellfire 2000 Club. Dan knocked on the door. His radio mike dug uncomfortably into his back and the reporter-light, mounted on the front of the camera, was making his eyes smart.

The evening, a birthday party for one of the members, was to be Dan's first filmed session with the group and he really had no idea what to expect beyond the fact that the dress code would follow a fetish theme. He'd deliberately engineered it so that, when he knocked on the front door, it was his genuine first encounter with the group at play. His reactions would be real, natural and all the more effective on screen.

Though it was hardly natural being followed around by two cameramen, a soundman, a boom swinger and a production assistant, not to mention his co-producer, Sarah, Dan was so used to the team that he hardly noticed their presence.

Dan spoke directly into the camera. 'I'm standing outside Madame Cyn's house. She's a founder member of the Hellfire 2000 Club, a group of individuals who are all active in the world of BDSM. That's Bondage and Discipline, Domination and Submission, Sadism and Masochism to you and me. I've been invited along to her birthday party. I can hear music coming from inside, and so far it all seems pretty normal. But I've been told I should expect the unexpected and I've also been warned that the evening is strictly for adults only. So, if you're of a squeamish disposition, perhaps you ought to change channels now. Let's ring the doorbell and see what happens.' Dan pressed the bell.

The team waited. Through the frosted glass, they saw a figure approaching down the hall in dark silhouette. The door was opened by a large middle-aged woman wearing a long black dress with a corseted bodice and a tall stiff collar that stood up behind her head. Her ample breasts were barely contained by the cups of her corset and wobbled precariously as she moved. Her long red hair was teased into an enormous lacquered edifice that puffed out around her face like a halo. She was heavily made-up with bright-blue eyeliner, glossy pink lipstick and harsh triangles of blusher on each cheek. To Dan's eyes, the overall affect was like *Dallas* on acid; straight out of the 1980s and rather scary.

'Dan, good to see you.' She stepped forwards and kissed him on both cheeks. She was doing her best to act naturally; her smile was stiff and forced and her eye-line deliberately avoided the camera.

'Happy birthday, Madame Cyn. Thanks for inviting me to your party.'

'Come on in.' She stepped aside and Dan and the team entered the house.

The team trooped down the narrow hall behind Dan and into the living room. He'd deliberately tried not to have any preconceptions but, if he'd been asked to visualise the scene in advance, Madame Cyn's living room wouldn't even have made the shortlist.

The décor was pink and the soft furnishings were Victorian and fussy, reminding Dan of the kind of brothel you only ever saw depicted in old Westerns where the whores sat around waiting for clients in frilly bloomers and corsets.

Dan could see Dave and Rick, the cameramen, panning around the room and taking it all in. Standing by the fireplace was a young couple in their twenties. Both of them had long dyed black hair flowing down to their waists and they were wearing identical black leather corsets. The woman wore a tiny silk thong but the man was naked underneath. Dan noticed his body hair had been shaved and he had a name in elaborate Gothic script tattooed above his bare pubis.

Their corsets ended under the bust and the woman's small pointed breasts were displayed. Her nipples had been pierced with thick gold rings. The man's were also pierced and he was wearing some kind of elaborate jewellery through them, like a filigree metal shield that completely covered his areolae and seemed to elongate his nipples.

Though Dan had never considered himself even the slightest bit bisexual, he found the man's appearance curiously appealing. Far from making him look feminine, the corset seemed to emphasise his manliness. Even though he had no body hair whatsoever – a look that Dan usually considered feminine – the corset seemed to accentuate his masculine shape and enhance the appearance of his cock, showing it off shamelessly. Even his long hair, tumbling over his smooth shoulders, seemed erotic, sensual and yet somehow butch.

Dan spoke to the camera: 'I must admit I'm finding it rather interesting. In fact I think I might even be getting the beginning of an erection and I'm honestly not sure if it's the boys or the girls that are turning me on . . .'

31

Across the room, talking to Madame Cyn, Dan spotted a man in women's clothes. He knew the group included a post-op male to female transsexual and at least a couple of other men who liked to cross-dress. He tried to work out if the person talking to Cyn was the transsexual or just a weekend transvestite.

The make-up was convincing enough, and he/she had all the feminine gestures off pat. He held his wineglass by the stem and sipped from it demurely. His nails were long and scarlet and his figure seemed curvy and suitably female, though Dan knew this could be achieved just as easily by artifice and underwear as by female hormones. But his make-up was thick and masklike with a five o'clock shadow clearly visible beneath the layers of foundation.

What did you do with your tackle when you put on a skirt? Dan wondered. There must be some way of strapping it down out of the way. There was clearly more to cross-dressing than putting on a bit of slap and shoving tissues down your bra. It all seemed like a lot of effort and, though Dan didn't think he could be bothered to go to all that trouble, he could just about imagine the sense of liberation and excitement of adopting the female role.

If he was honest, the sheer alienness of it was what appealed to him most; the otherness that women represented. He had no doubt that walking a mile in a pair of stilettos and a wig would be both exciting and surprising. Though the idea of actually changing sex held no appeal, like most men he had an innate curiosity about women's lives. If he could have spent 24 hours as a woman, he'd have leapt at the chance.

Though he supposed it made him shallow, the first thing he'd want to try was sex. Who wouldn't want to experience multiple orgasms and the ability to keep going as long as you wanted? And owning nipples that actually worked, surely that would be worth experiencing?

He watched the cross-dresser talking to Madame Cyn. In their heels, they were a similar height and, if he had to choose which of them had done a better job on their make-up, it would have to be the transvestite. Come to think of it, he had a better figure too, even if it was padding.

'I'm definitely beginning to get aroused,' he said into the camera. 'I think I need a drink . . .' He headed for the kitchen, followed by the crew.

The kitchen was fitted out in Shaker style and decorated in the same pink colour palette as the living room. There was a large conservatory attached to it where half a dozen people were sitting eating. Dan helped himself to a glass of red wine, filled a plate with food at the buffet, then went into the conservatory and sat down.

He turned to speak to the crew. 'Why don't you go and see what's happening in the other room? There's no point in you filming me eating. I'll come back through when I'm finished.'

They made their way back into the kitchen.

Across the conservatory a small skinny woman with cerise-pink hair stood talking to a man dressed like a highwayman. He wore knee breeches, silk stockings and buckled shoes and a ruffled shirt under a long brocade waistcoat, which did nothing to conceal his generous belly.

Though balding on top, his hair was long and caught back in a ponytail and held in place by a black velvet ribbon. Dan thought he must be at least fifty and the overall effect was more Sid James in *Carry on Dick* than Adam Ant's beautifully androgynous dandy highwayman.

The woman's hair was arranged in two bunches high up on her head and reminded Dan of drooping bunny ears. Her eyes were heavily outlined in kohl and her lipstick was a deep red, so dark it almost looked black. She was obviously wearing heavy foundation but seemed not to have applied any blusher, giving her a doll-like appearance.

She wore a leather or PVC corset in the same shade as her hair and, beneath it, a garment that could only loosely be described as a skirt made out of chiffon in rainbow colours. It had a jagged hem and stood out from her hips as if it was either starched or boned. Her fishnet tights had been deliberately torn in several places, allowing circles of pale flesh to be seen. On her feet were heavy knee boots with rows of buckles up the side in bright-red leather. Around her neck was a leather collar which was padlocked. It had sharp-looking spikes at least two inches long and Dan wondered how she avoided hurting herself on them.

He tried to work out if she and the highwayman were a couple. From their body language it was obvious they were on intimate terms, but he couldn't have thought of an unlikelier pair. He'd have expected her to go for someone more like herself, punky, gothy and young. But, in this world, maybe the usual standards didn't apply.

He watched the punky girl talking to the highwayman. He noticed that the man had a small riding crop dangling by a strap from his wrist. The tip of the crop – what he knew from his research was referred to as the slapper – was in the shape of a tiny human hand.

The girl turned to look at something out of the window and Dan noticed that her skirt barely covered her buttocks at the back. He could see them sloping outwards and disappearing under the jagged hem. As far as he could see, she wasn't wearing knickers. He could clearly see her naked fishnet-covered buttocks. Maybe, though, she was wearing a thong. Without thinking, he dipped his head and tried to see under her skirt.

The highwayman said something to the girl and she turned to look at Dan. Caught in the act, he straightened up guiltily and felt his face colouring. He shrugged apologetically and mouthed the word sorry. The girl walked over and sat down beside him.

'I take it you're Dan? I'm Poppy.'

'Guilty as charged. I'm sorry you caught me looking up your dress.'

'Only sorry I caught you?'

'Well, the view was rather spectacular to be honest. You see I was trying to decide if you're wearing knickers or not.'

'And what's the verdict?'

'The jury's still out. But I must admit I rather hope you're not, though I don't know what that says about me.'

'Just that you're a bloke. They all do it, they just aren't usually so blatant about it.'

'I really am sorry. Normally I'm much more gentlemanly. It's just that I feel a bit like a kid let loose in a toyshop. I don't think I've seen so much flesh or kinky clothing on display outside the pages of a porn mag or my own sordid imagination. I'm afraid I was a little overcome.'

Poppy laughed. She opened her handbag, which Dan noticed was in the shape of a coffin, and took out a cigarette. She lit it and inhaled deeply.

'They told me you were a charmer. I can see how you get people to make such fools of themselves on screen. Where's your camera crew by the way? I've been aching for the opportunity to show off.'

'I told them to go into the main room while I ate. Do you enjoy showing off?'

Poppy made a show of looking down at her clothes. 'Well, I'm hardly the retiring type, am I?'

'Do you go out like that? I mean to work and to the supermarket? Not that there's anything wrong with the way you're dressed, by the way. It's very original and, as a matter of fact, I find it rather exciting.'

'Actually, I do go to work dressed like this because my husband and I run a fetish furniture company and I have been known to push a trolley round Sainsbury's in my fishnets, but mostly I go for something a little more comfortable.'

'Is that your husband?' Dan nodded towards the highwayman.

Poppy laughed. 'No. That's just Nick. Or Master Nicholas, as he likes to call himself. You'd better watch out because he does tend to hog the limelight. He's been on the telly loads of times. The trouble is, he loves the exposure so much he never seems to realise they're using him.'

'I thought he looked familiar. But I hope you don't think I intend to make fools out of all of you. I'm honestly just curious about "the lifestyle" and I want to understand it. So much of the stuff you see about it in the media is exploitative and sensational, I wanted to take an honest look at it and the people who do it.'

'Fine with me, but it'll be hard not to make it seem sensational, I'd have thought. After all, most of what we do is incomprehensible and downright outrageous to a lot of people.'

'I suppose what I'm saying is that I don't want to make you look like weirdos.'

'No need to worry about it, Dan. We do a good enough job of that ourselves. To tell you the truth, I love outraging the vanilla world. I relish my status as a weirdo. If I had to choose between my life and a traditional wifey with two point four kids and nice little semi who only gets shagged once a month on a Saturday, or twice if Man U win a game, I'd pick mine every time.'

36

'Can I ask you a question?'

'Anything.'

'Are you dom or sub?'

'What do you think? And does it have to be one or the other? People always make that assumption but some of us just like pain but aren't really submissive and others switch depending on who they're playing with. It's not usually as clear-cut as you make it sound. But, go on, what do you think?'

'I'm completely confused now ... Dom, yes I think you're dom.'

'You're nearly right. I'm dom with everybody but my husband. He's the one and only man I've ever submitted to. It's just the way it works between us. Which are you?'

'I'm not sure to be honest. What do you think I am?'

'Sub, no doubt about it. You might not know it, but you long to kneel naked at the feet of a dominant woman and to feel the kiss of her whip. You want to feel the shame and helplessness as she punishes you and the frustration as she denies you orgasm. It's written all over you.'

'You think so?'

'Oh yes. Your cheeks have gone all pink and you're breathing's grown shallow. I bet things are even feeling a little cramped in your underwear by now, aren't they?' Poppy's eyes narrowed as she spoke. Her voice had grown husky and deep. She was looking straight at him and there was no mistaking the authority in her eyes. 'You can't deny it, you know it's true, come on, tell mistress.'

'Can I get back to you on that one?'

She burst out laughing. 'No need, sweetheart. Both of us know the answer already.'

When he'd finished eating Dan wandered back into the main room. The party seemed to have taken off. Madame Cyn was leading around a young man on the end of a leash. He was naked except for spiked leather bands around his wrist and ankle and the collar around his neck. He was extensively tattooed with a complicated black Celtic design down his arms and over his chest. The design went down into a point between his nipples then snaked a winding path across his abdomen, terminating just above his crotch.

Someone handed Cyn a long thin whip and she ordered the naked man to kneel. Dan took a quick glance at the cameramen to make sure they were getting it all on film and sat down to watch. The man got to his knees and bent forwards, resting his forearms on the floor and his forehead on the carpet. From where Dan was sitting he had a good view of the man's arse and his genitals dangling between his legs.

Cyn trailed the tip of the whip up the crack of his arse and the man's body jolted. She ran it up and down his cleft and around the dark bud of his hole. The man's body was trembling. He was breathing audibly and Dan could see his hands flexing into fists as the whip teased him.

Without warning, Cyn raised the whip into the air and brought it down across both buttocks. There was an audible swish then a sharp crack as it made contact. The man let out a deep guttural moan and Dan was unable to tell whether it was from pleasure or pain.

Cyn whipped him again, raising her arm above her shoulder and bringing it down with great force. The room was silent, all eyes on the action. The sound of the whip slashing through the air then slapping against flesh seemed to underline the intensity of the moment.

She delivered half a dozen blows in quick succession. Dan noticed that her breasts wobbled as she wielded the whip and she had grown breathless. There was a pattern of red stripes across the man's buttocks. Each time the whip made contact he moaned and his body jolted forwards.

38

Madame Cyn raised the whip high into the air. Dan could see a thin sheen of sweat across her collarbones. Her eyes were shining and intense. Her lips were parted. She brought the whip down with a crack that sounded like a gunshot and Dan realised he'd been holding his breath.

Dan's heart was thumping. Tingles of delicious pleasure trickled down his spine.

Cyn's hair had partially collapsed and the front had fallen over her face. One of her breasts had escaped the corset, its nipple hard and dark. She stood with her feet apart and delivered slash after slash across the man's reddened buttocks. He moaned loudly, a deep animal sound that seemed to come from his soul.

He was lost in the moment, Dan realised, responding purely physically. It didn't matter that he was in Cyn's chintzy living room in front of a roomful of people and a camera crew; as far as he was concerned he was alone with the whip and his own torment and joy. Though he still couldn't understand why anyone would want pain, it was clear to him that this was a transaction of mutual need.

Dan's cock was tingling. The hairs on the back of his neck were erect and sensitive.

Cyn dropped the whip and got to her knees beside the man. She spoke to him quietly. She kissed him, not a lover's kiss by any means, but the gesture seemed so intimate and personal that Dan felt like a voyeur intruding on a private moment.

Cyn helped the man to his feet and the crowd began to disperse. The camera crew moved over to Dan to get his reaction.

'Did that get you going?'

Dan turned to see a tall slender woman in a slinky black dress standing by his side.

'I'm not sure . . . yes, it did I suppose. But I'm sort of

horrified as well. I mean, why would anyone voluntary submit to that kind of abuse?'

'Did it look like abuse to you? He looked as though he was thoroughly enjoying himself to me.'

'He certainly did. That's why I'm confused I think. It was clearly consensual – and highly pleasurable. And yet, she was hurting him . . . giving him real pain. I'm having trouble understanding it.' Dan was conscious of the crew filming a few feet away, but the woman didn't seem at all bothered by their presence.

'I'm not sure any of us fully understands it. There are plenty of books about the psychology of kink but, ultimately, we just do it because it feels good.'

'And it feels good even if it hurts like hell?'

'Especially then. Pleasure and pain . . . the divine dichotomy.'

Dan thought she sounded vaguely American – or maybe Canadian, as her vocabulary was definitely English. Her hair was a sleek black asymmetrical bob. Her dress had a deep V at the front which dipped almost to her waist. Her breasts were small and pointed and the nipples were clearly visible through the silky fabric. The sleeves of her gown were long and flowing. The look reminded him of someone but he couldn't quite put his finger on it.

'Now I've seen it in action I can see that's possible but I'm not sure I'd want to try it for myself.'

'You never know, you might enjoy it. I'm Sadie, by the way.'

'Pleased to meet you, Sadie. Are you Canadian? I think I can detect a hint of an accent.'

'Wash your mouth out! I'm American, from New York State, though I've lived here nearly thirty years now. So, do you think you want to try it for yourself?'

'Personally, my instinct is to say no but, in the spirit of sharing and for the sake of the film, I'd consider it.'

'You should come to my dungeon and do some filming there. I'm fairly certain you'll find it illuminating.'

'You have a dungeon? How medieval.'

'More of a basement, really. It's where I see my clients. I'm a professional dominatrix.'

'Really? I thought they only existed in racy novels.'

'Not at all. We're very real and, since the Internet, pretty easy to find.'

'So what do you do to people?'

She shrugged. 'Whatever they want. Some want pain and there are various ways of delivering it. Others are attracted to humiliation and want to be led around on all fours like dogs and verbally abused. Some want to be dressed up . . . I have an extensive wardrobe. There's also a medical fetish room where I can do enemas and piercings and that sort of thing. The list is endless.'

'Do you stick needles through people's nipples and nail their scrotums to boards like in the film *Maîtresse*?'

'Yes, I do.' She looked him straight in the eye. 'Whatever they want, as long as I'm sure I can do it safely.'

'Wow. I must admit I thought that stuff was made up just for the movie.'

'Well, now you know. If you're serious about trying it for yourself, I'll give you a session in my dungeon.'

'And you're happy for the crew to come along and film there?'

'Sure. I've got several clients who'd be perfectly happy to take part. In fact they'd probably get off on it.'

'Thanks, we'll definitely take you up on that.'

'And will you be taking up my offer of a private session?'

'As long as you promise not to poke any needles in my nadgers.'

'Spoilsport . . . But, of course, I'll respect your limits. You'll be perfectly safe.'

41

'And you promise not to hurt me?'

She shook her head slowly. 'No, darling, I definitely will. But you've got to remember that, while I may hurt you, I'll never harm you.'

'OK, it's a deal. I'll ask Sarah, my producer, to set it up.'

'I'll look forward to hearing from her.'

'Can I ask you something?'

'Sure.'

'I met Poppy out in the conservatory and she said she thought I was a natural sub.'

'And you want me to say she got it wrong and you're obviously a big butch dom?' Sadie began to laugh.

'So you think she's right?'

She leaned forwards and put her mouth close to his ear. He could feel her hot breath on his neck. 'Let's find out, shall we?'

Sadie walked away and, as he watched her cross the room, it struck him who she had reminded him of: Morticia Addams. She had the same wardrobe and make-up and the same hint of danger and strangeness.

Across the room, Dan spotted Jim, the group's chairman. Apart from his leather trousers, he was dressed perfectly conventionally. In fact, he looked like a business executive desperately trying to dress the part but failing miserably. There was just something utterly wholesome and conventional about him. Dan nodded to the film crew and walked over to him.

'Hi, Dan. Are you having a good time?'

'It's certainly been interesting. I had no idea at all what to expect but it certainly wasn't this.'

'You knew about the dress code and you knew that there would be a few scenes going on, surely?'

'A scene is what you call a session, right? Like the beating Madame Cyn gave to the man on the lead.'

'That's the idea, or you might call it playing; people

often refer to gatherings like these as play parties.' Jim picked up his glass and took a sip.

'I can see I've got a lot to learn. You're right, I did know there might be some action, I just didn't realise how it would make me feel.'

'And how does it make you feel?'

'I don't know where to start.' Dan ran his fingers through his hair. 'Shocked, certainly. Appalled even – that people would do that sort of thing for pleasure. But I also find it strangely exciting. And, do you know, as I watched Madame Cyn and the slave I was honestly unable to distinguish between horror and arousal.'

'That must be very . . . I don't know . . . unsettling.'

'Yes, it is. I'm completely confused and not at all comfortable at finding violence arousing.'

'Is it violence, do you think, if it's consensual and mutually desired? Isn't it just extreme?'

'It's certainly that and I can see how powerful and intimate it is for the people involved.'

'Did Sadie talk you into trying it for yourself?'

'Yes, she did. How did you know?'

'She said she'd ask you and she seldom takes no for an answer. You're in for a treat; she's one of the best. You'll be in good hands.'

'I hope so. We were talking about that scene in *Maîtresse* where the Madame pierces the slave's nipples and hammers his scrotum to a board. I must admit it rather scared me.'

'Horses for courses. The slaves in that film were real clients of the Madame they used as advisor. They were queuing up to be abused on screen.'

'You mean they actually did it? It wasn't faked? Now I really am shocked.'

'All genuine. You see, we're an exhibitionist bunch by and large. A lot of us get off on public play and being seen. When they made *Preaching to the Perverted* people

43

in the scene were falling over themselves to be in it. And you can hardly watch late-night TV these days without stumbling across another documentary about S&M. We just love showing off.'

'That's what Poppy said to me.'

'Ah, so you've met the wife.'

'I have, but I didn't realise you were her husband. It all falls into place now. I made the mistake of thinking that Nick was her partner and she found it rather funny.'

'Nick? Now he's the biggest TV whore of us all. He just loves the limelight. You'll have to watch out, he can be a real scene stealer.'

'I'll bear that in mind. I've never asked, but I find I'm curious, why did you agree to do this film?'

'Because you seemed to want to look beyond the surface and see the people underneath. You aren't just interested in what we do but why we do it and how it makes us feel. It just seemed to us that you might really be interested in what makes us tick.'

'But you know my reputation. Weren't you concerned that I might be trying to manipulate you? That I might have the same agenda as everyone else? It might turn out to be just another freak show.'

'No, because you don't see us as freaks. You're fascinated by us, anyone can see that. You honestly want to understand.'

'Thanks, I appreciate your trust in me.'

'By the way, I bumped into Jo Lennox yesterday and she tells me you're hoping to do a film at Hall Croft? I hope you're not intending to turn it into a scathing exposé of private education, because anyone who tried to pull a fast one on Jo Lennox would live to regret it.'

'How do you know Jo?'

Jim laughed. 'Everyone knows her.'

'You're not saying she's a pervert?'

'No, I'm not.' Jim sipped his drink. 'Would you be surprised if she was?'

'I'm not sure. She's undeniably sexy and she certainly doesn't lack confidence, but she just seemed so respectable.'

'Assuming she is a pervert – and we're definitely speaking hypothetically here – you wouldn't expect her to go to work dressed in rubber, would you? I can't imagine it going down very well with the Board of Governors, for a start.'

'I suppose not. You've piqued my interest now. Come on, you've got to put me out of my misery.'

'You'll have to ask her yourself, I'm afraid. But I will say that, even though I'm a dom, if I ever found myself kneeling at her feet naked and quivering, I would count myself a very lucky man.'

Four

That night in bed Jo cuddled up behind Costas, his buttocks nestled into her lap. Her arm was wrapped around his chest, her hand in his. She could feel his hard muscles and smooth skin. She could feel the birdcage of his ribs rise and fall as he breathed.

Outside an owl hooted. Jo could hear Costas's watch ticking on the bedside table. She listened as his breathing slowed and sleep relaxed and softened his muscles. She closed her eyes.

When she woke up it was light outside and Costas was gone. Jo reached across the bed and stroked the dent his head had left in the pillow. She smiled to herself. The first time he'd disappeared in the night she'd worried that something was wrong but he'd assured her it was nothing personal. He just preferred waking up in his own bed.

She turned over and looked at the alarm clock's digital display. It was 5 a.m. Jo slid over to Costas's side of the bed where the sheets were cool and his smell still lingered.

More than an hour later she was still awake. Her logic told her it was still the middle of the night, but the bright sunlight streaming in through the open curtains told her senses it was daytime. She slid out of bed and put on her dressing gown and slippers. She fetched a towel from the bathroom and let herself out of the flat, leaving the door on the latch.

Downstairs, she pulled back the huge iron bolts on the front door and walked down the steps onto the drive. As soon as she reached the lawn, she stepped out of her slippers. The grass was cool and dew-damp under her feet. Jo could see the sun gleaming off the glassy surface of the lake.

She walked out to the centre of the bridge over the lake and put down her towel on top of the knee-high stone balustrade. She undid the belt of her silk robe and slid it off. The sun warmed her naked skin. A cool breeze stiffened her nipples. She stepped up onto the wall and dived into the green water, barely rippling the surface.

The lake was cold and silent and vast. She could hear the sounds of nature all around her; birds twittering overhead, the breeze rustling the leaves, the hoarse calls of the waterfowl.

She could smell the moist aroma of earth and the green vegetable scent of the waterweed. She moved silently through the water, doing breaststroke. On the bank a swan preened its wings.

Her wet body gleamed in the light. Her normally pale nipples were dark and wrinkled. She lay on her back in the water and looked up at the cloudless blue sky. High above, a flock of geese flew in formation. She could see the white vapour trail of a jet.

The sun hurt her eyes and she closed them. The water muffled and muted all sounds. She could hear the sound of her own breathing and blood pumping in her ears. She could hear the water itself lapping around her body.

Jo kicked her legs and languidly snaked her arms, steering herself in the direction of a wooden jetty that jutted out into the lake. She could feel the strength of the water as it resisted her limbs. As she neared the jetty, she rolled over onto her front and swam to the edge. She heaved herself up onto the wooden planking and climbed out.

Back in the house, she showered and washed her hair then made coffee and toast. She put her breakfast on a tray and carried it through to the living room. As she sat down on the sofa she noticed the DVD Dan had given her on the coffee table. She went over and switched on the TV and put the disc into the player.

Dan was definitely handsomer in the flesh, she reflected as she watched the screen. And he was much more manly and confident than he came across on TV. The self-deprecating humour was still there, along with that refusal to take himself seriously which she found so captivating and attractive.

He dressed better in real life, too, playing down his boyish gawkiness. He'd looked stylish and elegant in his simple black outfit and his slenderness had given him the look of a young Bryan Ferry.

It was easy to see how he used his natural charm and that appealing quality of innocence to manipulate his subjects. He looked so wholesome, so honourable, that somehow you just had to trust him. Jo could imagine their stunned, mystified faces as they watched the final film, unable to work out how he'd got them to make such fools of themselves. But, she was willing to bet, they'd grown so fond of him that they couldn't quite find it in themselves to resent it.

He was a dangerous man and a courageous one too. In one programme about naturists he'd spent the entire hour naked. As his own producer and director, Jo knew he could have insisted that the cameras shot him only from the waist up to preserve his dignity. Yet he allowed his body to be seen freely, indicating to his subjects and the viewer alike that he was entering into the spirit of things.

In one of the excerpts he'd received a Brazilian wax, the camera lingering over every detail of the process in vivid close-up.

Not that he had anything to be ashamed of on that score. His chest was surprisingly muscular for such a slender man and he had the solid shapely legs of a rugby player. His belly was flat and hard with an obvious six-pack and a trail of dark hairs leading down to paradise. His cock was thick and long and had a pleasing soft curve to it as it lay over his balls.

She found herself wondering if it grew much when he was hard because you never could tell. Sometimes a cock that was only a chipolata when flaccid would surprise you by turning into a python when roused. Likewise a promising package might barely grow at all. She closed her eyes and imagined a naked Dan looking down at her with his erection standing out purple and proud in front of him. Her belly seemed to turn watery and her nipples stiffened and tingled.

After Madame Cyn's party Dan went home with Sarah, his co-producer and 'fuck-buddy'. The term was Sarah's own. A middle-class public schoolboy like Dan would never have called a woman who was generous enough to sleep with him anything so derogatory. But Sarah was American; a loud down-to-earth New Yorker who was outspoken, direct and often foul-mouthed. A tough Jewish broad was how she described herself.

Half the crew were scared of her and she used their fear to her full advantage. Dan was happy to let Sarah play the dragon because it got results and freed him up to concentrate on the creative side. They were a good team at work and away from it, and they spent so much of their time together that the sexual side of their relationship had just sort of evolved.

It was friendly and undemanding and without strings. If they were both at a loose end they'd end up in bed together, and in the morning neither of them had to feel guilty, or make any promises they didn't want to keep. But that didn't mean it lacked passion. Sarah knew Dan better than anyone and vice versa.

Between the sheets she was as demanding, earthy and loud as she was at work, except that she nurtured a deep attachment to receiving erotic pain and verbal abuse. Dan knew she'd have died rather than let their colleagues know about her private preferences. Likewise, he could imagine their looks of wide-eyed shock if they knew how hard and excited he got when Sarah was bossy with him and demanded orgasm after orgasm without even thinking of giving him his turn.

As he sat in the passenger seat beside Sarah the fly of his trousers was damp from pre-come and his cock was tingling. Unconsciously, he stroked his crotch with the heel of his thumb.

Sarah laughed. 'There's no need to ask you if the evening turned you on. It was something, wasn't it?'

'Yes. It was certainly interesting.'

'Yeah ... it was so "interesting" that my clit ached the whole time and I'm sitting here in a puddle.' She smiled at Dan.

'I think the project's going to be much harder than I thought.'

'You're right about that. You looked hard to me most of the evening.' She glanced at his crotch.

'A lot of the time anyway. I don't know what I'm going to do if it keeps happening.' He looked at Sarah as she drove. She was frowning slightly, trying to focus though the dark. Her jet-black hair was cut into an elegant full bob that swung to her shoulders.

'You seemed to cope pretty well, making a joke of it like you usually do. But maybe you should do what teenage boys do before they go on a date, to keep their minds out of their pants . . .'

'What's that?'

'You know . . . don't tell me English boys don't do it. They masturbate. It's supposed to make them more relaxed. You could have a quick one in the loo before each take.'

'Good idea. I don't suppose you'd like to volunteer to help me out, would you?' Dan's eyes travelled downwards. Sarah's plain wrap dress clung to her curves and revealed several inches of deep golden cleavage. 'Strictly for the sake of the film, of course.'

'I don't remember reading that in my job description. We're here.' Sarah parked outside her house. 'Come on. I'm so horny it hurts.'

Sarah let them into the house and headed straight up the stairs. Dan followed, watching her plump buttocks twitch under the soft jersey fabric of her dress. Her figure was curvy and feminine, her legs long and shapely. Dan could see the soft arc of her calf bisected by the seam of her nylons and the taper of her ankle before it disappeared beneath the suede heel of her shoe.

Dan closed the bedroom door. Sarah was standing by the bed with her hands on her hips, smiling. Her brown eyes glistened in the light and her lips were slightly parted, revealing her perfect American teeth. Dan could see her chest heaving as she breathed.

'Why don't you take my clothes off for me?' Her voice was throaty and deep.

'I'll tear them off with my teeth if you like.'

Dan walked over to Sarah. He ran the tip of one finger down her chest and between her breasts. She sighed softly.

'Don't you dare . . . this dress cost me a fortune.'

She caught Dan's wrist and slid his hand under the

top of her dress. Dan cupped her breast, massaging it through the sheer silk of her bra. His cock tingled. He bent to kiss her throat. He drank in the warm womanly scent of her skin. She moaned.

Dan could feel his cock thickening. A slow shiver slid down his spine. He gave Sarah's neck a final kiss. He found the ties at the side of her dress and began to undo them with trembling fingers. He pulled the dress open and found another tie on the inside. He undid it and slid the dress off over her shoulders. Sarah executed a little shimmy, shaking her body and making her ample bosoms tremble, and the dress slipped off and pooled around her feet.

Underneath she was wearing a sheer lacy bra through which the swollen dark tips of her nipples were clearly visible. Dan was surprised to discover that she was wearing tights. When he'd seen the seams up the back of her legs he'd assumed that they were stockings. The tights were darker at the top, like a pair of knickers, and underneath she was naked. The neatly trimmed triangle of her pubes was clearly visible.

Dan stroked the curve of her belly with his fingertips then turned his hand and cupped her crotch. Sarah gasped. It was hot and damp and soft in his palm. He ran the tip of his fingers along the groove between her lips and he could feel the moisture welling there.

'You're already wet,' Dan's whispered.

'I told you, I've been wet all evening. I need to come.' Sarah laid her hand over Dan's, pressing his fingers against her crotch.

'You always need to come.' He slid his hand away and she sighed in disappointment. He reached behind her and unclipped her bra. He pulled it over her shoulders and down her arms. Her breasts swung free. Her nipples were hard and dark. Dan's cock twitched. He cupped her breasts and rubbed his thumbs across the tips. He bent his head and put his mouth close to her ear. He whispered, 'You're such a . . .'

'Don't tease me. Say it. You know what I want.' Sarah's voice was urgent and excited.

'You're such a slut.' Dan squeezed her nipples between thumb and forefinger. 'You're a dirty sexy slut who's obsessed with cock and you want to come all the time.' His balls ached. His erection was trapped painfully inside his underwear.

His mouth was millimetres away from her ear. He could feel her hair on his face. He could smell her skin. He pulled hard on her nipples, stretching and elongating her breasts.

Sarah let out a long moan of pleasure and pain. 'I need to come now.' The tone of her voice left Dan in no doubt that she expected to be obeyed.

He laughed softly. 'You need to learn to be patient . . .' He slid to his knees and pulled down her tights. He rolled them down slowly over her thighs. As he uncovered her crotch he could see the moisture on her lips gleaming in the light. Dan's heart was thumping. His crotch ached.

She had an hourglass figure that had always reminded Dan of Hollywood actresses of the 1950s like Jane Russell or Ava Gardner. She looked strong and powerful and all woman. He leaned forwards and laid a hand on each of her hips. He brought his face to her crotch and inhaled deeply. He opened his mouth and tongued the top of her cleft, finding her clit. Her body juddered. He laid a tender kiss on her pussy then sat back on his heels, looking up into her face.

Dan took off his glasses. He folded them and put them into his shirt pocket then unbuttoned his shirt with trembling fingers. He pulled the tails out of his trousers and tossed it aside. He stood up and unzipped his fly. He pushed his trousers and boxers down to his ankles, pausing to undo his shoes and kick them off. He straightened up, naked.

His cock was standing out in front of him, hard and purple. He could feel the blood pumping under the skin. Sarah took his hand and pulled him over to the bed.

She sat down then lay back and put her feet on the edge of the bed. She spread her legs. Dan gave his cock a long slow stroke. He sighed as the foreskin slid over his helmet and back. He dropped to his knees.

'I'm not quite sure what it is you want me to do.' He stroked her thighs with his fingertips and her body quivered.

She raised herself up on one elbow. 'Stop teasing. I want an orgasm and I want it now.'

Sarah's lips were swollen and dark. The cleft between them was purple and glistening. Her clit stood out, engorged and obvious.

'That's the trouble with you –' he ran his tongue along the length of her pussy, making her gasp '– you want it all and you want it now. You're a filthy, cock-hungry slut who's obsessed with her own cunt.' He covered her clit with his open mouth and circled it with the tip of his tongue.

He felt Sarah's body stiffen. He could taste her salty moisture. His mouth slid against her slippery flesh. Dan's cock was rigid.

Dan spread her lips with his fingers and lapped at her clit. Sarah was moaning and gasping. Blood throbbed in his ears. His balls ached.

Sarah's clit was hard and tense in his mouth. He reached up and found a nipple. He pinched it, twisting and pulling. She let out a long animal roar and arched her back. Delicious tingles travelled up his nape and over his scalp like ghostly fingertips.

He squeezed her nipple. Sarah moaned and thrashed. He wrapped his free hand round her hip and held onto her. Dan sucked on her clit and flicked his tongue over the sensitive tip. Sarah began to rock her hips. He matched her rhythm. Her pussy felt hot and slippery. Her clit twitched in his mouth.

He gave Sarah's nipple a final pinch and slid his hand back down between her legs. He slid two fingers inside her. He pressed his fingertips hard into her G-spot and she raised her bottom off the bed, gasping and panting. His cock was pumped with blood and heat.

He slid in a third finger and fucked her slowly as he sucked on her clit. Sarah's hips pumped, rubbing her crotch against his eager face. He lapped at her hot cunt. He could feel her muscles gripping his fingers.

Hot breath gushed down his nose as he licked her. He was tingling all over. His cock was on fire.

Sarah's body had begun to buck. The bed creaked and squealed. Dan held onto her hip. He pressed his face against her crotch, sucking on her clit. Her muscles gripped his fingers, hard as iron.

'I'm going to come . . . I'm going to come . . .' Her voice was high and urgent.

She began to wail. She ground her crotch against Dan's mouth. Her clit danced in his mouth. Her muscles gripped his fingers. His cock was rigid and tingling. Prickles of excitement slid down his spine.

The bed squeaked and shook. He struggled to keep his grip on her as she came. He kept his mouth fastened over her clit, sucking the orgasm out of her. He pressed the tips of his fingers against her G-spot. She sobbed and mewled. Her body was rigid and trembling.

As soon as her muscles began to soften Dan released her. He slid out his fingers and gave her clit a final kiss. Sarah lifted her head off the bed and looked down at him.

'What are you going to do now?' She sounded weak and exhausted.

'I'm going to fuck you.' He climbed onto the bed and Sarah slid across and lay on her back with her legs spread wide. He wrapped his fist around his cock and slowly stroked it. The tip was shiny and slippery.

He shuffled forwards until he was between her parted thighs. He put a hand under each of her buttocks and lifted her up until her crotch was level with his erection. He used one hand to position himself and rolled up his hips, pushing into her. He sighed as he entered her. She felt fiery hot and soft and wet.

Smudged mascara stained her face. Her normally sleek hair was messy and matted. Her nipples were thick and dark. Dan lifted her legs up over his shoulders and wrapped his arms round her thighs.

His body was rigid with excitement. He was tingling all over. He moved his hips, sliding in and out of her hot cunt. The out-stroke was long and delicious and slow. He could feel her muscles squeezing him. On the in-stroke his foreskin slid back, revealing the tip of his cock so that it prickled with pleasure and sensitivity. Heat and pleasure coursed through his bloodstream.

Sara slid her right hand between her legs and began to stroke her clit. Her eyes were closed. Her mouth was open slightly and Dan could see that her lips were puffy and dark. Now and again, he would get a glimpse of her glistening pink tongue between her perfect teeth.

The headboard banged rhythmically against the wall. Sarah was rocking her hips, bringing up her crotch to meet his thrusts. Her breasts wobbled. Dan's arms were wrapped around her thighs. He could feel the tension building in his gut. Where the back of her thighs slid against his body he was slick with sweat.

Sarah was gasping and moaning; hoarse animal cries of passion and hunger. She ground her crotch against his, her fingers clamped over her clit.

'You're a filthy, horny slut and you can't leave your cunt alone, can you?' Dan's voice sounded hoarse and breathless. 'I can feel your muscles gripping my cock. You're going to come soon. I know the signs.' Dan pumped his hips, pounding her. 'Your lips are all puffy and dark . . . you're panting and moaning . . . You're on the edge, I know you are. You're going to come any second . . .'

Her calves banged against his face. He held on, fucking her hard. His strokes grew shorter and more urgent.

'Yes . . . it feels so good . . . I'm going to come . . .' Sarah spoke in short strangled gasps.

Dan's balls banged against Sarah on every thrust. He could feel her fingers between their bodies as she worked her clit. She rocked her hips, grinding her crotch against him. Her tits bounced.

Sarah's moans began to rise in pitch and urgency. The sound seemed to fill the small room. Her body was rigid, her back arched. She let out a long single cry of alarm and relief. Dan felt her muscles gripping him as she came.

He held onto her slippery thighs and pounded her hard. His hips pumped. He looked down at Sarah as she came. Her mouth was open, her neck stretched back. She was beautiful and she was coming. He was making her come.

He gave one final deep thrust and exploded inside her. A hot wave of pleasure shot through him. He grunted through clenched teeth. He could feel his cock pumping out sperm inside her.

Sarah was thrashing and trembling as she continued to come. Her hand was clamped over her crotch. She was covered in sweat. Her chest heaved.

Dan's body was shaking. His cock tingled. Wave after wave of pleasure and release crashed over him.

When it was over they climbed under the covers and lay in each other's arms. The sweat had cooled on his body, chilling him. He pulled up the duvet.

'That was great.' Sarah's voice sounded dreamy. 'But you should have hurt my nipples more.'

Dan stroked her hair. 'I don't know. I give you two fantastic orgasms and you still want more. You're insatiable.'

'You say that like it's a bad thing . . .' She kissed his nipple.

Sarah quickly fell asleep. Her hair was spread out over Dan's chest, tickling him, but he daren't move. He bent his head and dipped his nose into the thick perfumed mass. He inhaled. He could feel her big breasts squashed against his side.

It had certainly been an exciting evening. He hadn't seen so much bare skin in one room since he'd made the film about the nudists. But the two projects couldn't have been more different. The naturists hadn't struck him as sexy at all, in spite of the acres of naked flesh on display.

He wasn't sure why but he'd found the corsets, leather and rubber a thousand times more sexy even though most of the partygoers had been respectably covered. If he was going to get aroused every time the cameras rolled he might have to take up Sarah's suggestion of a pre-filming wank.

He smiled to himself. He felt fifteen again; plagued by unwanted erections he felt powerless to control and was convinced everyone could see. He hadn't felt like that for years. But, as he thought about it, he realised that wasn't true. He'd felt exactly like that sitting outside Jo Lennox's office. Helplessly horny and certain she knew about it.

She was a fascinating woman. He wondered if it was true, as Jim had implied, that she was kinky. She certainly seemed dominant enough and she was undeniably sexy. But – other than wishful thinking – he had no reason to believe that she was even interested in him, let alone involved in anything perverse.

There was no reason why Jim shouldn't know her. After all even kinky people sent their children to school. But Jim had said '*everyone* knows her' which seemed to hint at something more, something Dan couldn't help finding intriguing and exciting.

He tried to picture her dressed in a corset, stockings and spike-heeled boots and, instantly, his spent cock began to stir. Dan gave it a lazy stroke. Sarah moved in her sleep, turning over so that her back was towards him. He curled up behind her. Her buttocks nestled into his lap and he closed his eyes.

Five

The taxi driver couldn't stop looking at her. Every time they stopped at a traffic light Jo saw him watching her in the rear-view mirror. She was going to her best friend's birthday party. Sam was a fetish fashion designer and she lived above her showroom in the King's Road.

Jo looked fantastic and she knew it. She was wearing a dress that Sam had made for her. It had a flouncy knee-length skirt and a sweetheart neckline. The waist was formed of a broad horizontal piece of leather that reached from the top of her hips to underneath her bust. It had been gathered into soft pleats, emphasising her curves and the soft swell of her belly. Underneath she wore a waspie corset that nipped in her waist.

Sam's assistant Victor had made a pair of shoes and a matching handbag and hat for her. She felt sexy and powerful and alive. She'd painted her lips in the same shade of scarlet as her outfit. The soft leather of her dress had grown warm in response to her body heat and lay against her skin like a soft caress. The corset gripped her body like a lover's tight embrace. She crossed her legs, conscious of the driver's eyes on her. Her stockings sighed softly as they slid against each other.

'Didn't your mother ever tell you it's rude to stare?' She met the driver's eyes in the mirror.

He shrugged. 'She did, but she'd obviously never met you. I just can't help myself.'

'I see . . . so you're blaming me? The sin of Eve and all that.'

'Let's just say that if Eve had looked like you I'd have eaten every apple on that tree.' The lights changed and the taxi began to move. At the corner, he turned into the King's Road

At Sam's showroom Jo was greeted at the door by one of Sam's models who reminded Jo of a human Barbie doll, tall, slender and impossibly big-breasted. She was dressed from head to toe in body-hugging rubber. On her head were a pair of pussy ears and she was wearing a long stiff tail.

'You've got a long climb ahead of you, I'm afraid. Third floor.' She handed Jo a glass of champagne. 'Fuel for the journey . . .'

Sam was Jo's oldest friend. She was half French and half Scottish and owed her gamine features and effort-less elegance to her French mother, and her heavy Glasgow accent to her father. She was a fashion designer, producing exotic sexy creations which were equally at home on the catwalk as at a fetish club.

Sam was a creature of contrasts. She dressed to reflect her ever-changing moods. One day it might be retro chic, the next it could be goth or punk. She changed her hair colour every few weeks, often dying it a vivid unnatural shade to match her current outfit.

Jo loved Sam's many contradictions; her stylish clothes made her seem doll-like and untouchable but she was earthy and foul-mouthed. She knew good wine but preferred a pint of heavy. She made clothes out of leather and yet she didn't eat meat.

To the outside world the two women could not have been more different. Jo had a respectable job and a status within the community whereas Sam made kinky clothing for people society preferred to ignore. But they shared a love of clothes and an utter disrespect for society's rules and roles.

The only difference between them, Jo often reflected, was that her work forced her to live a kind of double life. At school she was the respectable headmistress but on her own time she was every bit as rebellious, individual and dangerous as Sam.

Jo could hear a hubbub of voices and loud soul music as she climbed the stairs. On the first floor she bumped into Victor and his boyfriend J queuing for the loo.

'Jo. You look fab.' He air-kissed her.

'Hi, Victor. Hi, J. So do you two.'

Victor was dressed in a tiny pair of red leather shorts and an upper-body harness. J seemed to have been poured into a clinging black rubber garment that reached from his mid-thighs to his neck. His impressive muscles were emphasised by the outfit and, in the dim light, it seemed to be the same colour as his dark skin, giving the illusion that he was naked. It was so tight that Jo couldn't help wondering how, when he got to the front of the queue, he could possibly manage to pee.

She walked up the stairs towards the music. When she reached the third floor she looked around the room for Sam. The living room was decorated in purple and scarlet. There were silver stars on the ceiling and the furniture was an eclectic mixture of Victorian Gothic pieces and modern. For the party the room had been hung with hundreds of fairy lights, making it look exotic and mysterious, like the inside of a fortune teller's tent.

Jo spotted Sam on the other side of the room. She was dressed in a purple leather corset and matching spike-heeled boots which buttoned up the side like a Victorian lady's. She was wearing a multi-layered chiffon miniskirt in mottled shades of purple, lavender and pink. It seemed to have been starched and stiffened and it puffed out around her hips like a diaphanous cloud. On her back, she wore a pair of matching tiny fairy wings. She was carrying a sparkly silver wand. As Jo drew closer, she realised that the wand was actually a riding crop with a star attached to its tip.

Sam's black hair had been cut into an asymmetrical bob and the front had been dyed the same shade of purple as her corset and boots. When she spotted Jo she waved her wand.

'Hello.' Sam smiled. 'Do you know who you remind me of in that outfit?' Sam was staring at Jo, her eyes wide.

'Betty Grable?' Jo struck a pose.

'Almost. You look like a blonde Dita Von Teese. The way you clip up the front of your hair and everything.'

'Really? You think so? Thanks. She's really glamorous. And you look gorgeous too, Tinkerbell. Happy birthday.' The two women kissed. She handed Sam a wrapped gift.

'Thanks. We were still sewing on the wings when the first guests arrived.'

'Well, they look lovely. And they suit you. You look as though you were born with them.'

'Stick around. A few more glasses of bubbly and you might see me fly.' Sam took a glass of champagne from a passing waitress. 'Is it tomorrow you're meeting Dan Elliot?'

'Yesterday.'

'And? I hope he's as cute in the flesh.'

'Cuter as a matter of fact. On screen he deliberately cultivates his boyishness. In real life he's rather stylish and elegant. He's quite a man, actually.' Jo sipped her champagne.

'I see . . . he's obviously made an impression.'

'Yes, he has, I suppose. I rather liked him. In real life he's much more confident; a man in full possession of his personal power and authority.'

'Just the way you like them. The more powerful they are the sweeter it is when you get them to submit.'

Jo laughed. 'I must admit it does sound tempting. But I have no idea if he's even kinky.'

Sam's models, all dressed as cats, moved between the partygoers with trays of champagne and canapés. The other guests were a mixture of Sam's friends and her clients and the dress code reflected the fact. Most were conventionally, if formally, dressed for a posh night out, but at least a third of the guests were sporting the type of fetish fashion Sam was famous for.

It wasn't often, Jo thought, that you saw two such contrasting styles of dress in the same room; usually it was one or the other. It seemed to represent a collision of two worlds and, while Jo was comfortable in both, she had to admit that she felt more herself – more whole – when she was able to dress in the type of clothes Sam had made her.

The hat and the shoes made her at least eight inches taller. She towered over most men and, she had to admit, she rather liked it. The outfit made her feel sensual and elegant and strong. The corset pushed her breasts up and out and she was aware that men couldn't seem to take her eyes off them. A waitress went by and Jo helped herself to another glass of bubbly.

'Well, don't you look fantastic?'

Jo turned. 'Jim. Thanks. Good to see you. Where's Poppy?'

Jim was dressed in black leather trousers and waist-coat. 'She's around somewhere. She's fairly easy to spot. She's got green hair this week and an outfit to match.'

'I'll look out for her.'

'I must say you're looking particularly magnificent

tonight. I'm almost tempted to change the habit of a lifetime and beg to kneel at your feet.'

Jo laughed. 'Well, don't let me stop you.'

'Actually, I was saying something quite similar about you the other night. Were your ears burning?'

'You were talking about me? To who?'

'Dan Elliot. But don't worry, I didn't out you as a pervert.'

'Ah, yes . . . Dan.' Jo felt her cheeks flushing.

Jim smiled. 'I see he's had the same effect on you as he's had on my wife. He's very . . . charming, isn't he?'

'And by "charming" you mean?'

Jim shrugged. 'Clever perhaps. He's a powerful, intelligent man and he's fully conscious of his effect on women. The floppy-haired bumbling innocence is all an act, as I'm sure you know.'

'Yes I do. And I have to admit I prefer the strong confident Dan.'

'And we all know how much you like that in a man . . .'

Jo smiled. She sipped her drink. 'Perhaps. There's little point in mastering a man who's a wimp is there?'

'And you plan to master him?'

'I haven't decided yet.'

'Sorry, darling. I've been neglecting you.' Sam squeezed between a group of guests and stood beside Jo.

'No problem. Jim's been keeping me amused. I'm going to find myself some food in a minute.'

'I've got to go and mingle again. But . . .' She leaned close and put her mouth next to Jo's ear. 'Will you stay the night?' Jo could feel Sam's hot breath on her neck. A slow shiver of excitement slid down her spine.

'Of course I will.'

Sam kissed her neck then moved away.

Jim raised his eyebrows. 'I think I'd better go off and find my wife.' He turned to walk away then seemed to think better of it and turned back. 'Don't do anything I wouldn't do.' He winked.

Jo made her way over to the buffet. When she'd filled her plate she spotted an empty sofa and headed for it. As she sat down someone flopped down on the seat beside her. She looked up.

'Adam. You're a pleasant surprise.' Jo did a double take. Adam was dressed in a white pleated halter-neck dress and high heels. He was wearing a platinum blonde wig and his face had been made up in a fairly passable likeness of Marilyn Monroe. Jo felt her nipples stiffen. 'You should dress like that more often.'

'Thanks. I'm glad you like it.' Adam preened his hair.

She looked him up and down. The dress plunged into a deep V at the front, reaching down to the waist. Jo noticed that he was wearing falsies underneath, giving him the illusion of breasts and his figure looked unusually curvy and feminine. 'What are you wearing under that? You look as though you've got hips and boobs.' She reached out a hand to touch his hip but Adam slapped it away.

'Take me home with you after the party and you can see for yourself.' Adam softened and raised his voice, making it sound more feminine.

'I'd love to, but I've already promised to spend the night here, with Sam.'

'How about making it a threesome? All girls together . . .' Adam fluttered his fake eyelashes.

Jo looked at him. His make-up had softened in the heat and she could just see the beginning of a five o'clock shadow along his jaw. In spite of his feminine attire she could detect his masculine scent rising from his warm skin.

'OK. I don't suppose she'll mind. When I've finished eating I'll find her and let her know.'

'Why not ask her now? She's just there.' Adam

pointed to where Sam was talking to a man in a suit near by.

'Sam . . .' Jo called. Sam turned to look at them. 'Can we have a word when you're free?'

Sam nodded. She said something to her companion who looked disappointed and walked away.

'Thanks for rescuing me. He's a buyer for one of my major customers but he's the most boring man alive.' She looked at Adam. 'Who's your pretty friend?

'Sam, this is Adam.'

'We meet at last.' Sam and Adam shook hands. 'Jo's been singing your praises but she neglected to mention how pretty you are.'

'Would you mind if he joined us later?' Jo slid along the sofa so that Sam could sit down.

'Maybe . . .' She looked Adam up and down. 'What's his body like under that dress?'

'Hard and muscular. And he's got a fantastic arse . . . round and pert and covered in golden hair.'

'Actually, I was thinking about his cock.' Sam pointedly looked at Adam's crotch.

'It twitched when you said that.' He stroked himself with the heel of his thumb.

'Let me see . . . it's not the biggest one you've ever seen, but it's surprisingly thick and, when he's really excited, it gets so hard it looks as though it might burst and the tip goes a beautiful shade of purple. My clit's tingling just thinking about it.' Jo glanced at Adam. He looked humiliated and proud in equal measure. His cheeks burned.

'Oh, don't tease him, Jo. Can't you see he's blushing?'

'But he loves it. Like all men he's a narcissist. He loves being the centre of attention. See – he's positively glowing.'

'I cannot tell a lie. What man wouldn't enjoy two gorgeous ladies discussing the merits of his cock?' Adam looked from one woman to the other.

'But the best thing about Adam –' Jo lowered her voice '– is that he really loves cunt. He can't get enough of it. He loves the smell, the feel, the taste of it. He's only really happy when he's got his head between a woman's thighs, worshipping at the altar of his goddess.'

'I think we're going to get along.' Sam smiled at Adam. 'But, if you don't mind, I think I'm going to help myself to some food before it's all gone. See you both later.'

The party ended around 3 a.m. As Sam ushered out the last stragglers, Jo and Adam walked up the narrow staircase to the top-floor bedroom. Jo switched on the light.

Adam whistled. 'What a lovely room. It's sort of dreamy and magical.' Adam looked around.

'I think you've been in that wig too long. You'll be sewing your own curtains next.' Jo pulled off Adam's wig and tossed it on a chair. She ruffled his blond hair. 'That's better, though the make-up will have to go. And didn't you promise to show me what you had on underneath your dress?'

Adam put both hands behind his back and unzipped his dress. He pulled the halter over his head and the dress slid onto the floor. Underneath he was wearing two flesh-coloured fake breasts complete with rosy nipples. They appeared to have been glued to his chest. She watched as Adam peeled them away from his body.

'That's a relief. They're terribly itchy.' He scratched his chest.

On his lower body he was wearing a garment which reached from his thighs to his waist. It seemed to be made out of thick Lycra like the stout support knickers women sometimes wore to look smooth under tight clothes. But Adam's underwear had clearly been padded on the hips to give him a feminine shape and had extra Lycra at the top to nip in his waist.

Jo ran her hand down the curve of his hip. Adam turned around and stuck out his bottom and that, too, was softly padded. 'I see. Cunning. But I think I prefer you as a man, so off it comes.' She folded her arms, waiting to be obeyed.

Adam slid the garment down over his hips. It was obviously very tight and clingy and he had to struggle to get it down. He slid his hand inside and fiddled with something for a moment then manhandled his cock and balls over the top of the panties. He sighed in relief.

'I was wondering where that had gone.' Jo stroked a fingertip down the length of his cock. Adam gasped.

'There's a cache-sex inside. It holds it all out of the way.'

'Isn't that uncomfortable?'

'You get used to it ... After a while it's rather pleasant as if it's being gripped in a tight fist.'

'Like this?' Jo wrapped her hand round his cock and squeezed. Adam exhaled. Jo could see a pulse beating in his throat. 'It's growing in my hand, so you obviously like it.'

'Yes ... yes, I like it.' Adam's words tumbled out in a sibilant rush.

Jo released him. Adam went into the bathroom and Jo took off her dress, hat and shoes. She slid off her French knickers and tossed them onto the chair. She climbed onto the bed, rearranging the pillows so that she could sit up. Her skin felt sensitive and alive. Already her crotch was tingly and tight.

Sam's bedroom had been decorated in red with touches of gold leaf. Jo always thought it was like living inside a Klimt painting. The bed was a magnificent Gothic affair with black wrought-iron rails and finials.

Above the bed was an enormous painting of a naked man bending over kissing the booted feet of a woman. Just the man's head and shoulders were in the painting and the woman was only visible as far as the knee. The boots were of shiny patent leather and had a complicated series of buckles up the side. The heels were a slender vicious steel spike, like a six-inch nail. Jo knew that Sam had made the boots for the artist, Jude Ryan, and that the painting had been her thank-you present.

The door opened and Sam came into the room.

'I thought they'd never go. Where's Adam?' She sat down on the bed.

'In the bathroom washing his face. Oh – there he is.'

Adam was standing in the bathroom doorway.

'And he's pleased to see me . . .' Sam pointed at his cock. It was thick and half hard, its tip purple. 'I'm beginning to feel a little overdressed.' Sam tossed her wand onto the bed and unzipped her skirt. She let it drop onto the floor and began to unhook her corset at the front. A pair of surprisingly large breasts tumbled free, tipped by dark thick nipples.

Her big breasts seemed to unbalance her petite frame. Jo always thought Sam looked as though she'd topple over at any minute. She was wearing a tiny purple silk thong. Adam stepped forwards and knelt in front of her. He slid the thong down slowly over her hips and thighs. Jo could see his eyes shining as he gazed at her crotch.

Sam lifted each foot in turn and Adam removed the thong. He raised the wispy garment to his face and inhaled deeply. His cock was fully hard now, almost flat against his belly.

'If you like it that much, maybe you should put it on.' Sam stroked his short hair.

'I doubt if it'll fit.' Adam was still holding the panties to his face.

'Put it on anyway . . .'

He got to his feet and stepped into the thong. He struggled to pull it up. Adam was stocky and his thighs were muscular from his weekly soccer games. Jo could see the waistband of the thong digging into his flesh as he pulled it up his legs. She wasn't even sure she'd be able to fit into Sam's undies herself. Adam fiddled with his crotch, trying to fit his cock and balls inside the inadequate panties.

'I suppose that will have to do.' Sam ran a fingertip over his crotch. He gasped. Jo could see that Sam's nipples were erect, tiny raised pinpricks were standing out around the edge of her areolae. Adam's body was taut with excitement. His fists were clenched by his side.

'I think Adam should show Sam his gratitude for allowing him to wear her panties. What do you think, Sam?' Jo's crotch blazed with heat and pleasure. Her nipples tingled.

'Good idea. But actions speak louder than words . . .' Sam sat down on the bed. She lay back and put her feet on the edge, her legs spread and her crotch obscenely on display. Adam stepped forwards and dropped to his knees. He used his fingers to spread her lips and covered her cunt with his mouth. Sam gasped.

Sam's eyes were closed. She was panting audibly. Jo could hear Adam's excited snuffly breathing. She leaned forwards and looked at his crotch. There was a big dark spot of pre-come on the front of the panties.

Jo slid across the bed and lay down beside Sam. She put her mouth close to her friend's ear. She could smell the perfume rising from her skin. She recognised Anais Anais and the unmistakable scent that was all her own. She was breathing heavily, making little grunting noises as Adam's mouth worked its magic.

'Does that feel good? He's good at it, isn't he? He knows just how a woman likes it.' Jo whispered into her friend's ear. 'At first he sort of circles your clit without directly touching it. He gets you all worked up by licking along the length of your slit then sucking your lips into his mouth. Then, when you start to moan and wiggle he goes straight for the target . . .' Jo's crotch felt warm and liquid. Her nipples ached. 'He flicks the tip of your clit with his tongue then sucks it all the way into his mouth, making you gasp and sob. Can you feel it? Can you?'

Sam made no answer but she arched her back and let out a long deep moan. Jo stroked her friend's cheek with a fingertip. She trailed it down Sam's throat and over her breasts. She circled each nipple in turn, barely making contact. Sam thrust out her chest.

Jo rubbed her thumb across the tip of Sam's nipple. Sam gasped. Jo pinched it between thumb and forefinger. She pulled on it gently, elongating it. Sam began to moan. Her closed eyelids fluttered.

Adam was making excited little grunting noises as he licked. Jo could hear obscene wet squelching noises as his mouth moved against Sam's crotch. She knew his cock would be hard and painful, pumped with blood and heat.

Excitement pumped around Jo's bloodstream. Her clit was aching. She rolled Sam's swollen nipple between her fingers. Sam let out a long deep moan. Her head thrashed against the duvet, matting her hair. Her hips rocked.

Jo leaned close and whispered in her friend's ear. 'You're getting closer, now, aren't you? You're grinding your hot cunt against his mouth. You're covered in sweat.' She brushed Sam's hair off her face. 'Your nipples are tingling . . . your clit's hard and throbbing . . . can you feel it?' She pinched Sam's nipple hard, squeezing and pulling it.

Sam roared. Moist hair clung to her face. Her hips moved rhythmically.

Jo sat up. She ran her fingertips up and down Sam's torso. She looked at Adam and she could see a dark flush of arousal on his cheeks. The tip of his erection was poking out the top of his thong. His damp body gleamed.

Moisture welled between Jo's legs. Waves of shivery tingles slid up and down her spine.

Sam's head thrashed. Her feet dug into the mattress as she raised her bottom off the bed, rubbing her crotch against Adam's face. He wrapped his arms around her hips and held on tight.

Jo could see him unconsciously wriggling his hips, trying to gain some relief for his aching cock. She could see a little dark spot of mascara that he'd missed at the corner of his eye. A bead of sweat ran down his face.

Sam's hips moved frantically. The bed rocked and creaked. Jo laid her palm tenderly on Sam's cheek. She leaned close for a kiss. Sam's eyelids snapped open for a moment then languidly slid closed again. Sam's mouth was hot and wet. She tasted of brandy and chocolate. She slid her mouth down Sam's face, over her neck and chest until she found a nipple.

She felt Sam's body begin to tremble and buck. The bed was creaking and rocking. Jo's clit ached, demanding attention.

Jo's fingers found Sam's other nipple. Sam arched her back. Adam's face was clamped between Sam's spread legs. Jo could see him struggling to hold on as Sam writhed and thrashed. Heat and excitement pumped round her body.

Sam began to make a high keening noise which, Jo knew, signalled imminent orgasm. Her hips bucked as she ground her crotch against Adam's face. Her nipple in Jo's mouth was stiff. Jo fingered the other nipple, squeezing and stretching it so hard her knuckles turned white. Tension pulled at her belly. Ghostly fingers trailed over her scalp.

Jo sat up and looked at Sam. Her face was flushed and pink. Her heavy mascara had softened and smeared. Light gleamed on her closed eyelids. Jo used both hands to tease Sam's nipples.

Sam was practically screaming now. Her normally sleek hair was tangled and messy. Her hips moved, her breasts bounced. A tight fist of excitement pulled at Jo's belly. Her nipples burned.

Sam's whole body stiffened. She was coming. Jo pinched her nipples, digging in her fingers and pulling on them. The screaming became urgent and frenzied. Sam brought her bottom up off the bed, pressing her crotch against Adam's face.

Jo turned to look at him. She could see muscles and tendons standing out in his forearms as he tried to hold onto Sam. His body glistened.

Though his cock wasn't visible, Jo knew it would be rigid and purple. She pictured a bead of pre-come glittering in its single eye. She bet he was desperate to plunge into Sam and take his pleasure.

Jo's heart pounded. Sam circled her hips, grinding her crotch against Adam as she came. Her bottom was raised off the bed. She was screaming, a single high note of pleasure and exhilaration. Jo pinched Sam's nipples.

Without warning Sam brought up her hands and covered Jo's and she pulled them away.

'Stop . . . stop. It's too sensitive.' Sam's voice was weak and breathless. She pulled away from Adam. She propped herself up on her elbows, smiling. 'Well . . .' Sam's voice was breathless and weak. 'Aren't you a clever boy?'

Adam sat back on his heels. 'Happy birthday.' He pushed his damp hair off his face. He looked at Jo then down at his cock. 'Can I do anything for you, Jo? Even though it isn't your birthday?'

'Climb up here and lie down.' Jo slid across the bed.

'If you two don't mind, I'm going to take a shower . . .' Sam stood up. 'Oooh, my head's all swimmy and my legs feel like rubber.' She walked haltingly towards the bathroom.

Adam stood up and slid off his panties. He lay down on the centre of the bed. His erection was huge and purple, pointing at the ceiling. His hard muscles gleamed. His face was flushed. Jo's nipples were tingling and sensitive. Her crotch was tight and aching.

She got onto her knees and straddled his body. She used both hands to position his cock. She let out a long deep sigh as it began to fill her. It was fat and hard and hot. She felt it sliding past her muscles, enlivening and exciting every nerve ending.

'I don't think I'm going to last very long. Watching you with Sam has got me all worked up.' Jo wriggled her hips.

'Me too. I'm fit to burst. And you look so horny in just your corset and stockings.' Adam ran his hands along her thighs.

'Thanks. But I'm not sure you deserve to come, actually.'

'Don't be cruel . . .' He rubbed her nipples.

'Why not? We both know it's what you like.' Jo rocked her hips, riding his cock.

Jo's crotch felt liquid and tight. Adam's cock stretched and filled her. She could feel his thighs, hard and thick between her legs. The corset clasped her middle in its firm grip.

Adam stroked his fingertips up and down her thighs. She bent forwards and kissed him. His mouth was hot and wet. She could feel his beard stubble against her skin. Her breasts were squashed inside the corset. Her nipples tingled. Adam put his hands on her buttocks. He rocked his hips up to meet her thrusts.

Heat and arousal pumped round her bloodstream. His mouth was meltingly soft and fiery hot. His stubble rasped her skin. She rode his cock.

Wet skin slid against wet skin. Adam's fingers dug into her buttocks. She gave him a final kiss and sat up. She pushed down the front of her corset, freeing her breasts. She grabbed his wrists and pulled his hands up to her chest. His fingers found her nipples.

She gasped as he began to pinch. Her nipples burned with pleasure and pain. Every sensation seemed to be instantly transmitted directly to her crotch.

'That looks like fun.' Sam came out of the bedroom and sat down on the bed. 'I'll have to try it myself later.' She slid across and knelt beside Jo. She ran her fingers up and down Jo's back. Jo sighed.

She moved slowly up and down. Adam's thick cock slid inside her. He pinched her nipples hard, pulling on them and elongating her breasts. She was tingling all over. Sam's fingers stroked her back, barely making contact. It felt shivery and tingly and intense. Her nipples prickled in response.

Jo's crotch felt hot and tight. Her clit was sensitive and hard. She tilted her hips backwards and forwards as she rode him, causing delicious friction.

Adam rotated his hips up to meet her, following her rhythm. He looked up at her, his eyes shining and intense. Her breasts bounced. Adam gave her nipples a final squeeze and put his hands back on her hips. She felt him bending his knees. He brought his hips up hard, meeting her thrusts.

Sam's hand slid down her spine and onto her buttocks. She ran a fingertip down the cleft between Jo's cheeks, making her moan. She stroked each buttock with the flat of her hand. She kneaded and squeezed.

'Does that feel good?' Sam's voice was thick with arousal. She slid her hand underneath. Jo felt Sam's fingertips on her cunt. She gasped. She felt Sam's fingers circling the edge of Adam's cock. Jo's body quivered.

Sam's fingers explored the cleft between her buttocks. They teased the margin of her arsehole.

Jo was trembling all over. She was breathing in huge noisy gulps. Her nipples ached. Adam's cock felt huge and hot and hard inside her.

She felt Sam's slender fingertip sliding past her sphincter. She let out a long strangled sob. Her clit instantly responded. It tingled and burned. She leaned forwards and gripped the top of the bed's iron rails.

Adam looked up into her face. She ground her crotch against his, pulling on the rails for leverage. The bed creaked and rattled. Sam's finger fucked her arse. She could feel Adam's balls against her buttocks.

Her long hair fell forwards into Adam's face. A strand went into his mouth and he turned his head to free it. He looked up at her, his eyes narrowed and his lids gleaming in the light.

She was tingling all over. Her hips hammered. She felt Sam slide a second finger into her arsehole. Her back arched, her body bucked. The headboard banged against the wall.

Adam was grunting and panting. His eyes glittered. His fingers dug into her flesh. His cock was rigid inside her.

Her breasts bounced. She pulled hard on the rails, grinding her crotch against his. Sam's fingers fucked her arsehole, matching the rhythm of Adam's cock. She was vibrating with pleasure and excitement.

Jo was sobbing and moaning. The bed clanged against the wall. Adam's hands pulled her onto him. His hips pumped. She rode his cock. Sam's fingers slid in and out. The dam burst.

She pulled hard on the rails. She ground her crotch against his. Adam gripped her buttocks, his hands locked and rigid. He gave a final deep thrust and circled his hips, pumping out hot sperm. She quivered and shook.

'I can feel you coming . . .' Sam circled her fingers inside Jo.

Adam gazed up at Jo, his eyes wide and glassy. Wave after wave of pleasure gripped her, each more intense than the last. Tingles rocketed up and down her spine. Her muscles gripped his cock.

A final intense wave of pleasure gripped her. She gazed down at Adam. Her hair covered his face and he was glistening with sweat.

'I love it when you come for me . . .' His voice was hoarse and breathless. He circled his hips.

She collapsed on top of him. He reached up and pushed her hair out of her eyes. He wiped her damp face with his fingers. She bent her head and kissed him softly on the mouth then slid off his cock. Sam lay down beside them.

'Well. Don't you look a happy boy?' Jo kissed Adam's nipple. 'Like a cat with two tails.'

'No . . . more like a tail –'. Sam stroked his softening cock '– with two cats.'

Six

On Saturday while Jo was eating breakfast Costas let himself into the flat.

'I've brought up the post. You've got an interesting-looking parcel.' He put the mail on the table and went over to the cupboard for a cup. He poured himself a coffee and sat down.

Jo picked up the package and turned it over in her hands. 'I think I know what it is . . .' She slit the padded envelope open with her knife and tipped out the contents. A pile of novels slid onto the table.

Costas picked up one of the books. 'Oh, it's your author's copies of your latest book. It looks good.'

Jo had been writing erotica since her teens and had been published in *Forum*, *For Women* and a couple of specialised fetish magazines. Five years ago, Costas had suggested that she have a go at writing a novel. At first, it had seemed an impossible task but, after a couple of chapters, she seemed to find her voice.

It was liberating and exciting to be able to describe human sexuality in more depth than a six-thousand-word story normally allowed. She could give her characters real depth and complexity. She could explore the erotic journey that they made together and show how each step of the voyage brought them closer to the terrifying bottomless intimacy which, Jo knew, lay at the heart of kinky relationships.

Her first book had been a modest success and, with each successive novel, her popularity had increased. Rosalind Quirt, as she called herself, had a dedicated and growing group of fans.

Jo often wondered if any of the parents or governors had read her books. She imagined them being aroused by her words, maybe even masturbating as a result, never even knowing that it was Jo's writing that was turning them on. It gave her an illicit thrill and delicious feeling of power.

She drained her coffee cup and picked up a book. On the cover, a woman stood with her back towards the camera. Only her parted legs and bottom were in the picture. She wore long shiny boots and a tiny pair of leather shorts. Her hands were behind her back and she was holding a vicious-looking riding crop in both hands. Between the A of her parted legs could be seen the figure of a shackled hooded man on his knees.

'You're right. It looks great. Pass me that pen and I'll sign one for you.' Jo ate the last bite of toast and wiped her fingers clean on her napkin.

'Thanks. I always find your books . . . inspiring.' He passed her the pen.

She opened the book and leafed through it until she found the dedication page. She signed it and handed it to Costas.

'Oh, you've dedicated it to me! Thanks.' He smiled at her. 'I had no idea you'd done that . . . "for Costas Metaxas, my friend and muse". I really am honoured.'

A few days later Dan and the crew turned up at Sadie's house to film one of her sessions. Dan had tried not to have any preconceptions about the day, but, as they turned into her street in a quiet suburb of Wembley and drove slowly along trying to read the numbers on the doors, the well-kept Victorian terraced houses gave no hint that one of them housed a modern dungeon.

When they found the right number they parked the van and Dan got out and walked up the path, leaving the crew to unload the gear. Because space was tight in Sadie's dungeon they'd decided to use a single camera, rather than the usual two. You got better coverage with two cameras and didn't have to spend time doing cutaways, but a single operator and soundman would be less intrusive and wouldn't interfere with the flow of the session.

He rang the bell and almost immediately he saw a dark figure approaching down the hall. The image was indistinct and distorted by the frosted glass of the front door, but he didn't think it was Sadie. The figure was too broad and it seemed to have an odd lumbering gait.

The door opened. Dan was right; it wasn't Sadie. It was a tall chubby middle-aged man dressed in a pair of black rubber shorts and an upper-body harness. Around his ankles he wore metal shackles connected by eighteen inches of sturdy chain. No doubt that explained his unusual walk, Dan thought. Though he couldn't have explained why, the sight of the man's get-up quickened Dan's heart and made his cock tingle.

'Good morning, Mr Elliot. Mistress Sadie has instructed me to take you to her dungeon.'

'OK.' Dan looked back down the path to the van. 'I don't think my colleagues are quite ready, though.'

'I'll come back for them, sir. My orders are to take you directly to the mistress.'

Dan stepped into the hall. The man turned and walked towards the back of the house and Dan immediately realised that two round panels had been cut out at the back of his shorts, exposing a circle of pale hairy buttock on each side. His ankle chain clanked as he moved and he was forced to walk in short shuffling steps.

The man opened a door under the stairs and motioned Dan to go through. Inside there was a steep flight of steps. Dan held onto the handrail and walked down carefully and the man followed after him. At the bottom there was a closed door. Dan tried the handle but it appeared to be locked.

'It's got an electronic lock ... let me.' The man reached forwards and punched a six-digit code into a numerical keypad. Dan heard the lock click open and the man turned the handle. 'Mistress Sadie is waiting for you in the room at the far end. I'll go and get your crew.'

Dan stepped through the door. Inside it was dimly lit by wall sconces that mimicked flaming medieval torches. The walls had been painted to resemble stone and the floor had heavy rough flagstones. He could smell something perfumed and exotic, incense probably, or scented oil. He began to walk along the short corridor and was surprised by how loud his feet sounded.

There was a door on either side of the hall, the first was ajar and Dan could see that it was a changing room, like in a sports club with lockers and benches. He opened the other door and saw a basic bathroom, with a sink and separate shower and toilet cubicles and a pile of fluffy towels in a rack.

The door at the end of the corridor was wooden and heavy with black wrought-iron banding and studs, like an ancient door to a church or castle. Dan wouldn't have been the slightest bit surprised if it creaked like a sound effect from a Hammer horror movie when you opened it. Ever since he'd passed through the electronic door his heart had been beating double time and his mouth had gone dry.

He stood in front of the door, suddenly apprehensive. Barging straight in seemed insensitive and presumptuous but knocking and waiting seemed timid and unmanly. He didn't want to make the wrong impression before he'd even got to the dungeon. He knocked on the door, rapping it hard with his knuckles in what he hoped was an authoritative fashion and immediately opened it.

'Come in, Dan. I've been waiting for you.' Sadie got up from her seat and walked towards him. She was wearing a long flowing black dress. He noticed that she'd been sitting on a sort of throne, with a padded red leather seat, carved wooden arms and a high back.

The room's walls had been painted in the same stone effect as the hall. Here and there, huge iron rings had been set into the wall, reminding Dan of the kind of prison you saw in old movies where the unfortunate starving bearded inmates were shackled by their elevated wrists.

One wall was completely concealed by red velvet curtains. Dan assumed this was where the window must be and he could understand that the ingress of natural light would totally ruin the mood. On the wall opposite the curtains there was a St Andrew's cross and row upon row of vicious-looking implements: whips, crops, chains and pieces of equipment Dan wouldn't even have been able to name hanging on hooks.

In the centre of the room there was an enormous piece of furniture that he couldn't immediately identify. The main body of the item was of padded leather. Halfway down the front legs there was a smaller padded platform. Straps and buckles seemed to dangle from every part of the piece.

Dan tried to work out how they all worked and eventually realised that it must be a whipping bench. The victim lay over the bench with his knees supported by the smaller platform and the straps were used to fasten him in place. He allowed himself to imagine himself bent over it with his naked arse thrust high into

83

the air and his belly gave a little involuntary lurch and his cock twitched.

'This is fascinating.' He looked around the room. 'It's very atmospheric, I must say. It definitely puts you in the mood.'

'I'm glad you think so because I've got a proposition to make.' Sadie smiled at him and, though it seemed warm enough, there was something in her eyes that made him feel like a fly caught in the spider's web.

'That sounds ominous . . .'

She smiled again. 'I hope not. I'm sorry to spring this on you at the last minute, but you remember you agreed to filming a session as my client?'

Dan nodded. His heart was pounding and a small vein in his temple had begun to twitch.

'Well, I've been thinking and, if you agree, I think it would be a good idea if you also undergo a private session with me. No cameras, no one else, just you and me and our imaginations.'

'But I've already agreed to let you dominate me, what difference does it make if we film it or not?'

'All the difference in the world. The cameras will make you feel safe. You'll put on your charming boyish persona and none of it will be real. I want you to know what it feels like to really surrender – to submit to me and to my desires. I want you to taste your own fear and to learn how exciting that is.' She gazed at him, her dark eyes shining. 'It's not too much to ask surely?'

Dan stared back at her. His stomach felt fluttery. He could hear his own heart beating. 'OK. Why not?'

'Excellent . . .'

The door opened and Dave and Dennis came in carrying their kit.

'Good morning, gentlemen. I'll leave you to set up while I get changed. I'm expecting our guests at noon. I hope that gives you enough time?'

'Should do. Can you just walk me through which bits of . . . er . . . equipment you'll be using so I know what to light?' Dave, the cameraman, looked around the room.

'Of course. Normally we keep the lighting quite atmospheric in here but Dan's explained that the cameras need plenty of light. We'll be using the whipping bench, of course, and the St Andrew's cross. During the second session I'll be using the examination chair.' She pointed to the corner where there was a huge medical-type chair with straps and leg stirrups. 'And for general stuff we tend to use that space over there.' She pointed to an empty space in front of the curtains. 'Is that all right?'

'Sure. I can use a redhead and a couple of dedos and I'll use some spun to diffuse the light. Should be fairly straightforward and won't take me too long. Thanks.' Dave went over to the equipment and began to erect a light stand.

An hour later the cameras were ready to roll and Sadie's slave had informed them that the clients had arrived and were waiting in the changing room.

Dan always felt psyched up and excited before a shoot, as if anything might happen, and he'd never felt that more than today. He'd never thought of himself as narrow-minded or innocent, but since he'd started working with Hellfire 2000 he'd found himself permanently wide-eyed and perpetually aroused.

Dan was already wearing his radio mike and Dennis, the sound engineer, was fitting Sadie's. She'd got changed and was wearing a skin-tight leather cat suit and clinging pointy-heeled boots. The suit had a long zip up the front and it was undone almost to her waist. Around her hips was a thick leather belt from which hung half a dozen whips and crops. It reminded Dan of Batman's utility belt. Dennis fixed the radio mike's transmitter to the back of the belt and clipped the mike itself to the top of her cat suit.

'Right. Can you just say a few words – to give me a bit of level?' Dennis went over to his portable mixer. 'Just tell me what you had for breakfast, or recite a bit of poetry, anything you like.'

'There is a young woman named Sadie,
Whose tastes are decidedly shady,
She'll often enjoy
An obedient boy
To dress up and pretend he's a lady . . .

Will that do?'

Dennis laughed. 'Fabulous, thanks. Right, I think we're ready when you are now, Dan.'

'Thanks.' Dan stood in front of the camera. 'OK, Sadie. I'd like to do a piece to camera first, if you don't mind, then we can begin?'

'Sure. What do you want me to do while you're doing that?'

'How about if we bring the clients in and you're doing something with them in the background? It'll add atmosphere.'

'Sure.' Sadie went over to the door and opened it. 'Slave, I'm ready for them now,' she shouted down the corridor.

She held the door open and, a moment later, the slave appeared followed by a man in full tarty drag including a wig and make-up and a hooded man in a body harness. The slave led them into the room and over to the area in front of the curtains. He pointed at the floor and both of them got to their knees.

'Great. Now if you'll just go over and stand by them and give them some silent orders, that should look great for the camera . . . thanks.' Dan stood by the slaves. 'And I'll do my bit here. Is that OK for you, Dave?'

'Yep.' Dave put the camera on his shoulder and walked over to them. 'OK. We'll start rolling and you start when you're ready.'

Dan faced the camera. He waited until Dave gave him the nod that he'd begun to roll.

'This is Mistress Sadie's dungeon. She's what's known as a professional dominatrix. You'll remember that I met Sadie at Madame Cyn's party and she invited me along to do some filming here. We're going to see a couple of sessions today, with a variety of clients, all of whom have kindly given us permission. As you can see, the clients are masked or otherwise disguised to protect their identities. I've got no idea what to expect, but I'm pretty certain it's going to be an eye-opener.'

Dan took a step closer to the camera and leaned forwards as if he was sharing a secret. 'Apart from anything I'm as nervous as hell because Sadie's somehow got me to agree to a private session with her so what happens here today might be a little taster of what I can look forward to and, frankly, I'm not sure if I'll be able to handle it. Anyway. Let the fun begin. Sadie . . . it's over to you.' He stepped out of shot.

Sadie touched the transvestite on the shoulder. 'Will you get up and stand over there, please?' He got to his feet and walked over to the whipping bench. He was wearing a floaty turquoise top and a shiny PVC miniskirt with a deep slit up the back. When he reached the bench he turned and clasped his hands in front of him, awaiting further orders.

The man in the harness remained on his knees, looking up at Sadie. He was already breathing heavily. Sadie removed an implement from her utility belt. She pressed a button at the top and it extended and Dan saw that it was a retractable riding crop.

Sadie swished the crop noisily through the air. The hooded man flinched. Dan could see him blinking through the mask's small eyeholes. His breathing had grown noisy and the leather around his mouth seemed to alter the sound and make it seem urgent and amplified.

'Bend over.' Sadie pressed her hand down on the back of the man's neck and he eagerly complied, thrusting his arse high into the air.

Sadie began to walk around the man. Her stiletto heels clacked noisily against the flagstones. She used the tip of the crop to trace along his spine and down the crack of his arse. She extended one foot, placing it right under his nose. He seized it between both hands and began to lick, panting and slobbering as he covered the leather with his eager tongue.

Dan could see that the man's body was trembling and that the upturned soles of his feet were stained with dust from the floor. Sadie withdrew her foot sharply and the man gasped in shock and disappointment. For a moment he didn't move, his cupped hands still in position, then he put both palms flat on the floor and lowered his head.

Sadie walked to his other end and brought the crop down across the meat of his buttocks. It swished through the air and landed with a crack, knocking the man forwards with a grunt. Dan glanced at Dave to make sure he was getting the shot and saw that he'd moved round and was zooming in on the man's beaten arse.

She hit him again. The crop cracked and a raised dark stripe instantly appeared. Dan's heart seemed to be in his throat. He watched as Sadie lifted the crop high into the air. She brought it down and it landed with a crack that made the man grunt and his body judder.

Dan wasn't sure if it was the pain that had made him grunt or pleasure. Both, he supposed, though it was

88

hard to imagine how that much pain could feel good, even though the evidence of his own eyes clearly told him that it was. The man's arse was criss-crossed with angry scarlet stripes now and a few dark bruises were already visible.

Sadie lifted the crop. Dan could see her chest heaving. There was a fine sheen of sweat on her exposed cleavage. She lowered the crop, delivering a stinging blow that resounded around the bare room and made the man gasp and jerk forwards and Dan realised he had been holding his breath.

She retracted the crop and hooked it back onto her belt. 'I think that's enough for now. Straighten up please.'

The man slowly raised himself up onto his knees and gazed up at her. Sadie beckoned to the slave. As he walked the short distance to her, Dan noticed that he was no longer wearing his ankle cuffs and chain. When he reached her side he bowed respectfully and stood to attention. 'I'd like you to piss on him, please. I think he needs cooling down a little.'

'Yes, mistress.' The slave unzipped his shorts and pushed them down over his buttocks. He slid his hand inside and pulled out his cock. He stepped up to the hooded man and took up the universal stance of a man about to relieve himself. Dan couldn't help noticing that he was particularly well endowed and, for a moment, experienced a sharp stab of envy until he realised that, as Sadie's slave, he was probably seldom permitted to use the monster on her or even allowed relief.

'I'm sorry, mistress –' the slave's voice sounded frustrated and ashamed '– but I'm having trouble going.'

'So I see . . . too aroused no doubt. But I suggest you try to do as I've asked. I'll be punishing you later for failing to obey instantly. If you fail completely the punishment will be twice as harsh.' Sadie's voice was cold and severe. Dan felt an icy shiver slide up his spine.

'Yes, mistress.' The man closed his eyes.

A moment later he sighed and the urine began to flow. It trickled down the hooded man's body and tinkled onto the stone floor. Dan heard him gasp and he began to shake his head as the urine stung his eyes.

Sadie stood several feet away, out of range of the splashing urine, and watched, expressionless, as the slave pissed. The slave gazed down at the man, his eyes shining with intensity and excitement. When he'd finished he shook his cock and squeezed his foreskin over the tip, shaking off the last drips.

'Now, I think our guest ought to thank Slave for giving him such a nice shower. Open wide . . .'

The hooded man shuffled forwards and raised his head. Dan took a step closer. He could see the man gazing up at the slave. Dan could hardly breathe. Time seemed to have slowed down. The sound of his own heartbeat throbbed in his brain.

The client opened his mouth and the slave slid the tip of his cock along the man's lower lip. For a second, an image flashed into Dan's mind of a believer kneeling at the altar rail for the communion wafer. The man stuck out his tongue and began to lick. Dan saw the slave's legs quiver as the supplicant's tongue made contact with his tender flesh. The hooded man opened his mouth and swallowed him to the root. The slave tilted back his head and moaned.

'You're a cock-loving cissy, aren't you?' Sadie's voice was full of contempt. 'Not a man at all.'

Dan's watched the man and the slave, each lost in his own pleasure. He tried to imagine himself in the scenario, first imagining himself as the slave, receiving pleasure from the faceless client, then as the hooded man, stinking of piss with his mouth full of cock. He couldn't decide which was the lesser of two evils. All he knew was that his heart was beating so loudly he was sure it must be audible over his radio mike. His cock tingled.

'Can you see how much he loves it, Dan? How much he loves me to humiliate and abuse him.' Sadie bent down and fingered the man's nipple. His body juddered but he didn't stop sucking.

The kneeling man's hand slid unconsciously to his crotch. His fingers pulled at the studded metal codpiece. Dan was pretty sure that he must be hard underneath it. He knew that, if it were him, he'd want to rip off the leather and free his erection. He'd begin to wank, stroking it urgently in his tight fist as the slave fucked his face and he wouldn't stop until he'd shot his hot seed all over the stone floor.

Dan heard the clack of Sadie's boot heels against the flagstones. The kneeling man was so focused on sucking the slave's cock and fingering his own crotch that he didn't notice Sadie approaching and removing a long swishy cane from her utility belt. She flicked the cane's slender tip across the back of the man's fingers. He snatched back his hand, grunted and spat out the slave's cock. He hung his head.

'Sorry, mistress.' His voice was full of shame and contrition.

'I should think so. Go over there.' She pointed. 'Now!'

The man began to stand up, but Sadie pushed him back down.

'On your knees.'

The man crawled slowly away, his head hanging in shame. When he'd reached the whipping bench Sadie walked across and spent a moment cuffing him to one of the bench's many restraints. She had chosen one close to the ground so that the man had no choice but to bend forwards, his head practically on the floor. When she'd

91

finished, Sadie stood up and delivered two stinging strokes of the cane across the man's upturned arse.

'Thank you, mistress.' The man's voice was quiet and Dan thought he sounded broken and ashamed.

'You.' Sadie pointed at the transvestite. 'Follow me.' Sadie walked back over to the slave and he followed. 'Kneel down.'

The transvestite looked down at the floor, clearly conflicted. 'But . . . the floor is dirty, mistress.'

'I'm well aware of that but when I issue an order I expect it to be obeyed.'

He got down on his knees. Dan noticed that he achieved the manoeuvre with considerable elegance in spite of his high heels.

'Wank into his face please, slave. And get a move on, because I haven't got all day.' Sadie walked over to her throne and sat down, affecting boredom.

The transvestite waited, his face upturned and expectant. The slave gripped his cock in his fist and began to wank. Dan saw his eyes close as he slid his foreskin backwards and forwards over his swollen helmet. He could see that the slave's balls were already riding his shaft and the tip of his cock was glistening with pre-come.

Dan saw Dave step closer to them, focusing in on the scene. Dennis shadowed his steps so as not to disturb the cables that linked his mixer to the camera. Dan's cock was half hard. Sweat prickled in his armpits.

The transvestite wore a long blonde wig. He was elaborately made up with green eye shadow and exaggeratedly arched Elizabeth Taylor eyebrows. His lips were a shiny tarty red and they glistened in the bright lights. Dan could see his stocking tops and a couple of inches of pale thigh peeking out from under the hem of his skirt.

The slave was wanking furiously. He was grunting and panting. His half-lowered shorts cut across the bottom of his buttocks. A smudge of fading bruises marked the outer edge of one of his cheeks and a fresher series of stripes could be seen at the top of his thighs.

Dan's face felt hot. His crotch ached. He noticed that the slave's legs seemed to be quivering. He was rubbing his cock in short urgent strokes. He reached down with his other hand and began to stroke his balls. The transvestite's eyes glistened. He licked his painted lips.

The slave began to gasp and shake. He pulled back his foreskin with a sudden urgent motion and Dan saw his cock begin to twitch and spurt. A strand of thick creamy come splashed onto the transvestite's face, right across his mouth. A second squirt splashed across his cheek.

He knelt motionless with eyes closed as rope after rope of hot sperm landed on his face. His hands, resting on his parted thighs, were clenched and trembling. An obvious erection stuck up under the front of his skirt.

The fine hairs on the back of Dan's neck were erect and tingling. When the slave stopped coming he didn't move. He looked down at the transvestite, cock still in hand as he got his breath back.

'Rub it into his face please,' Sadie called over from her chair, her voice sounding distracted and bored.

The slave released his cock and rubbed his sperm all over the transvestite's face, smearing his make-up. Soon his face was a filthy mess of colour and gleaming sperm.

When the slave was finished he looked at his dirty hand in disgust then pulled up and zipped his shorts. Sadie walked slowly over to the two men. She unhooked the cane from her belt and used its slender tip to lift the front of the transvestite's skirt. She turned to the slave.

'What's the meaning of this? Our guest is improperly dressed. You know perfectly well that you should have given him a cache-sex to wear. If I'd wanted to see his worthless cock and his pathetic little erection I'd have said so.'

The slave looked at the floor. 'I'm sorry, mistress, I forgot.'

'I'm not interested in your excuses. That's a second demerit you've earned yourself and, I assure you, my punishment will be severe. Now take these two out and bring in our next guests.'

The slave escorted out the two men. Sadie turned to Dan. 'I know he misbehaves because he wants me to punish him and he knows that I know ...'

'So how does that work? If you punish him because he wants it isn't he the one in control? What do they call that? Topping from the bottom?'

Sadie nodded. 'Yes, that's right ... A slave usually wants a particular kind of punishment and that's what he hopes he'll get so I always make sure that my punishment is something he neither expects nor desires. Believe me, he knows which one of us is really in charge.'

'I don't doubt it.'

Sadie was smiling slightly as she spoke. Her eyes were huge and brown and they seemed to see straight into his soul. Dan couldn't imagine that anyone would be brave enough to defy her, let alone attempt to manipulate her. He looked away.

'If you'll excuse me, I've got to go and change.' Sadie walked away.

A moment later the slave appeared leading a man on a lead. He was wearing a hospital gown. At the back it didn't quite meet so that six inches of buttock was clearly visible. Dan could see that the man already had an erection. The slave led him over to the medical chair and began to fasten him to it with the leather restraints.

The straps and buckles were made of thick leather which creaked as the slave fastened them and lined with sheepskin. When the slave had finished with the patient's wrists he lifted his legs into the stirrups and fastened the restraints at his ankles.

He folded back the bottom of the man's gown, exposing his cock, then draped his legs and belly with green cloths, as if in readiness for surgery. Dan could see that the man was trembling with excitement. The slave picked up something metal from a trolley beside the chair and began to fit it to the patient's mouth. It took Dan a second to realise that it was a gag, the kind used to force a patient's mouth open during dental surgery.

The door creaked open and Sadie entered the room. She was wearing a rubber outfit which Dan immediately recognised as a parody of a nurse's uniform. The dress barely reached her bottom, and beneath it she was wearing black fishnet stockings. On her feet were shiny patent leather black lace-up shoes with heels so high and slender that Dan wondered how they could possibly support her weight. She clacked across the room and the patient's eyes followed her, full of excitement and trepidation.

The final client of the day had been an adult baby. The slave had dragged in an enormous cot and the bonnet-wearing baby had climbed contentedly into it and promptly wet his nappy. Sadie had changed into a flowery matronly dress and she chatted and cooed to the man in baby talk, changing his soiled nappy and dressing him in frilly girly dresses and bibs. At the end of the scene she had unbuttoned her dress and offered him her nipple. He had nestled in her arms, his eyes closed and one hand cupping her breast. It had looked so satisfying, complete and intimate that it was only after the slave had escorted the man out that Dan realised there had been no sexual contact at all.

'I hope you've got enough material.' Sadie closed the door behind the departing client.

'Plenty, thank you.'

'And what did you think?' Sadie smiled, her eyes full of mischief and curiosity.

'I can't even begin to answer that . . . some of it was frankly disgusting and some of it was unexpectedly erotic but all of it was fascinating . . .' Dan hesitated. 'Can I ask you a question?'

'Of course. After what you've seen today you can't possibly believe I have anything to hide.'

'No, you've been incredibly open. The last man . . . the adult baby. When you breastfed him it was – I don't know – utterly captivating. And I couldn't help wondering . . . are you actually lactating?'

Sadie smiled. She leaned in close and Dan could smell her perfume. 'Actually I'm not . . . though I rather sense that you'd prefer it if I was. I hope you're not disappointed.'

Dan laughed. 'I can see I've got a lot to learn. Can we have a chat in a minute? I've got a few questions.'

She nodded. 'Sure. Give me ten minutes and then come up to the kitchen. It's on the floor above us at the back of the house. I'll put the coffee on.'

'See you soon.' He watched Sadie walk away. He looked over at Dave and Dennis and saw that they were watching the day's filming on the portable monitor. They wouldn't miss him for a minute. He left the room and headed down the corridor to the toilet. He locked himself in a cubicle and unzipped his fly. He manhandled his cock, pulling it up over his boxers.

He wrapped his fist around it. It was already half hard, pumped with blood and tingling. His skin felt alive and sensitive. His crotch ached. He pumped his cock and it began to grow, thickening and lengthening until it felt as hard as rock in his hand. His helmet was purple and tight and glistening. He felt his scrotum contracting and thickening as his balls hugged his shaft.

Heat and excitement pumped through his veins. He was gasping and panting. Dan could feel his arse muscles contracting and hardening. His hand pumped rhythmically, slapping noisily against his body on the down-stroke.

He closed his eyes and imagined himself on his knees, naked in front of Sadie. He pictured her cold cruel eyes on him and the hint of a sneer on her beautiful lips. Perhaps she would extend her booted foot towards him, inviting him wordlessly to kiss and lick the gleaming leather.

He knew that he would eagerly comply, lavishing the leather with his wet tongue as hungrily and willingly as any one of her clients – even though he'd never so much as contemplated such a thing before today.

It made no sense, but he didn't care. It felt good. Her vicious heels, her imperious voice and her absolute expectation of obedience all somehow combined into a single image of perfect womanhood for Dan.

He wanked his cock frantically. He allowed himself to imagine what Sadie might look like beneath her rubber and leather. The cat suit had left nothing to the imagination. He knew she was slender but shapely and that her breasts were small and pointed. Her prominent nipples had been clearly obvious and he wondered if she liked them to be sucked and bitten like Sarah did. Or maybe she preferred them to be teased and coaxed with the tip of a finger.

Dan imagined kneeling at her feet and slowly peeling down her cat suit. He pictured himself pulling the clinging fabric down over her hips and thighs, revealing the flat plane of her belly and, a moment later, the dark V of her crotch, with its neat trimmed triangle of hair.

His cock was rigid. Shivers travelled up and down his spine. He imagined Sadie's beautiful disapproving face looking down at him as he handled his cock. Would she

97

sneer and look away or would he see interest, even arousal shining in her eyes? He pictured her parted lips, puffy and berry-dark as she watched him wank and her heaving chest, betraying her arousal.

His thighs were trembling. The air was filled with the sound of his urgent breathing and the rhythmic slapping of his hand. He screwed his eyes up tightly, focusing his attention inwards and imagined her hand sliding down the zip of her cat suit and dipping under the leather to finger the hot groove between her legs.

His heart was pounding. His crotch ached. He thrust his hips forwards and brought his hand down hard. He grunted and gasped. His cock throbbed in his hand. He arched his back. Relief and satisfaction flooded through him. Spunk splashed against the toilet door.

When he'd got his breath back he used toilet paper to clean himself then carefully wiped the evidence off the door. He put his cock away, let himself out of the toilet cubicle and washed his hands. He walked back down the corridor on unsteady legs and let himself into the dungeon.

As he closed the door behind him he was greeted by the sound of Dave and Dennis giving him a slow handclap. He looked from one to the other, mystified.

'What's up?'

'Sorry, Dan, but you've still got your radio mike on.' Dennis tapped the mixer. 'We heard everything.'

Seven

Dan joined in the laughter. He should have remembered about the mike but his urgent need to relieve his excitement had been the only thing on his mind. He told the crew to pack up and head home in the van.

He climbed the stairs and found Sadie sitting at the kitchen table. She'd taken off her mummy dress and was wearing a clinging long-sleeved black T-shirt and a long purple velvet skirt over a pair of black ankle boots. The dark outfit emphasised her slenderness and, Dan thought, gave her the look of a healthy vampire.

'Sit down and I'll pour you some coffee. How do you take it?'

'Black, no sugar. Thanks.' He sat down.

Sadie poured coffee into a mug from a gleaming chrome cafetière. She pushed a plate of chocolate brownies across the table.

'Chocolate is my major weakness. I simply can't resist it.' She selected an enormous slice of brownie and bit into it with a sigh.

'You don't strike me as the kind of woman who limits her indulgences.' Dan sipped his coffee.

'Appearances can be deceptive. I'm quite a health fiend, actually. I work out every day and I've been a vegan for years.'

'Well, I am surprised.' Dan nibbled at his brownie. 'What you do is so ... I don't know ... excessive. I'd have pegged you for a sybarite.'

She shrugged her shoulders. 'Maybe I am. Can't a sybarite care about her health? And you shouldn't make the mistake of believing that the way I am with my clients is the real me. It's just an act ... you, of all people, ought to understand that.'

'I do, of course. You're putting on a sort of performance for the clients. The real you is much more warm and human.'

Sadie laughed. 'I wouldn't be so sure. I'm pretty dominating in real life too. The only difference is that it's real, not a mask or a stereotype. But tell me, Dan ... what did you think of today? I know it turned you on – I happened to be in the dungeon when Dennis realised what you were up to so he turned up the volume and we all listened.'

Dan felt his face colour. 'You heard that?'

'Don't worry about it ... If it hadn't aroused you I'd think you were a eunuch.'

'Thanks. It's all very unsettling. I'd never have dreamed that kind of stuff would affect me.'

'Wait until you try it for yourself.'

'Yes ... To be honest I found it all fascinating. Some of those fetishes are truly bizarre and yet, because of you, I could see their power and appeal. Not that I think I'd want to try them for myself. Not all of them anyway.'

'But some you might?' Sadie sipped her coffee. Her dark eyes never left his face.

'Maybe. I guess I'll just have to put myself in your capable hands.'

'You can trust me. I promise.'

'I know that but I appreciate the reassurance.'

'Tell me, Dan ...' She offered him another brownie.

'What particularly turned you on today? There must have been moments that really pushed your buttons?'

'Of course. I was close to erection several times.' He met her gaze.

'Care to tell me when?'

He shook his head. 'After a couple of glasses of wine, maybe ... Tell me, the things you do to your clients, do they really turn you on?'

'Some of them turn me on more than others but fulfilling a client's fantasy – even if it doesn't happen to be one of my own – is always exciting.'

'So do you ever take the obvious next step?' He drained his cup.

'You mean do I ever fuck my clients? No. I'm not a prostitute. But, occasionally, a private relationship develops with a client that might lead to sex. Want a refill?' She pointed at his empty cup.

'Please. Like the slave, for example? Was he a client at one time?'

Sadie nodded. 'That's right. He doesn't pay me any more and he has certain privileges in return for helping me out during scenes.'

'And do those privileges include sex?'

Sadie raised an immaculate eyebrow. 'You want to know all my secrets yet you refuse to reciprocate. Don't you think that's a little ungentlemanly?'

'Meaning you want me to spill the beans about what turned me on?'

She nodded. 'I will if you will.'

Dan looked at her. Her hands were curled around her cup, her long red nails tapping the porcelain. She seemed down to earth and open and, somehow, reassuring.

Dan began to speak. He used every ounce of his will to meet her gaze. 'There were two things that really turned me on, but don't ask me why. The first was when your slave came in the tranny's face and then rubbed it in and the second was when you breastfed the adult baby.'

'I see. That's interesting. And do you think you can explain why?'

He took a long swallow of his coffee. 'Well, I think it must have been the degradation of the first one. It ruined her – or his – make-up. It was an act of defilement yet the fact that he so obviously desired it was a huge turn-on.'

'I think I can understand that. Don't you like it when a girlfriend lets you come on her face?'

'Of course. Because it makes me feel completely accepted and also it tells me that she's absolutely filthy and uninhibited and wants my spunk on her.'

'There you go then, not so strange.'

'Maybe . . . but the breastfeeding I can't explain so easily. Though, I suppose, it looked intimate and tender and I could see the absolute submission and regression of the baby.'

'Well, when you think about it, breastfeeding is the most intimate thing you ever do for anyone, perhaps more intimate than sex. It's a very powerful primal relationship of mutual need. You seemed quite disappointed when I told you I wasn't really feeding him.'

'Do you think that means I've got an Oedipus complex?'

She laughed. 'I've obviously given you a lot to think about, Dan.'

There was a knock at the door and they both turned to see the slave enter the kitchen.

'I've put away all the toys and cleaned the dungeon, mistress.'

'Thank you, slave. Now, if you don't mind, please remind me how many times you let me down today.'

The slave stood in the doorway, his hands clasped in

102

front of his crotch and his head cast down. 'Three times, mistress.' He didn't look up.

Sadie shook her head. 'Do you imagine I can't count? We both know it was two. And now I'm even more angry with you so I'm going to give you the ultimate punishment.' She turned back to the table and began to sip her coffee.

The slave began to shake his head as if in fear. 'Please, mistress. Anything but that.'

'You know the arrangement.' Sadie didn't even bother to look at him. 'I demand honesty at all times. If you attempt to elicit an extra punishment by inflating your number of offences just because you enjoy being whipped I have made it clear that I will punish you very severely. Wouldn't I be a fool, under the circumstances, to give you a punishment you'd enjoy?' She waved the back of her hand at him, as if in dismissal. 'Those are the rules. You live by them or you leave.'

'I'm sorry, mistress.' He looked at his feet.

'Now go home. And make sure you're not late in the morning.'

Dan watched as the slave turned and left the room.

'Did you forget to punish him? And what was he was so terrified of?'

Sadie laughed. 'I punished him, all right. Not getting punished is what he most fears. That causes him far more pain than any beating I could give him.'

Dan was in the back of a taxi on the way home when he realised that Sadie had never actually got round to telling him if she had sex with the slave. He began to laugh.

A week later Dan and the crew turned up at Sadie's dungeon to film his own session. Sadie answered the door wearing a simple black dress and no make-up.

As he followed her along the hall and down the stairs Dan felt a curious mixture of trepidation and excitement. She led him down to the changing room in the basement.

'I've laid out an outfit for you to wear. If you put it on, Slave will come and fetch you when we're ready for you.'

'I'll need my radio mike.'

She nodded. 'I'll let Dennis know. How are you feeling?' Sadie sat down on the bench.

'OK I think. Excited mostly.' He sat down beside her.

'That's good. I just wanted to remind you that I said I'll look after you and I mean it.'

'Thanks. I know I can trust you.'

'All right then. I'll go up and get changed now and I'll see you later in the dungeon.' Sadie left the room.

Dan looked down at the items Sadie had left out for him to wear. On top of the pile was a studded black leather collar. He picked it up and fitted it to his own neck. It felt tight and heavy, circling his throat like the span of a lover's fingers. He felt his heart quicken.

The next item on the pile was a body harness. If he hadn't seen one being worn on his previous visit to the dungeon he wouldn't have had a clue what it was or how to put it on. As it was, he had to spend several minutes holding it up and turning it around and around until he finally worked out where each of the straps was meant to go. As he unbuttoned his shirt he realised that his hands were trembling.

When he was naked he picked up the harness and began to put it on. All of the leather bands converged at a big silver ring which sat in the centre of his chest and a similar arrangement at the back which rested between his shoulder blades. There were two straps that passed over each shoulder and connected to the ring at the front with press-stud fastenings and a strap that circled his chest.

Hanging downwards from the central ring at the back

was a single long strap which was supposed to pass between his legs and up the front to connect to the chest ring. He bent forwards and reached between his legs, catching hold of the last strap.

As he pulled it forwards he realised that there was another ring, roughly level with his crotch. Dan stared at the silver ring. He could see that it was supposed to encircle his genitals, but he hadn't got the first clue how to get them through it. Then he remembered a film he'd made about a gay stripper who'd told him that the correct way to put on a cock ring was to slide your balls through first and then your dick. He'd seen the man execute the manoeuvre and it had looked simple enough, if a little eye-watering.

He held the back of the ring carefully against his perineum and pushed first one and then the other ball through it. He gasped as the icy metal made contact with his skin. So far, so good. There didn't seem much room left for his penis but he could see how it was supposed to work. He pulled down on his scrotum with one hand, anchoring everything inside the ring and maximising the space available to thread his cock through. He managed to lift the tip over the top of the ring and he tugged gently on his foreskin, pulling his cock fully through the ring.

Dan pulled up the last strap and fastened it to the chest ring. The leather harness creaked as he moved. The crotch straps pulled slightly on the cock ring making him acutely aware of his genitals. Maybe it was the air conditioning, but Dan felt goose pimples rising and his nipples growing erect.

He looked down at the last item on the bench. It was a studded leather jockstrap with a rigid codpiece like a cricket box. He put it on, passing the rear strap up between his buttocks before fastening the belt around his hips. He was looking around the changing room for a full-length mirror when the door opened and Dennis came in. When he saw Dan he did a double take.

'I've got to hand it to you, Dan, I couldn't do what you do for a million quid. I've come to fit your radio mike.' He held it up.

'I must admit, I think this is the weirdest thing I've ever done. And it's all in the name of art.'

'Art?' Dennis laughed. 'Well, you're certainly making an exhibition of yourself. But at least it's all done in the best possible taste. Turn round and I'll hook this onto your . . . belt or whatever you call it.'

After Dennis left, Dan sat down on the bench waiting to be summoned by the slave. Without his own clothes he felt vulnerable and unprotected. He hadn't realised how much of his on-screen confidence came from the wardrobe.

The cock ring pressed against his body as he sat. He could feel the tip of his cock brushing the interior of the leather codpiece.

The door opened and the slave stood in the doorway. He was dressed in red leather shorts and a matching harness. He pulled something out of his pocket and Dan instantly realised that it was a dog lead. His stomach flipped like a fish at the end of a hook.

The slave clipped the lead to a D-ring on Dan's collar and tugged on it sharply, indicating that he should get to his feet, then began to pull the lead downwards, making the collar dig into the back of Dan's neck. Alarmed, Dan looked into his face. The slaved flicked his eyes downwards to the floor and Dan understood that he was to get onto his knees.

He got down on all fours and the slave turned and began to walk away. Dan followed, shuffling on his hands and knees like a dog. The flagstones were cold and hard against his knees and he made slow progress. He felt apprehensive and humiliated before he'd even reached the dungeon. The slave opened the heavy wooden door and led him into the room at the end of his lead.

Dan was instantly struck by the brightness of the camera lights in the room after the relative gloom of the corridor. Using his peripheral vision he was able to see Dave and Dennis standing by the curtains, the camera already rolling. Mercifully he was spared the embarrassment of seeing the expressions on their faces.

He followed behind the slave as he led the way over to Sadie's chair. By the time they'd reached it he was breathless and sweaty and his knees were killing him. He could feel his face burning and his crotch ached.

The slave handed the loop of the lead to Sadie. As she took it Dan could see that she had long leather sleeves which dipped over the back of each hand in a V and fastened to her middle finger with a loop. He took in her long scarlet fingernails and the smooth white skin of her hands. He daren't look up to see the rest of her outfit but he could see high-heeled black boots which laced up the front. Dan's heart was thumping.

Sadie extended one leg, lifted her foot and placed it directly under Dan's nose. 'Kiss my foot.' Sadie's voice was clear and imperious. Dan leaned forwards and pressed his lips to the top of her boot. He could smell the leather and a hint of something grittier and unpleasant. She pushed him away with her foot, forcing him back on his heels.

It wasn't a violent movement, yet the force behind it took his breath away and shocked him to his core. 'The sole . . . a worthless trainee slave like you is only worthy to kiss the sole of my boot.'

He leaned forwards and rubbed his lips against the dirty leather, kissing it as tenderly and eagerly as he might a pair of cherished lips. The leather felt rough and dirty against his skin. He could feel his cheeks burning.

Sadie withdrew her foot. She stood up and tugged on Dan's lead, forcing him to look up at her. As her outfit came into view he inhaled sharply and his cock tingled inside the codpiece. The boots reached her thighs, clinging to her shapely legs and making them seem impossibly long. She was wearing a long black leather skirt which hung to her ankles and was split at the front to the waist. A froth of black lace was visible at her crotch. Above the waist she was wearing a kind of corseted bodice which thrust her breasts upwards and outwards. Over it all was a floor-length cloak with a high collar which stood up dramatically behind her head.

'You look magnificent . . . mistress.' Dan had spoken without thinking. He wasn't sure he was even allowed to speak but he hoped that giving Sadie her correct title might make her overlook the transgression.

'I don't recall giving you permission to speak, but thank you. Follow me.' She turned and walked away and Dan followed, on all fours, at the end of his taut lead. Unable to focus on anything other than the floor in front of him, it wasn't until they'd almost reached it that he realised she was taking him over to the medical chair.

An instant rush of heat crashed over him. 'Can I change my mind now?' He looked over his shoulder at the camera and put on a mock-terrified face.

He felt Sadie's warm hand on his shoulder. 'It's far too late for that, I'm afraid. Now climb aboard and we'll have some fun.' She patted the chair.

'Fun for you maybe . . .' Dan got to his feet. He sat down in the chair. 'Christ, it's freezing . . . it's torture.' He wriggled and mugged for the camera.

'Stop making a fuss and sit still.' Sadie began to fasten the wrist restraints.

The sheepskin-lined cuffs felt soft and itchy. She buckled them tightly. Sadie operated a lever tipping the chair back, then lifted each of Dan's legs into the stirrups. She fastened the ankle cuffs. When all four of the restraints were fastened Dan struggled and wriggled, making the leather creak.

'I'm absolutely helpless now.' He looked up at Sadie's face. 'You will be gentle with me, won't you, mistress?'

Sadie picked up an item from the trolley beside the chair. She held it up for him to see. It was a leather blindfold, lined with the same white sheepskin as the chair restraints. She pressed it up against his eyes and buckled it behind his head.

'Can you see how many fingers I'm holding up?' Sadie asked.

'No. Can you see how many I'm holding up?' Dan made a fist with his right hand and extended his middle finger towards the ceiling.

'If you continue to misbehave you'll make me angry.' Sadie had put her mouth right beside his ear. He could feel her hot breath on his skin. 'And you really won't like me when I'm angry.'

'Oooh, now I'm really scared. Do you go all green and huge like the Incredible Hulk?' He wriggled against his bonds.

'If you don't behave I'll have to gag you.' She caught his face in her hands. Her tone of voice left him in no doubt that she was genuinely annoyed and that she knew he was playing up for the cameras.

'Sorry, mistress, I'll be a good boy, I promise.'

'I'm glad to hear it.'

Dan heard her move around the chair and stand between his legs. She reached forwards and ran the tips of her nails slowly down the front of his body. He shivered. She began to rake her nails down his sides, each pass a little harder than the first.

Soon Dan was wriggling and thrashing his head. 'It burns ... it tickles ... it's terrible. Stop, please stop.'

Deprived of his vision, every sensation seemed magnified and intense. He could feel the cool air against his body. He could feel the smooth leather of the chair against his back. He was conscious of Sadie's breathing and could hear Dave and Dennis moving quietly around the room.

Sadie began to scratch his legs. She ran her talons along the length of his inner thighs, digging them in deep. His body jolted. He clenched his fists. His skin was on fire. The sensation was unbearable, a mixture of heat and itchy tickling that was impossible to ignore.

She began to tease his belly with her nails, circling his navel and running them along the top of his codpiece. Dan felt his cock responding. His skin instantly rose into goose pimples.

Her hands slid up his torso and she began to circle his nipples with her nails. Dan pictured the gleaming red tips moving across his chest. She used the point of one nail to flick across the tip of his nipple. He gasped. She increased the pressure, scratching the tip of his nipple harder and harder until he began to wince and bite his lip.

Sadie began to tease both nipples at once. They prickled and throbbed with pleasure and pain and every sensation seemed to be directly transmitted to his tingling cock.

'That really hurts.' His voice was a strangled whisper.

'But does it feel good too?'

'It does, strangely enough. Do you think that means I'm a pervert?'

'No . . .' Sadie shook her head. 'You've got a long way to go yet.'

Without warning she gripped each of his nipples between thumb and forefinger and began to squeeze. She gradually increased the pressure. Dan imagined her eyes shining with passion and excitement. The pain was

110

intense and pure and overwhelming. He felt heat and exhilaration crashing over him.

'That's incredibly painful . . .'

She squeezed harder. Dan wondered if she had begun to smile as she watched him squirm in pain, her gaze never wavering.

'You're a vicious bitch and I don't think I like you any more.' Dan spoke through his clenched teeth. She gave his nipples a final squeeze and released them. She laughed.

Dan heard Sadie lean over and pick up something from the trolley. She put it into his hand and he fingered it, trying to identify it.

'What's that? Is it a clothes peg? I'm not sure I like the thought of that. I didn't realise you were planning to do your laundry.'

Sadie took the peg. 'It's a simple object, really. Nevertheless it can deliver quite a sting. You can use them anywhere. Nipples . . .' She brushed the tip of the peg across his sore nipple, making him gasp. 'Testicles . . .' Dan's eyes widened beneath his blindfold. 'But I find it's more fun if you're inventive.' He heard her pick up something else from the tray.

She was standing between his parted thighs. He felt her pinching up a section of skin on the inside of his thigh with her fingertips then a strong pinching grip as Sadie attached the peg to it.

He grunted as it bit into his flesh. It was tight rather than painful, but distinctly strange and not a little alarming. He heard Sadie pick up another peg. She pinched the skin directly beside the first and attached the second peg. She repeated the procedure over and over. The sensation intensified with each new peg as the skin was stretched tighter and tighter and the pressure grew more painful. He was trembling and shaking. Sweat was pouring down his body.

Dan counted each peg, gasping in pain as they bit into his flesh. When she stopped he had ten pegs stuck to the skin of his inner thigh. Sadie ran her fingertips across the ends of the pegs rippling and jiggling them and moving the biting ends that gripped his stretched skin. He grunted.

He felt a rapid burning pain as all the pegs were ripped away from his body in a single sudden movement. 'Ouch, ouch, ouch. You're so mean. What was that?' Dan lifted his head up off the chair.

'It's called a peg zipper. I fixed the pegs over a length of ribbon and then tugged on the ribbon so that they all ripped off at once. It's supposed to feel intense.'

'You can say that again. Oww ...' Dan gasped as feeling began to flood back into the spots where the pegs had been.

Sadie bent down and gently kissed each of the peg marks in turn. He felt her silky hair trailing along his inner thigh. He felt her hot breath and her warm lips. Inside his codpiece his cock twitched.

She straightened up and unbuckled his ankle restraints. She walked round the chair and undid his wrist cuffs and then took off his blindfold. Dan opened his eyes slowly, blinking in the bright light.

'Now stand up please ... but slowly, because you might feel light-headed.' She pulled the lever, raising the chair to the upright position. Dan got to his feet and Sadie picked up the dangling end of his lead.

She led him over towards the whipping bench. She fastened the end of his lead to a hook on the bench and walked over to the door. Her stiletto heels clacked noisily against the stone floor. Dan watched her backside undulating as she crossed the room. Her back was ramrod straight and her carriage was regal and imperious. Dan felt a little flutter of excitement under his ribs and his heart quickened

She opened the door. 'Slave ... bring in our other guest now, please.' She held the door open and Dan saw the slave lead someone out of the changing room by a lead. Like him, they were moving slowly on hands and knees so it took Dan a few moments to realise that the client was a woman. He could see long blonde hair pulled back in two plaited pigtails, a white shirt and striped tie and a short grey pinafore-type garment which he worked out must be a gymslip.

The slave led her into the room. As Dan watched her slowly moving across the stone floor he realised that she had an enormous chest and that her shirt was unbuttoned down to her cleavage, the tie had been pulled down and loosened so that its knot rested directly between her magnificent breasts. She looked up at him and smiled. When they had reached the bench Sadie walked over and took the handle of the lead from the slave.

'Mount the bench, please.' Sadie patted the leather top of the whipping bench.

The girl stood up. She spent a second rubbing her reddened knees. She stepped up to the bench and knelt down on the lower platform then leaned her body along the bench's length.

The slave moved around fastening the sheepskin-lined restraints. There were straps for each ankle and wrist and similar restraints for the back of the knee and each thigh. He fastened a strap around the girl's upper arm and then laid a broad foot-wide band of leather across the small of her back and buckled it up. Dan assumed it was designed to protect the kidneys from damage, as well as anchoring the victim firmly to the bench.

Dan could see that the girl's cheeks and lips had grown dark and her breathing had grown noisy. She clenched and unclenched her fists and he realised that, apart from lifting her head, it was the only movement she was now capable of.

Sadie walked slowly over to the side of the room. The sound of her heels seemed to echo ominously. Dan noticed that the girl had turned her head and was following Sadie with her eyes.

Sadie chose a long vicious-looking cane and she walked back over to the bench with it. Dan saw that she was holding the cane across her body, between her two hands and she flexed it from time to time, bending it into an arc.

He hardly dared to breathe. He could hear the girl panting and the leather creaking as she resisted her bonds. Dan was already half hard.

'Would you be kind enough to lift up her skirt for me?' Sadie flicked the bottom of the girl's skirt with the tip of her cane.

Dan stepped forwards and, with trembling fingers, lifted up the skirt of the girl's gymslip. He folded it up over her back and smoothed it down neatly. Underneath she was wearing big navy-blue school knickers. He looked up at Sadie.

'Now I'd like you to pull her knickers down to her knees. She's got to be punished and we need to be able to see the target.'

The moment she had made the request Dan felt his cock responding. He leaned forwards and hooked his fingers under the top of the girl's knickers and pulled them down. The girl pressed down with her knees and raised up her hips slightly so that he could slide them down over her bottom and thighs.

Her arse was round and creamily perfect and, as he pulled her knickers all the way down, he caught a glimpse of her swollen shaved pussy.

'Oh no . . . I think I'm getting an erection!' He turned to the camera. 'I can just see the headlines. BAFTA-winning presenter gets a stiffy on national television.'

Dan played the rest of the session for laughs. He

covered his eyes in mock fear and alarm when Sadie delivered a vicious caning to the restrained girl. He could clearly see that, for her part, the girl was enjoying every moment of it. She grunted and sighed each time the crop made contact and he could see her hips rocking back and forth as she brought up her buttocks to meet the crop.

He watched the whole scene with a throbbing erection concealed behind his codpiece. The cock ring pressed pleasurably against his perineum and squeezed his scrotum as he became aroused.

When Sadie had finished caning the girl she ordered the slave to release her and take her over to the medical chair. Dan watched as Sadie walked back over to the equipment racks and hung up the cane. She selected a thin riding crop with a narrow loop of leather at its tip and walked back over to the bench. It wasn't until she tapped the bench's broad leather back with her crop that Dan realised she intended to use it on him.

He swallowed melodramatically and did a double take for the camera. 'I hope you're not going to leave marks on me, only I play football every Sunday and it'll be really difficult to explain a striped arse to the other lads.'

'I'm sure you'll think of something . . .' Sadie slapped the bench with the shaft of the crop and it landed with a loud crack.

Dan turned to the camera and pretended to bite his nails. He climbed up onto the bench.

The leather was cold and clammy against his skin. The slave began to fasten the restraints. As Dan felt the cuffs being buckled up, his sense of helplessness and excitement grew.

Dan struggled against his bonds, but he was powerless. The leather creaked and the straps dug into his flesh but he could barely move. He hung his head and waited. He could smell the leather and the sharp tang of his own sweat.

He had no idea where Sadie was and he daren't lift his head to look. He heard her heels clacking against the floor and he worked out that she was walking around the bottom of the bench behind him. She took up position on his left side.

Dan held his breath and closed his eyes. He waited for the sound of the crop swishing through the air and the moment of pain that would follow. He could feel the tip of his cock rubbing against the rough leather inside his codpiece. He heard Dave and Dennis's trainered feet moving softly across the floor. He imagined the camera focusing in on his soon-to-be striped behind.

He lifted up his head and looked over his shoulder. 'Does my bum look big in this?' Out of the corner of his eye he saw Sadie's arm rising into the air. He heard the crop swishing through the air and he gasped and his body juddered as it landed across both buttocks. It stung and burned, a moment of agony that quickly dissolved into something he could only describe as pleasure. He lowered his head.

The crop swished and slashed across his behind. He felt the sharp throb of pain and, a moment later, a hot flash of excitement and contentment crashed over him. He imagined dark red weals forming on his skin and the camera focusing in on every shameful detail.

His cock was rigid and throbbing. Sadie gave him three strokes in quick succession. His body jolted forwards and the front of his thighs banged against the bench. The impact moved his erection inside the codpiece, making it tingle.

Sweat poured down his face and into his eyes. Sadie whipped him over and over again. His body juddered and shook. His arse was burning, tingling, throbbing.

He lost count of the strokes but he could hear Sadie panting from the effort and grunting from exertion. The leather beneath him was slick with sweat and he was itchy and uncomfortable beneath the sheepskin-lined restraints. He heard the crop clatter to the floor and Sadie bent down beside his head. She pushed his wet hair off his face and wiped the sweat off his brow with her fingers. She leaned forwards and laid her forehead against his.

The sound of her panting throbbed in his ears and he could feel her hot breath on his face.

'Well . . . we're not making wisecracks now, are we?'

When Dan had showered and changed Sadie took him up to the kitchen for coffee and brownies. She poured a slug of brandy into his first cup and he gulped it down. She watched him drink, an expression in her eyes that he couldn't read. She sipped her own coffee and nibbled at a brownie silently, never taking her eyes off him.

He drained his cup and slid it silently across the table for a refill.

'Do you want brandy in it this time?'

'No thanks.' He watched her pouring the coffee. She refilled her own cup and put the pot down. 'You've been staring at me . . .'

'And now you're staring at me.' She set his cup down in front of him.

'Trying to work out what you were thinking.'

'Did it occur to you to ask?' She smiled.

'OK. So what were you thinking?' Dan picked up his coffee and blew on it.

'What a complex man you are . . . and what a showman.'

'Thank you – I think.'

'Oh, it's a compliment I assure you. I live half my life behind a mask. I can hardly blame you for retreating

117

behind yours.' She sipped her coffee. 'But you do realise you won't be able to play it for laughs when it's just you and me? Then, it will have to be real.'

Dan nodded. 'Yes. I promise. I'll be myself, no mask, no pretence. Just you, me and the chains.'

'Do you know, Dan, that millions of people indulge in kink every day without the need to even give it a name. They come from every walk of life, classes, races and backgrounds. Everybody's doing it, have done for centuries. Don't make the mistake that whips and chains are what makes a person kinky.'

'I'm not sure what you mean.' Dan selected a brownie.

'How many relationships do you know where there's a real power dynamic? One person has it and the other hasn't and that's the way they both like it yet neither of them has ever heard of domination or submission and has no desire to be addressed as master.'

'I think I understand. One of my women friends recently got married to a much younger man. He'd been in the army and he seems to really like being told what to do and, fortunately, she's always been bossy. I thought it odd at first, yet it seems to work for them.'

'That's it exactly.' Sadie opened a drawer and took out a novel. She laid it on the table in front of him. 'I'd like to give you this.'

He picked it up. 'What's this? *Discipline* by Rosalind Quirt. Great cover – that woman could be you.' He held it up for her to see.

'Wash your mouth out, she's got a much bigger behind than me.' She closed the drawer. 'You should enjoy it and, you never know, it might give you some insight. And, incidentally, I happen to know that you've met Rosalind . . .'

Dan frowned. 'I can't think of anyone with that name.'

'It's a nom de plume – a quirt is a type of whip. But I promise you have met her.'

'It's not you is it? Or Madame Cyn?'

'I'm not telling. You'll have to work it out for yourself.'

Eight

Jo parked her car beside Sam's at the rear of the showroom. She'd come to discuss her costume for the Torture Garden Summer Ball. It was one of the biggest fetish events of the year and Jo always liked to wear something spectacular.

She got her things together and went in through the back door. Sam was in her office, bent over the drawing board. She looked up and smiled.

'Hello, darling. Is it that time already? I'm working on the new collection, I must have got carried away.'

'I'm late actually. It's nearly lunchtime so I bought us cakes from the Hampstead Tea Rooms.'

'Great. I'll put some fresh coffee on.' She got up. 'Why don't you pop along to the shop for a minute? There's a friend of yours there.'

'Who?'

'Go and find out . . .' Sam left the room.

Jo went out into the corridor, walked towards the front of the building and let herself into the shop. She could see Victor standing by the window with two customers.

'Hi, Victor. Sam says there's someone I know in here.'

Before Victor had a chance to respond, the female customer turned to face her.

'Do you think she means us, Jo?'

'Jade. Sorry, I didn't recognise you. And Peter . . . hi. How are you both?'

'We're fine thanks.' Peter was wearing a pair of leather trousers and a tight T-shirt with a series of parallel slashes across the chest. On his feet were heavy thick-soled knee-high boots which buckled up the side. His black hair reached to his waist. Jo glanced over at Jade. She was dressed identically except that she was wearing a skirt. Both of them wore heavy black eyeliner.

Jade picked up a purple rubber miniskirt. 'Isn't that just divine? We've come to choose some new outfits. We've brought Dan Elliot along.' Jade pointed at the changing room. 'He's making a film about our group.'

'Ahh . . . that must be who Sam was talking about. I'll go and say hi. Excuse me.' Jo walked over to the curtained-off changing room. She hesitated. She peeked over the top of the cubicle and saw Dan trying to pull up the top of a clinging rubber all-in-one outfit. The legs finished at mid-thigh level, like cycling shorts, and the top was scooped low in the front, scarcely covering his nipples. The sleeves went all the way down to his wrists and Dan was struggling to get the arms pulled up and over his shoulders.

'Do you need a hand?'

Dan turned, startled. 'Oh, it's you. What on earth are you doing here?'

'Sam Baillie is my best friend. Didn't you know?'

'I didn't realise.' He looked down at his outfit. 'I'm supposed to be finding something to wear to the Torture Garden. For my film.'

'I see.' Jo kept her face deliberately neutral.

Dan pulled at his outfit. 'This is like trying to struggle into a giant condom.'

'Let me help.' She pulled aside the curtain and stepped into the cubicle, closing it behind her. 'It's not that difficult really, but sometimes it's useful to have a

121

third hand. It helps if you put talcum powder on first, so there's less friction.' She used both hands to pull up the sleeves.

'But you'd get powder all over the outfit, surely?' Dan stood still and allowed himself to be dressed.

'Yes. You have to polish it afterwards. They sell special spray. It's called Pervoshine – and I promise you I'm not making that up. There. You're finished. It looks . . .' She began to laugh.

'It's not me, is it?' He looked at his reflection in the mirror.

'Not really. I think it's because you're so tall and slender. It makes you look a bit like a dildo. And that's not a good look.'

He sighed in disappointment. 'I'm overheated and exhausted. I've been squeezing myself into these ridiculous outfits for hours.' He began to peel down the rubber.

'You need the help of an expert.'

'That's why I came here with Jade and Peter.' He lowered his voice. 'The trouble is that the two of them look good in anything. When I first met them they were naked except for matching corsets and they both looked fantastic. But they seem to have no idea what will suit me.' Dan had managed to extricate his arms from the costume and began pushing it down over his torso.

'I was talking about Victor – he's Sam's assistant and a really good designer in his own right. He'll sort you out. You finish taking that off and I'll go and get him.'

'Thanks.' He frowned. 'You seem to know an awful lot about this fetish stuff. I'm beginning to wonder if you might be kinky.'

'Are you? That's interesting. Let me get Victor.' She pulled back the curtain a slit and carefully let herself out of the cubicle.

Jade and Peter were looking at a rack of uniforms with Victor.

'When you've got a minute, Victor, could you give Dan a hand? I think he needs a bit of guidance.'

'Sure. These two can take care of themselves.' He turned to Jade and Peter. 'Excuse me, but I'm needed elsewhere.' He walked across the shop. He gripped the edge of the curtain. 'Are you decent? Because I'm coming in, ready or not.' He ripped the curtain aside.

Dan was sitting on the bench beside his discarded street clothes. At first Jo thought he was naked but she realised he was wearing a tiny thong. He noticed that she was looking at him and he shrugged.

'When in Rome . . .' He turned to Victor. 'I'm putting myself totally in your hands.'

'And it's not even my birthday.' He looked Dan up and down. 'The first thing we need to do is measure you. We need to find you something that makes an asset of your figure. Off you go, Jo. I can handle this.'

'Thanks. Sam's probably waiting for me anyway.'

Victor swished the curtain closed.

'I'll come back and see you later Dan,' she called.

After lunch Sam showed Jo the sketches she'd made for her costume. There were half a dozen designs, all broadly following a forties theme, as Jo had requested. They were all fantastic but she'd managed to narrow it down to two.

The first was a rubber version of a military uniform with epaulettes and flapped pockets and a belted jacket. Sam had given the figure in the drawing a swept-up forties hairdo.

The second echoed the New Look; the post-war reaction to the austerity of the war years. Sam had designed a long skirt supported by dozens of petticoats and a fitted jacket with shoulder pads. Underneath there was a waist-nipping corset to give the right silhouette and there was a small hat to finish off the outfit. It was designed to be made out of supple calf leather and the overall effect combined retro elegance with extreme fetish.

'They're both gorgeous. I can't make up my mind. What do you think?' Jo pored over the drawings.

'Well, I think you'd look gorgeous in either but, if I were choosing, I'd opt for the more practical option. The uniform's rubber and you'll get pretty sweaty and uncomfortable in that after a couple of hours in a hot nightclub. The other one's leather and you can wear something cotton under the jacket. It'll be cooler and more comfortable and you'll still look absolutely fantastic.'

'Yes, you're right. OK then. I'll go for the New Look outfit. Now all we have to decide is the colour. Black's always good.'

'True, but I was thinking of something more eye-catching. Half the people there will be in black. How about –' Sam got up and rummaged through a pile of fabric samples before handing Jo a swatch of bright-red leather '– this.'

'It's wonderful. So soft and fluid. And the colour . . . I think I have a lipstick in exactly this shade.' She handled the square of leather.

'And it will really suit your pale colouring. We should be ready for a first fitting in a month or so.'

'Thanks, Sam. I'm really looking forward to it. You spoil me.'

Sam waved the compliment away with the back of her hand. 'You're welcome, but I'm going to have to chuck you out I'm afraid. I've got a buyer coming in half an hour and I need to prepare.'

'No problem. I've got to get going anyway but I promised to go back and see how Dan's getting on first.'

Sam raised an eyebrow. 'You seem very interested in Dan . . .'

'Do I? Well, he's an interesting man.'

'So it appears. Are you going to do his film?'

'I haven't decided but I'm definitely coming round to the idea.'

Back in the shop Jade and Peter were strutting around in front of the mirrors, modelling matching rubber nun's habits. Dan was standing beside the counter with Victor looking down at something spread out on the surface.

'Hi. Did you sort something out?' She walked over to the counter.

Dan looked up and smiled. 'Yes, thanks. Victor's been great. Come and have a look.'

Jo looked down at the drawing. The figure Victor had sketched bore an impressive resemblance to Dan even though the face had no features. He seemed to have captured his body shape and stance perfectly. The figure was wearing a tight pair of shorts, military boots and a garment on the upper body that looked like a combination of a body harness and a gladiator's breastplate.

'It's great. I told you Victor was a genius.'

'And you were absolutely right. He's been fantastic and he hasn't touched me up once.' He winked at Victor.

'As if . . . but you should consider yourself lucky I didn't have to measure your inside leg. Now, if you'll excuse me I should see how the terrible twins are getting on.' He walked away.

'Thanks a lot for helping me out.' Dan smiled and Jo felt her crotch soften and her nipples peak.

'You're welcome. How's the filming going?'

'Great, it's been a real eye-opener. The other day I had a session with a pro domme.'

'Really? What was it like?'

'Do you know, I don't think I have the words to describe it. It was . . . fascinating, exciting, terrifying, surprising.'

125

Jo scanned Dan's face as he spoke. His eyes were shining and there were dark spots of colour on each cheek. 'And did you enjoy it?'

Dan frowned. He seemed to be considering his answer. 'I think I did. Some of it was incredible. But, if I'm honest, it scared me – I mean I liked it so much that it scared me – so I played up for the cameras as a way of maintaining control and I rather wish I hadn't.'

Dan stroked his chin with a fingertip as he spoke and she noticed that he had a tiny depression, a hint of a dimple, in the centre of his chin. A tingly flush of excitement crept up her throat and over her face.

'Interesting. You could try it again maybe, and this time just allow yourself to surrender to it. You never know, you might like it.' She met his gaze.

'Actually, I'm going to. Sadie made me promise to have a private session with her. It was a condition of the filming.'

'No cameras? Just the two of you?'

Dan nodded. His mouth was on the edge of a smile and his eyes stared into hers. 'Do you think I'm crazy?'

'No. I think you're rather brave, actually. And an extremely interesting man.'

Dan feigned shock, holding onto the edge of the counter and fanning his face as if he was about to faint.

Jo laughed. 'Are you free tomorrow night, Dan?'

'Yes, I am.'

'How would you like to come to dinner? Nothing fancy, but it'll be home cooked.'

'I'd love to. Thanks. What time?'

'Shall we say 8 p.m.? If you give me a call when you get onto the school grounds I'll come down and meet you at the front door.'

'OK, thanks. I'll look forward to it.' Dan picked up a novel from the counter.

'What are you reading?' Jo took the book.

126

'Oh, it's something Sadie gave me. She thought it might be educational and she also said that I'd met the author.'

Jo laughed. 'Yes, you have. As a matter of fact, you're talking to her.' She handed it back.

'You're Rosalind Quirt?'

She nodded. 'But obviously it's a side of myself I keep strictly separate from my work, and I'll be grateful if you'd do the same.'

'Of course. It goes without saying.' Dan lowered his voice and leaned in close. 'You've just got to be kinky . . . Everyone I meet seems to know you, I bump into you in here and now I find out you write erotica . . . come on . . . I won't tell.'

'Writing about something doesn't necessarily mean you do it.' She smiled. 'Do you think PD James actually kills people or that Anne Rice is a vampire?'

'But the other things . . . you've got to admit they're big clues.'

Jo shrugged. 'Maybe, maybe not . . .'

'You're not going to tell me, are you?'

She slowly shook her head.

Jo stood in the doorway watching Dan's car snake its way along the drive. It was a beautiful evening. The sun glistened on the surface of the lake and the rolling parkland looked lush and green.

She was wearing a simple cotton dress covered in tiny printed flowers and a pair of high strappy sandals. She'd dressed for the weather though, as she'd stood in her bedroom in her underwear trying to decide what to put on, she'd realised that she was as keen to impress him as a teenager on a first date.

As Dan's car neared the school she was surprised to realise that it was an ordinary compact car like a Corsa or a Fiesta. She would have expected something more ostentatious or sporty. But, when she thought about it, Dan had already proved himself to be a man capable of surprising her.

Jo could hear the wheels of Dan's car crunching over the gravel now. The sun glinted on the windscreen. He spotted her and raised a hand in greeting and she thought she saw him smile. She waved back.

He stopped in front of the entrance and Jo walked down the steps to meet him. Dan climbed out of the car and walked towards her, smiling.

'Good evening. You're so lucky to live here. It's like your own stately home, isn't it?'

'Yes it's great. I love it when the kids are on holiday and I have the place all to myself.' She stopped in front of Dan and he laid a hand on each of her upper arms and bent his head to kiss her gently on both cheeks. He smelled of shaving soap, fresh and clean. Jo felt a slow wave of shivers creep up her neck and over her scalp.

'You must feel like a queen, living here alone.'

She laughed. 'Well, not entirely alone. A few of the staff live here all year round but most of them go on holiday during vacation, so at the moment it's just me and my second in command, Costas. But come up and see the flat. I have a fantastic view.' She led him into the house.

Upstairs Jo took him on a quick tour of the flat, showing him the view from the various rooms. Finally she led him into the living room.

'You were right about the view. The lake looks like something out of a fairytale. The kind of place you might meet a frog who's really a prince.' He smiled at her.

'Well, there are plenty of frogs – I swim in the lake every morning during the summer – but I've never been tempted to kiss any of them.'

'Now that I would like to see . . . you in a skimpy

costume slipping through the water like a mermaid.' His eyes were shining.

Jo slowly shook her head. 'No costume, I'm afraid.'

Dan's eyes widened. 'In that case I think I'll get up early tomorrow and sneak into the grounds with a pair of binoculars.'

Jo laughed. 'I hope you're hungry. The food's nearly ready, we're having lemon linguine. I'll put the pasta on and pour us both a drink while we're waiting.' She went into the kitchen. As she dropped the dried pasta into the boiling water she realised that Dan had followed her. She smiled.

'Is there anything I can do? I'm quite domesticated.'

'You could open the champagne. You'll find it in the fridge.' She stirred the pasta.

Dan found the champagne. He looked at the label and whistled. 'Are we celebrating something? Or do you drink vintage champagne every day?'

'Not every day, but I love it and I'm far too greedy to save it for special occasions. And, anyway, this is an occasion . . . you're here.'

'I'm flattered.' Dan smiled. 'Where are the glasses?'

'In that cupboard behind you. I'll get them . . .' She set the kitchen timer. 'We've got ten minutes, let's go through to the other room.'

Back in the living room Jo watched as Dan removed the foil and wire from the bottle and expertly eased the cork out. He poured the champagne and handed her a glass. He sat down beside her and picked up his own glass

'To your good health.' He clinked her glass with his own.

'To pleasure.' She took a sip. The champagne was cold and crisp.

'That's an interesting toast.' Dan put down his glass and leaned back against the sofa cushions.

'You've got no objection to pleasure, surely?' She set her glass down on the coffee table.

'Not at all. I'm a hundred and ten per cent in favour of it. It just seems rather ... I don't know ... out of keeping with the image of a respectable headmistress.' He took off his spectacles and polished the lenses on the bottom of his shirt. It was a simple gesture but Jo knew he was deliberately avoiding her eyes.

'Do I look like a stereotype to you? A wizened old maiden lady with a bun and a squint and no idea what makes young people tick?'

Dan shook his head. He'd finished cleaning his glasses but he sat with them in his lap. 'No, far from it. From the moment I first met you it was obvious that you're utterly unique.'

'Thank you. But you think me too hedonistic for a headmistress? Is that what you're saying?'

Dan put his glasses back on. He looked at her for a long moment. Finally he spoke. 'I suppose I'm just saying that you constantly surprise me. For a start, you've got to admit there's a bit of a conflict between the job you do and the way you look.'

'How do I look?' She leaned forwards and picked up her glass.

Dan ran his hand through his hair. 'I seem to have dug a bit of a hole for myself. Perhaps I should stop before it gets any deeper.'

'No. It's all right. Go on. I'm interested.' She sipped her champagne.

'Well ... do you know who you remind me of? Only you're blonde of course, so the comparison's not quite perfect ... you look like a kind of cross between Nigella Lawson and Dita Von Teese, sultry, slightly bossy and a wardrobe out of the 1940s.'

'Actually, you're the second person to say I remind them of Dita Von Teese.'

'So it's not just my fevered imagination then.' He smiled.

'Apparently not and it's a very flattering comparison. Thanks.' Jo ran her fingertip around the top of her glass. She could feel heat in her cheeks and she knew they'd be stained with red. 'And I surprise you in other ways, too?'

'Yes.' Dan picked up his glass but he didn't drink. Jo was certain it was a delaying tactic. 'You know I'm working with Hellfire 2000 at the moment and every single one of them seems to know you. Then I find out you're Rosalind Quirt.' He stroked the condensation away from the outside of his glass with a fingertip, deliberately avoiding her gaze.

'And you think this all means that I must be kinky?'

He nodded. 'Well, are you?'

The timer pinged in the kitchen and Jo put down her glass. She stood up. 'It looks like I'll have to answer that later. If you'd like to take our glasses and the bottle into the dining room I'll be through in a second with the food.' She went into the kitchen.

After the meal they drank their coffee in the living room. Jo had taken off her shoes and she sat at one end of the sofa with her legs curled under her. Dan sat at the other, one arm along the back of the cushions and his long legs crossed. He looked boyish and handsome and relaxed.

Dan swirled the brandy in his glass. 'I suppose, when you think about it, writing novels is a bit like what I do. You hide behind your characters, but you also reveal aspects of your true self by giving your own attributes to them.'

'And you hide behind the version of Dan you've created for your films. I suppose I can see the parallels.'

'Yes, but it's a bit more than that, I think. The on-screen Dan is a mask, yes, but he's also, in a way, a shield. Something to hide behind and keep me safe when I reveal my true self, my true feelings. Isn't writing something like that?'

Jo took a long swallow of her brandy. She felt the hot liquid sliding down her throat, warming and relaxing her. 'Yes, I suppose you're right. It's a safe way of sharing myself with the world because, by the time anyone reads it, I've made a clean getaway.'

'And, as you write under a pen name, no one knows it's you anyway.'

'Well, a few people do, obviously. You among them, now.'

'And, I promise, it's a secret I intend to keep.'

'Thanks.' She watched Dan sipping his drink. She noticed his Adam's apple bob and his eyes narrow as he swallowed. Under her clothes, her nipples tingled. She looked away. 'Tell me, Dan. Were you involved in kink before you started the film?'

'No, not at all. Never even fantasised about it. No – I tell a lie . . . When I was a teenager I used to have a recurring dream about Margaret Thatcher. She was always dressed in an academic gown, like the masters at my public school wore, and she used to make me pull my trousers down and masturbate while she made derogatory comments.'

Jo noticed that Dan was blushing. She laughed. 'Interesting.'

'I have no idea what it says about me though.'

'I think it probably means that you're far too posh. You can't imagine lads who went to comprehensive schools dreaming about Maggie, can you?'

'Are you sure you'll be all right? We could call you a taxi.' Dan was standing on the top step as Jo held the front door open for him. It was almost midnight. Lit from behind, Jo's hair looked like spun gold.

132

'No, I'll be fine. There's no point in me risking getting stopped for being over the limit and I only live ten minutes away. The walk will do me good. I only drove over because I was running behind. I'll come back in the morning for the car if you don't mind.'

'Of course not. I'm not in tomorrow, unfortunately, otherwise you could have popped up for a coffee.'

'Another time then. Or perhaps I can return the compliment and cook for you one evening.'

Jo smiled. 'I'd like that. Goodnight then.' She stepped forwards and laid a hand on his upper arm. Even through his shirt, his skin felt soft. She looked up at him.

Dan put his hands on her waist. He could feel her body heat through the thin cotton of her dress. Her waist felt impossibly small and he could feel the beginning of the swell of her hips. He bent his head and kissed her. Her lips were soft and warm and her face felt silky and smooth against his face.

He pressed his body against hers. He could feel her breasts pressing up against him and the soft curve of her belly. He brought up a hand and stroked her hair. His heart was pounding and his armpits prickled with sweat. He ended the kiss and stepped back.

'Well.' Jo reached out and took his hand. 'I can't remember the last time I had to stand on tiptoes to kiss a man. It makes a welcome change.'

Dan enjoyed the walk home. The air cleared his head and the simple repetitive motion seemed to soothe and relax him, ready for sleep. It wasn't until he put the key in his front door that he realised that Jo had yet again managed to avoid telling him whether or not she was kinky.

Nine

Dan had arranged to visit Sadie for his private session early on Sunday morning. As he climbed into the car he felt vulnerable and uncertain but, nevertheless, there was a hard little kernel of secret excitement in the centre of his chest.

The rest of the team knew nothing about his bargain with her, and he'd deliberately avoided mentioning it to Sarah, though that didn't make sense really because they'd been lovers for years and trusted each other with their secrets. But, somehow, it just felt too personal, too vulnerable.

Jo alone knew about the visit, though he still couldn't work out why he'd mentioned it to her in the first place. At least he knew he could trust her. After all, she'd admitted she was Rosalind Quirt and had trusted him to keep her secret.

For some reason he felt that Jo would understand anything he said. She'd never judge him or try to impose her own values. He laughed softly. Though he didn't believe in fate, he could almost believe that life seemed to be throwing the two of them together. She cropped up everywhere he went, like a bad penny.

There was something about Jo that Dan found comforting and reassuring and that's what made it so easy to talk to her. But another part of her – the part that made his heart beat twice as fast as usual and his cock tingle – was surprising, challenging and slightly dangerous; as if anything might happen when he was with her. He couldn't wait to talk to her about his session with Sadie. He didn't doubt that he'd find her insights interesting and perceptive.

As he turned into Sadie's road, for a moment he considered turning around and driving home again. But he knew that if he wanted her continued cooperation and her respect he couldn't back out. He parked the car and locked it. At the bottom of her path he paused for a moment.

As he stood with one hand on the gate, it came to him with a shocking clarity just what it was he was afraid of. The utter panic that filled him, that made his hands shake and his heart pound, was caused by a fear that he'd actually like it.

If he enjoyed the session, as he feared he would, he'd be completely defenceless before her. She'd know his most secret desires and the balance of power would be changed forever. He shut the gate behind him and walked up the path.

He rang the bell and waited. After a few minutes he saw Sadie approaching down the hall. She opened the door silently and he stepped inside.

She was wearing long black gloves, thigh-length spike-heeled boots and a skimpy garment shaped like an all-in-one swimming costume, except that it was made out of shiny PVC. It clung to her lithe body like a second skin. It was cut high at the legs, almost to her hip bones, and Dan was fairly certain that her pubic hair must have been removed because the gusset was only about an inch and a half wide.

'I want to start by making it clear that, if we go ahead today, there's no turning back. This is real ... it's private and absolutely confidential, but it is real. No masks, no playacting, no place to hide. So it has to be what you want. Do you understand?'

Dan nodded slowly. 'Yes. That's what I want.'

'Very good.' She smiled. 'Then I'd like you to take your clothes off please – all of them. You can leave them on that chair.'

Dan began to unbutton his shirt. His fingers were clumsy and slow. He undid his cuffs and pulled off his shirt. He went to toss it on the chair but Sadie shook her head slowly and he understood that he was to fold it. He took his time folding it neatly then laid it on the chair.

He toed off his shoes then bent down to remove his socks. He could feel icy fingers sliding along his spine. His cock was tingling. He undid the button at the top of his fly and unzipped his trousers. He deliberately turned his back to her to hide his growing erection. He slid them down over his hips and bent to take them off.

He pushed down his boxers, pausing to extricate his hard-on, then slid them down and stepped out of them. He turned slowly round with both hands cupped over his crotch.

'Move your hands, please. I know you've got an erection, there's no point hiding it.'

'Sorry . . .' Dan's voice sounded quiet and wavering. 'Mistress,' he remembered to add. He uncovered himself and stood with his hands down by his sides. She ran the tip of one gloved finger along the underside of his cock, lifting it up then releasing it so that it waved obscenely.

'You've got nothing at all to be ashamed of . . . quite the contrary. It's a very impressive example as a matter of fact. Though, as far as I am concerned, your cock is of no interest whatsoever. It's mildly useful in helping me to gauge how much you're enjoying my attentions, but you needn't imagine you're going to be allowed any relief. Do I make myself clear?' Sadie looked him straight in the face.

'Yes, mistress.' He avoided her eyes, uncertain if it was permitted or not. His erection still stood out at half-mast.

'Now, I want you to get down on your belly and crawl to the dungeon like the worm that you are.' Sadie's voice was hard and full of contempt.

Dan slid to his knees and lay down flat on the floor. Sadie walked away from him.

Dan slithered slowly forwards on his belly. His skin rubbed painfully against the carpet. He made slow progress, alternately moving his arms and legs like a lizard. He struggled to keep his head high, so that he could see Sadie. He saw her open the door at the top of the stairs and pause, waiting for him.

He could smell the gritty aroma of the carpet and his own sweat. He was panting from exertion and every movement felt as though he was dragging his body over coarse sandpaper. When he reached the top of the stairs Sadie began to descend, expecting him to follow.

Dan negotiated the steps with difficulty. He held onto the edge of each stair with both hands and slowly lowered himself. He felt completely unstable with his feet so much higher than his head and his body at a 45-degree angle.

His body banged painfully against the steps. His glasses had slid down his nose and the front of his hair had fallen in his face. When he reached the bottom of the stairs Sadie was waiting for him, holding the door open. He crawled through it and into the corridor. The flagstones were icily cold and he flinched.

Dan followed Sadie down the corridor. The flagstones didn't scratch him like the carpet but they were so smooth and cold that his sweaty body kept sticking to them, making it difficult to move. His neck and shoulders ached from the effort of holding his head up. When he finally reached the dungeon and Sadie allowed him to stand up he was dirty, scratched and exhausted.

He stood to attention in the centre of the room, waiting for orders. Sadie went over to a trolley at the side of the room and picked up her utility belt. She wrapped it around her hips and buckled it up. Dan didn't dare turn his head to look, but he tried to identify the implements that hung from it. She wheeled the trolley across the room and put it beside the whipping bench then came back into the centre of the room and stood in front of Dan.

'I want you to know that I don't do this for all of my clients, Dan. But since you've agreed to this session – not because you chose to, but because I forced you into it – I thought I ought to reciprocate the enormous trust that you've shown to me. Normally I'd consider this sort of thing too personal, too vulnerable to do with a client but I thought it was important to show you that I appreciate how defenceless you're making yourself for me.' Sadie began to unzip something at the top of her costume and Dan realised that there was a zip running underneath the cups of the bra part of her outfit. She undid both zips and the bra cups came away in her hands.

She held them in front of her breasts for a moment then smiled at Dan and tossed them aside. Dan felt a rush of excitement crashing over him. Blood pounded in his ears. Her breasts were small and pointed, her nipples the colour of milk chocolate. Her areolae were quite small but the nipples themselves were thick and long. Sadie began to walk over to him.

'Thank you, mistress. It's a beautiful gesture. I'm honoured.' As Dan gazed at Sadie's nipples he felt his cock gradually stiffening and rising until it pointed almost to the ceiling, but this time he wasn't ashamed.

Sadie smiled. 'Will you mount the whipping bench for me please?'

Dan climbed up onto it, laying his body along it and lowering his arms, ready for the restraints.

The leather felt cold and clammy against his skin. Sadie fastened the restraints. He felt the blood rushing to his head and his nose growing blocked as he hung his head.

His cock was rigid and aching. His heart thumped. As Sadie fastened the final strap across the small of his back he felt utterly powerless and unbelievably excited.

He closed his eyes and waited. His skin already felt hot and uncomfortable beneath the restraints. He could feel his erection trapped between his body and the padded leather bench.

Dan assumed that Sadie was selecting a suitable weapon to whip him with. He strained his ears but all he could hear was the distant sound of traffic and the sound of his own frenzied breathing. He heard Sadie's heels clacking against the flagstones and braced himself in the expectation of pain. There was a soft slithering sort of noise like clothes being removed. Dan struggled to make sense of it and realised she was taking off her gloves. She picked up something from the trolley then walked around him until she was standing directly behind him.

Dan suddenly felt vulnerable and afraid. The bench was raked slightly so that his head was lower than his bottom. It forced his arse upwards and spread his legs apart. He knew that his rear end would be obscenely on display and totally exposed. A cold shiver slid along his spine and the hairs on the back of his neck began to prickle.

'Have you ever been fucked in the arse, Dan? Perhaps you're one of those men who likes a woman to strap on a cock and take him like a girl.' She stroked along the crack of his arse with a fingertip and the shock of it made his body quiver.

'No . . . no, mistress. Never. Some women like to slide in a finger while they're sucking you, that's as far as I've ever gone.' Dan's body was rigid with excitement and anticipation. His cock had begun to leak pre-come, wetting his belly and the leather beneath him.

'That's not very adventurous. A funny thing happens when a woman fucks a man. The balance of power completely changes. The woman feels masterful and aggressive and the man becomes passive and receptive. It can be quite mind-blowing.'

'Are you going to fuck me?' Dan could hear the anxiety in his own voice.

Sadie laughed. 'If I want to, yes. Haven't you realised yet? I can do whatever I want.' She walked slowly around the bench, her heels clip-clopping against the floor. She bent down and put her face beside his. He lifted his head, trying to look at her. 'And there's not a damn thing you can do about it.'

Dan's cock tingled. Sadie reached out and pushed the damp hair away from his face. He gazed at her, hardly daring to breathe. She stood up and walked slowly back to the other end of the bench.

He felt the flat of one warm hand on his buttock and, a second later, something cold and slippery being spread around his arsehole. She was lubing him. His body tensed and he let out a long excited sigh.

The lube squelched noisily as she worked it in. He could feel her fingers circling his hole. His body was tense and trembling. Heat burned in his crotch.

Sadie pressed a fingertip inside him. It slid past his sphincter, bringing his nerve endings to life. His body jolted forwards and his erection rubbed against the wet leather.

She pushed her finger all the way in then began to slide it out again. Dan clenched and unclenched his fists. His arse felt alive, tingling with pleasure and excitement. Sadie pushed in a second finger and he gasped.

Dan was panting and moaning. He could feel his nipples, hard and sensitive, against the slick leather.

140

Sadie curled her fingers and pressed their tips against his prostate and his body shuddered.

He could feel his muscles gripping her fingers. His cock was squeezed pleasurably between his body and the bench. His arse tingled and prickled with unfamiliar excitement.

Sadie slid in a third finger and Dan felt his muscles stretch. The sensation of fullness and intrusion was incredible. Each tiny movement of her fingers inside him caused dozens of delicious pinpricks that sent ripples all the way to his toes.

He felt her other hand cupping and stroking his balls and he let out a cry of shock and appreciation. Her hand slid beneath him, palm uppermost and squeezed his erection. Dan gasped. Her fingers withdrew from his hole and, for a moment, he felt abandoned. Then he felt something thick and slippery pushing against his opening. Not a finger this time, it was hard and cold and sort of rubbery.

It began to slide inside him and Dan felt his muscles opening to accommodate it. Sadie squeezed and stroked his erection as she pushed it into him. It must be a dildo, Dan thought, the silicone type that's moulded to look like a cock. He closed his eyes and panted as it filled him.

He could feel it sliding past his excited, electrified nerve endings, unleashing a wave of shivery tingles. Sadie's slippery hand was warm around his cock. The dildo slid all the way in and Dan screamed in pleasure and intrusion.

He ached for release. Sadie's hand on his erection was both fabulous yet tantalising. She squeezed and stroked but there was no rhythm to it. He struggled against his bonds. The straps creaked and his body slid against the slick leather.

He realised that by flexing and unflexing his thigh muscles and pushing down with his knees he could achieve a small backwards and forwards movement that would rub his cock against her hand.

He dug his knees in and thrust his body forwards, banging against the bench. Sadie slid her hand away from his cock and Dan moaned in frustration. 'Please! Let me come.' He humped the bench.

Sadie slid out the dildo and Dan heard her walking around the bench and dropping it onto the trolley. She bent down beside Dan. She gripped him by the hair and lifted his head. She twisted her hand, pulling viciously on his hair to turn his face to look at her. 'I must say, I'm disappointed. I made it perfectly clear that you shouldn't expect any relief and yet you demand an orgasm before we've even started properly. And, if that wasn't enough, you don't even bother to address me as mistress. It will never do.'

'I'm sorry, mistress. I was excited. I got carried away.' Dan's neck ached from the unnatural position.

Sadie shook her head in disappointment and Dan felt an irrational stab of shame.

'Excuses are meaningless. I demand obedience and I accept nothing less. I'm afraid I have no alternative but to punish you.' She dropped his head in disgust.

Dan heard her feet clip-clopping against the stone floor. He realised that she was walking over to the racks of tools and he turned to look. He knew there were many vicious-looking weapons hanging there and he didn't relish the thought of being on the receiving end of any of them. He'd seen a cat-o'-nine-tails, a bullwhip, a thick bunch of twigs bound with a cord, like a traditional birch, and various types of horsewhip.

He thought he knew he could cope with the crop, because she'd used it on him last time and he'd occasionally been caned at school, so that held no particular fear. He found himself worrying that he wouldn't be able to take the pain and that he'd be letting her down. His body was rigid with trepidation and excitement and his cock was rock-solid.

Sadie selected an implement and began to walk slowly back to the bench. As she drew nearer he saw that she was holding a long slender whip with a sort of knotted tassel at the end. She walked right over to him and ran the tip of the whip along his cheek.

'This is a dressage whip. It's used during competition to get the horse to make precise, specific movements. Naturally its bite has to be accurate and incisive.' She rubbed the tip of the whip across his lips. 'I think you'll find it memorable.' She stood up and Dan listened to her heels as she walked to the other end of the bench.

He could hear her breathing behind him and he pictured her standing with her legs apart, arm raised high into the air as she waited for the perfect moment to lower the whip.

Dan heard a loud whoosh as the whip swished through the air, followed by a resounding crack as it hit him. His body jolted forwards and there was a moment of stinging, burning pain that instantly seemed to melt into delicious pleasure.

Sadie delivered half a dozen strokes in quick succession. The whip swished and cracked. Dan's buttocks burnt and tingled. The moment he'd registered the pain it somehow transformed into intense pleasure and satisfaction.

He heard her raise the whip and he tensed his body in expectation of pain. Instead he felt her slide her hand, palm uppermost, between his crotch and the bench. She curled her fist around his erection and slid her hand backwards and forwards, wanking his cock.

He gasped. He could hear the pre-come squelching as she handled him. He could feel the heat of her hand. He used every ounce of his self-control to remain still as she stroked his cock. She gave it a final squeeze and released it then immediately brought the crop down across the meat of his buttocks and he moaned and shuddered in pain and relief.

The whip swished through the air and landed with a brutal crack. His body shuddered. She lashed him repeatedly with barely any pause between the strokes. He was overwhelmed by sensation, an overlapping chaos of helplessness, pain, pleasure, excitement and release.

Dan could imagine red stripes forming and blue bruises beginning to appear. After his last beating he'd been marked for days and, this time, he didn't doubt that he'd bear Sadie's signature for at least a week. His cock ached and tingled. Each blow of the whip rubbed it against the slippery leather.

Sadie delivered a final stinging blow and dropped the whip. Dan felt her hands on his arse. She ran her fingertips over his weals, stroking and soothing them. Dan was exhausted and breathless. He lay limp against the bench, his head hanging and his eyes closed.

She began to unbuckle the restraints, bending down to undo the straps on his wrists and arms. Dan turned to look at her. Her hair was untidy and damp and there was a fine sheen of sweat on her face. She saw Dan looking at her and she smiled.

'You took that well. Did you surprise yourself?' Before Dan could respond she stood up and began to unbuckle the waist strap. 'Stand up . . . slowly though.' Sadie went over to the medical chair. Dan straightened up and waited for his head to clear. 'Come over here when you're ready.'

Dan walked over to Sadie on unsteady legs and sat down in the medical chair. She hoisted his feet up into the stirrups and began to fasten the restraints at his wrists and ankles.

Sadie operated the lever that tilted the chair back and Dan experienced a moment's disorientation and lightheadedness. Excitement and trepidation fluttered beneath his ribs.

She turned to the trolley and there was a metallic clinking sound as she picked something up. 'Open your mouth for me, please.'

Dan complied. Sadie held up the item for him to see. He squinted, trying to identify it. It was the metal medical gag he'd seen her use on her client.

She began to fit it to Dan's mouth. The metal arms felt cold against his skin. It forced his mouth wide and already his jaw was beginning to ache. Sadie locked it in place. With his mouth wide open the sound of his breathing seemed to become transformed into an urgent heartbeat.

He felt defenceless. Unable to speak and with his legs spread wide by the stirrups, it seemed as if his very manhood was at risk. Yet heat and blood pumped around his body enlivening and arousing every particle of him.

Sadie ran her fingertip up the front of his torso and his body trembled. The restraints creaked. 'I'm going to shave you.' She picked up an old-fashioned shaving mug and brush from the trolley. 'It's quite a simple thing –' she began to lather the brush '– yet I think you'll find it powerful. By stripping you of hair I'm demonstrating my mastery over you and I'm actually altering your body.'

Dan gazed at the shaving mug. He watched the white foam as if he were hypnotised and the brush was the instrument of his subjugation. His crotch was tingling and tight. His chest heaved.

She began to smear the cold foam over his chest. He didn't have much hair there, just a small patch in the centre, but Sadie took her time spreading the soap. The brush felt soft and tickly against his skin. She brushed his nipple and he gasped.

She lathered up his belly and crotch. It tickled and tormented him. Dan began to wriggle, making the restraints creak and complain and Sadie paused.

'If you fidget like that when I'm shaving you there's liable to be an accident. I suggest you learn to keep still.'

She began to soap his crotch. Dan made a supreme effort to remain motionless. The gag made his face ache and he was unable to swallow his own saliva. The sound of his own frantic breathing throbbed in his brain.

Sadie set down the shaving mug and picked up something from the trolley. Dan turned his head, trying to look and his eyes widened in alarm. It was a cutthroat razor. Sadie opened it and the blade gleamed in the light. A jolt of electricity shot up his spine.

She began to shave his chest, expertly sliding the blade over the skin. She wiped away the foam and hair with a towel. The razor was icy cold and he could feel its sharp edge.

Sadie seemed totally absorbed. The razor slid through the foam, leaving pale bare skin in its wake. When his chest was denuded she began to shave his belly, using her other hand to stretch his skin for the blade.

The closer she came to his crotch the harder he found it to sit still. He barely dared to breathe. The blade made his skin tingle and the air felt cool and strange on his newly bare flesh.

She began to shave away his pubic hair, using short regular strokes. The blade quickly became clogged with hair and she wiped it frequently on the towel. She moved his penis around, pushing it out of the way, or pulling it taut with the precision and indifference of a barber at work.

Dan was half hard. Having her handle his cock was exquisite torture. The clinical treatment and her utter indifference were at once shaming and utterly exciting.

When she'd finished she set the razor down and wiped

the remaining lather off his body with a damp towel. Dan looked down at himself. He was as smooth and hairless as a Las Vegas showgirl. His cock lay sideways, resting on his thigh, thick and slightly curved, still semi-erect. Without the hair Dan felt it looked somehow obscene and shameful.

He looked up at Sadie. From his unnatural position she seemed exceptionally tall and somehow magnificent. He gazed up at her. Her hair was ruffled. Her cheeks were stained dark and she was breathing noisily through parted lips. She looked rumpled and slightly sleepy and it came to Dan that her messy hair looked as though she'd been rolling around in bed.

She smiled at him and an instant rush of heat crashed over his face. His cock stiffened. Sadie turned away from him for a moment and he heard a match strike and, a moment later, smelled the characteristic burning odour.

She turned and stepped between his spread legs and Dan saw that she was holding a long fat candle as thick as her wrist and six inches tall.

She raised it up into the air, as if it were some part of a sacred ceremony. It took Dan a second to realise that she was holding it directly above his cock and he began to struggle and shake his head. Sadie smiled and slowly tipped the candle.

Hot wax began to drip onto his crotch. There was a second of searing pain as the wax hit, then endorphins began to flood through his body like a drug rush.

He stared at his crotch. Blobs of hard and hardening wax covered his cock and balls. Drips landed on his belly and thighs. He was erect and tingling. A bead of hot wax dripped onto his exposed helmet and he grunted. The gag distorted the sound into a strangled animal cry. Waves of sensation whooshed round his body and thundered in his ears.

Layer after layer of wax fell onto his crotch. The hardening liquid took on a milky hue, darkening as it cooled. It pulled at his skin, making him itch and tingle. Heat and pleasure gushed over his face as if he'd opened the door of a hot oven.

His crotch was completely encased in wax. He could no longer see the shape of his genitals, there was just a lumpy mound of wax, its surface uneven and covered in drops and drips. There was an overall sensation of warmth, but the wax near his body was cold and hard.

His fists were clenched. Every muscle in his body was tense and rigid. His erection felt huge and painful, tight and pumped with blood. He wanted to come so much that the thought throbbed in his brain like a mantra.

Arousal pumped around his body like infected blood. His whole body was an erect cock, aching to come. His toes ached with frustration. His tongue seemed to fizz and buzz with the need for release. Goose pimples made his skin tingle and spark with desperation.

'I bet you want to come now, don't you?' Sadie blew out the candle.

Dan began to nod his head, repeating the movement over and over again in case she was in any doubt. Sadie laughed.

She began to peel off the wax. She rolled up the edges and slid her fingers underneath and pulled it off in a single piece. There were several blobs of stray wax on his belly and thighs and Sadie picked each of them off and dropped them onto the trolley.

When she'd finished, Dan's erection pointed at the ceiling, swollen, dark and purple-tipped. Sadie spit on her palm and wrapped her fist around it. Dan let out a stifled moan of relief. She wanked him slowly several times. It was exquisite and tantalising.

Sadie released his cock. She held onto the arms of the

chair and climbed up onto them so that she was kneeling astride him. Dan longed to touch her. To put out his hands and cup her round buttocks. To lean forwards and suck a nipple in his mouth then slide his hands lazily up her body to stroke her hair. He struggled in frustration. Perfume wafted up from her heated skin. It smelled sultry, heady and somehow soporific, as if he was under her spell.

She reached up and took off his gag. His jaw ached in relief. She used her fingers to wipe away the saliva then pushed his damp hair away from his face. She smiled. For a moment, he thought she was going to fuck him, to sit down on his cock and ride it for her pleasure, but she never moved. She just knelt astride him with his head in her hands, smiling down at him.

Sadie raised herself up on her knees and leaned her body towards him. She brought her nipple to his lips, still holding his face between her soft hands. Dan opened his mouth. Her nipple was thick and hard and hot. Her sweet womanly scent filled her nostrils. He sucked hard on her nipple, rubbing his face against the soft mound of her breast. His cock tingled.

'I bet you want to come now, don't you?' Sadie's voice was soft and tender.

He reluctantly released her nipple. 'Yes, please.' He went back to sucking.

'Sorry, darling, that's not part of the deal. I'm going to release you now and, when you're ready, you can shower and change. Let yourself out.' She climbed off.

On the drive home, Dan didn't know what to think. He hadn't really expected her to let him come, but then he hadn't expected her to mount him and let him suck on her nipples either.

The session had been surprising and shocking and utterly unimaginably arousing. His cock was still half hard and he was having to make a supreme effort to concentrate on the road when all he wanted to do was pull over to the kerb and relieve himself.

What had shocked him most, he realised, as he turned out of her road, was the way she had simply abandoned him at the end of the session. He'd expected her to invite him upstairs for coffee and brownies as she had done in the past but she'd simply told him to let himself out. He felt rejected and disappointed and somehow unworthy.

He'd been looking forward to the opportunity to talk to her about his experience in the relaxed surroundings of her cosy kitchen but instead he was driving home still horny and with everything buzzing around in his head.

Then it came to him that she'd deliberately not invited him upstairs because she wanted him to feel like a client. Sadie's responsibility only extended as far as the financial transaction. The client's arousal, his emotional responses to the session were his own affair. He laughed softly to himself.

He drove straight to Sarah's as fast as the speed limit would allow. He rang the doorbell, praying that she was home. When he saw her approaching down the hall, he undid the button at the front of his trousers and unzipped his fly.

'You're a lovely surprise.' Sarah smiled. She was still in her dressing gown.

Dan stepped into the hall and closed the door behind him.

'And here's another one.' He pushed his clothes down to his knees, freeing his erection. 'Get on your knees.'

Sarah smiled. She slowly slid to the floor. She gripped his cock at the base and Dan gasped. She swallowed him. Her mouth was hot and silky. She cupped his balls, gently rolling them inside their sac. Her head bobbed. She flicked her tongue over the sensitive tip and pressed it against the eye.

Dan was breathing hard. He tingled all over. Sarah stared up at him, an expression of pure bliss on her face.

Her dressing gown had fallen open and he could see her cleavage and the top of her breasts.

He was rigid with tension, vibrating with excitement and arousal. Her mouth moved rhythmically. She stroked his balls. He rocked his hips, establishing a rhythm. Snuffly breath snorted out of her nostrils. Dan handled her hair, pulling it away from her face and holding it back. The shape of her mouth around his cock looked utterly obscene, expressing both surprise and compliance.

She began to deep throat him. He let out a long low moan. He could feel her hot breath against his naked pubis and her chin bumping against his balls. His thigh muscles were taut and quivering. The knot of tension in his belly grew hard and dense.

He held her hair away from her face, giving him a full view of her mouth on his cock. Her eyes closed and she sucked hungrily. He thrust his hips, fucking her between the lips.

He was gasping and moaning. Sarah was making little satisfied mewling noises. Her dressing gown had slid off her shoulders, exposing the top of her arms and her long slender neck. Her dark hair bobbed and danced.

Heat and excitement boiled in his gut like lava. He was panting like a steam train. He was going to come. He shortened his strokes and Sarah followed suit. She sucked on his cock, tightening her mouth around it and Dan let out an involuntary grunt of pleasure and surprise. She pulled softly on his scrotum.

He fucked her face in short urgent strokes. Icy shivers slid along his spine. The tension burst. He gave a final deep thrust and arched his back. He began to howl in triumph and release.

He was coming in her mouth, pumping out streams of hot sperm. She swallowed it all, making soft little murmurs of satisfaction and pleasure. It kept on coming, like a tidal wave, knocking the breath out of him and making his knees wobble.

His fingers gripped her hair, pressing her face against his throbbing cock. He howled out his pleasure and relief, head thrown back and eyes closed. When it was finally over he looked down at Sarah and smiled. He stroked her hair.

She gave his softening cock a final reluctant kiss and released it. 'Well, now, you were a horny boy.' She sat back on her heels and looked up at him. 'And you seem to have had a shave. I can't help feeling there's something you're not telling me . . .'

Ten

A week later Dan and the crew went with Hellfire 2000 to a party thrown by the artist Jude Ryan to celebrate her new exhibition. Dan did a piece to camera and wandered around the gallery looking at the sexually explicit exhibits. He found himself particularly drawn to the sculptures. Mostly they featured naked men and women in chains, cuffs or ropes.

There was a life-size bronze of a naked woman on all fours, her head raised as if gazing into the eyes of her lover. Her breasts hung beneath her, nipples erect, and it was obvious to Dan that her chest was heaving with excitement. He bent down and put his face inches from hers. He almost expected to feel her hot breath on his skin.

'Do you like it? It's called "Surrender". It's one of my particular favourites.' She held out her hand. 'I'm Jude Ryan.'

Dan looked up and saw a tall woman with long dark hair. 'Yes . . . yes. I do.' She was wearing a simple red dress that emphasised her curves. He got to his feet and only then did he notice that she was holding a slender black leash at the end of which knelt a man who was gazing up at her with exactly the same look of adoration as the sculpture. He shook her hand. 'She looks almost real. How do you do that?'

She laughed. 'That's where the talent comes in. Though the three years at art college helps too. Apparently you're going to interview me later. I'm looking forward to it.'

'Me too.' He noticed that she had striking eyes. They seemed full of life and humour. They were compelling and hypnotic.

'But, if you'll excuse me, I'll have to move on. I've just spotted the art critic from *London Now* and I ought to butter him up.' She smiled at Dan and turned away.

Dan watched her walk across the room with the young man following at her heels. From the ease with which he moved on hands and knees Dan thought he must have had plenty of practice.

He left Dave, Rick and Dennis to get some shots of the partygoers while he went off to the buffet. He'd loaded up his plate and was looking around for somewhere to sit when he heard a familiar voice.

'If I didn't know better I'd think you were stalking me.'

'Jo.' He turned to look at her. 'I could say the same of you.'

Jo picked up a morsel from the buffet table and popped it into her mouth. She was wearing a black dress with a fitted bodice and a sweetheart neckline. Around her throat was a simple black ribbon and her hair had been swept up and twisted into a French pleat. Her skin was pale and flawless and Dan thought her décolleté looked as though it had been dusted with iridescent powder. Her lips were glossy and red.

Jo shrugged and smiled enigmatically. 'I'm here because of Sam. She and Jude Ryan are old friends. Do you like her work?' She tapped her fingernails against her wineglass.

'I didn't know it until today but yes, I do. It's very . . . powerful.'

'And so is she. Have you met?'

'Only briefly but I'm supposed to be interviewing her later. I'm looking forward to it.'

'And did you meet Michael?' Jo smiled and Dan thought he could see a playful glint in her green eyes.

'Is that the man who was kneeling at her feet at the end of a lead? She didn't introduce us.'

'Yes, that's him. He's an artist too.'

'Really? I didn't know that.'

'He used to be famous for graphic images of men dominating women. Quite cold actually ... I always thought there was something hard and soulless about them. Unlike Jude's work ... there's something quite moving and ... I don't know ... tender about her art. But Michael's work totally changed when he met Jude.'

'That sounds intriguing. What does he do now?'

'Exactly the opposite. He's got an exhibition coming up, you should go. He creates beautiful heartbreaking images of submissive men surrendering to powerful beautiful women. They're quite something.' She leaned in close. 'As a matter of fact I've got one of his sculptures in my bedroom.'

'I see.' He lowered his voice. 'And do you find it inspirational?'

Jo laughed. 'Still trying to get me to admit to being kinky, I see.'

'You can hardly blame me for trying. Are you saying Michael was dominant before he met Jude?'

She nodded. 'He was famous for it.'

'But, surely, we know our own natures. It's not possible to change from one extreme to its opposite just like that. He must have been submissive all along.'

Jo shrugged. 'That's certainly what Jude believes. He was always submissive, he just didn't know it until he met her and she unlocked that part of him.' She sipped her drink, never taking her eyes off him.

Dan leaned in close. 'And what do you think?' He could smell her perfume and feel the heat rising from her skin.

Jo looked at him silently, her beautiful lips curved into a smile but her brow creased by a frown. Finally, she spoke. 'I'm a chameleon. I spend my days being competent and professional and my evenings putting myself into my characters' heads. I think we are all capable of feeling and believing an infinite variety of things. What we are is fluid not fixed.' She paused to sip her wine.

'With certain people, or in certain circumstances, we may be one way yet another person brings out something completely different in us. A dominant powerful woman may meet a man who she longs to kneel before even though she's never felt that way about another soul. It's how the two of them connect.' She was smiling as she spoke and her cheeks glowed pink.

'That's interesting.' Dan couldn't take his eyes off her.

'Haven't you ever had a partner with a particular sexual interest which you'd never considered? It might be spanking, or sodomy, or dressing up. You go along with it because you don't feel strongly either way and you want to please her and much to your surprise you turn out to love it and you want to do it from then on, with other partners.' She looked into his eyes, waiting for an answer, and Dan felt a slow slither of pleasure slide along his spine.

He nodded. 'Yes, I have, as a matter of fact. I have a lover who likes her nipples abused and, at first, I was frightened of doing it but now I love it. She bucks underneath me like a volcano and I love being able to let go – to not worry about hurting her or going too far. It's a special and intense thing between us and I'd be sorry if it had to stop.'

'There you are then. And, perhaps, when you've had

your session with Sadie you'll discover a few more things about yourself that you didn't know.'

'As a matter of fact I've already had it.'

'Really? I'd really like to know what you thought of it.' She swirled the wine in her glass. 'But if you think it's too personal, I'll completely understand.'

'No, no . . . I'd love to talk about it. How about if you come to dinner at my house. Shall we say Friday at eight?'

'Yes, I'd like that. Thank you.'

'And perhaps you'll finally put me out of my misery about whether or not you're kinky. After our dinner the other night I realised that we'd barely even spoken about you.'

Jo laughed. 'I promise you I'm not being deliberately mysterious. I tell you what . . . I'll give you twenty questions on Friday. I'll even play truth, if you like. I've nothing to hide.'

'Really? That's not how it seems.'

Jo shrugged. 'You just haven't asked me the right questions yet. But you're an investigative reporter. There's plenty of time before Friday for you to come up with a suitable list. You can probe as hard as you like. I always enjoy a good grilling.'

Dan opened his mouth to speak but Jo interrupted. She laid a hand on his arm. 'I've got to go, I'm afraid. I've got another appointment and I don't want to be late. See you on Friday.' She squeezed his arm and walked away.

Dan walked down the hall to answer the doorbell. At the bottom of the stairs he paused and looked at himself in the full-length mirror. He'd dressed simply in black jeans and a plain long-sleeved T-shirt. He'd shaved for the second time that day and his hair was still slightly damp from the shower. It looked wavy and unruly. He ran his fingers through it, pushing it back off his face.

The bell rang again and he hurried down the hall and opened the door. 'Jo. Sorry to keep you waiting.'

He held the door open and she stepped inside. She was wearing a black silk shift dress printed with enormous scarlet daisies. It scooped low in the front and Dan could see the top of her breasts and the dark hollow between them.

'No problem. I wouldn't want to interrupt an alpha male's grooming ritual.'

The hall was narrow so that their bodies were practically touching. She looked up at him. Dan felt his cheeks colouring. He closed the door.

'You saw me looking in the mirror?' He felt foolish and wrong-footed and not for the first time in her company. The quivery feeling of disquiet beneath his ribs was beginning to feel like an old friend.

She nodded. 'But don't worry. I take it as a compliment.' She sniffed the air. 'And is that Antaeus I smell? You've obviously made an effort. Does that indicate an eagerness to please, do you think?'

He laughed. 'You're suggesting I have a submissive nature? You're not the first woman to bring it up, actually. Come through to the kitchen. We can have a glass of wine while I prepare the starter. It's this way.' He walked towards the kitchen.

'Sure. What are we having?' Jo followed him down the hall. Her high heels clip-clopped noisily against the wooden floor.

'Nothing fancy. Chilli and garlic prawns to start and fillet steak and salad to follow. Sit down and I'll open the wine.' He pulled out a chair and Jo sat down.

They enjoyed a relaxed meal at the kitchen table. Jo cleared away the plates from their first course while Dan prepared the steaks. He could feel her eyes on him as he cooked and he could feel the fine hairs on the back of his neck growing erect.

She was funny and sharp and disarmingly honest and Dan found himself stealing furtive glances at her like a fourteen-year-old with a crush on his teacher. He was fairly certain that she'd noticed, though she didn't seem to mind. In fact, he thought he'd noticed a look in her eyes, and a slight difference to the way she carried herself; as if she was fully aware of his admiration and accepted it as her due right.

'This crème brûlée is delicious. I love it but I always think it's too fiddly to make yourself.' Jo ate a mouthful of her dessert.

'I can't claim any credit, I'm afraid. Marks and Spencer's.' Dan noticed that she narrowed her eyes in pleasure when she ate.

'Really? Well, you'd never be able to tell.' She scooped up the last spoonful and ate it slowly. 'I could easily eat another one.'

'I only bought two. But you're welcome to the rest of mine.' Dan slid his half-eaten dessert across the table.

'Why don't we share it?' She cracked the crisp sugar with her spoon and dipped it into the creamy custard beneath. She brought the loaded spoon to her lips and sucked it clean, never taking her eyes off Dan.

She filled the spoon again and held it out for him. He leaned forwards and wrapped his hand around hers and pulled it to his lips. He sucked the crème brûlée off the spoon.

After the meal, Dan carried their coffee through to the living room on a tray. Jo sat on the sofa with her legs crossed at the knee. Dan followed the curve of her calf with his eyes all the way down to her narrow ankle. Her stockings were black and sheer. They glistened softly in the light. Her instep was high and curved and he could just see a hint of the top of her toes.

He picked up his coffee and sat back. When he looked at Jo the expression in his eyes instantly told him that she knew he'd been admiring her legs. He shrugged and smiled.

'I've been on tenterhooks all evening waiting to hear about your session with Sadie.'

'Ah yes . . .' Dan smiled. 'It was extremely memorable.'

'But in a good way, I hope?'

'Yes, I think so.' He put his cup down on the coffee table. 'I don't think I'd admit this to another living soul but I found it all incredibly intense and erotic even though – and this is the strange part – it was also totally humiliating. In some ways I felt utterly powerless and emasculated, yet at the same time it was totally liberating and exciting. Do you know what I mean?' He was conscious of Jo's eyes on his face.

She nodded slowly. 'Yes, as a matter of fact, I do.'

'I don't understand it, really, but somehow the whole experience has made me feel sort of liberated and fearless. I didn't have to worry about my performance, or her responses, I just surrendered. I felt as though there were no barriers between the two of us so there was no barrier to pleasure and no end to it.'

Jo nodded. 'There's a saying among kinky people. "When the ropes are on the outside the ropes on the inside dissolve."'

'Yes . . . yes, that's how it was.'

'Well, it sounds very exciting for you.'

'It was. It was . . . incredible . . . I know I keep saying that, but it was. Though, seeing Jude Ryan and Michael together the other night has made me realise what was missing from the experience.'

'That sounds intriguing. What was missing?' Jo sipped her coffee.

'Intimacy . . . commitment, connection, that indefinable something that makes it personal and real. For the first time I can see that kinky sex is not just consensual abuse but intimacy, trust . . . love even.'

160

Jo put down her cup on the coffee table. She turned to face him, tucking her legs beneath her on the sofa. 'And does that mean you want to explore that for yourself?' Jo's voice sounded soft and casual but the expression in her eyes was deadly serious.

Dan could hear his own heart beating. He looked at Jo. Her eyes glistened. He allowed his gaze to slide down her creamy throat to the curve of her breasts. Finally he spoke. 'I think there's a part of me that longs to experience it even though I understand that, if it's real, the fear and difficulty will be as intensified as the pleasure. But, yes, I think I would. With the right partner.'

He looked at her face again. She was smiling. For a moment, she met his gaze, her eyes shining and intense, then she looked down into her lap.

'I hope you haven't forgotten that I agreed to answer your questions. I'm ready for my interrogation. You can even shine a light in my eyes, if you like, to create the right atmosphere.'

Dan didn't even have to think about his first question. 'Are you kinky? And, if so, are you dom or sub?'

'Do I have to be either? I hate labels. If I have sex with women does that make me bisexual? I don't think so. If you put labels on your sexuality you have to try to fit yourself into someone else's definition. I prefer to think of myself as open to any experience that's pleasurable or interesting.'

'Isn't that avoiding my question? Even if you don't label yourself, surely you must have preferences.'

'I'm sorry. It's not my intention to evade any of your questions. You've shared your soul with me, I'll do the same.' She reached down and removed her shoes. She dropped them onto the floor with a thud. Dan knew that she was deliberately teasing him by making him wait for her answer. She massaged her feet for several seconds before carrying on.

'I'm mostly dominant, though it wasn't always the case and, occasionally, I switch with one of my lovers. But not because I feel submissive ... I just enjoy the pain and surrender. My first kinky experiences were submissive and I'm sure it was allowing myself to do it that put me in touch with my personal power and helped me, in a way, to find out who I really am.'

'So what sort of thing do you do sexually?' Dan noticed that her feet were unusually small for a woman of her height. He had to fight the urge to touch them.

'Let me see. I'm pretty open, really. Whipping, fisting, cutting, toilet games. I like to strap on a cock and fuck a man because nothing brings home to a man quite how powerless he is more than that.' She smiled as she spoke and Dan knew she was deliberately trying to shock and arouse him. And it was definitely working.

'So, what's the most extreme thing you've ever done, do you think?'

She shrugged. 'I suppose it depends on what you mean by extreme and what your particular limits are.'

'Well ... have you drawn blood – like that scene in *Maîtresse*?'

She nodded slowly. 'And I enjoyed it. Edge play produces extreme emotional and physical responses and can create and deepen an intimacy to a degree that most people can never even imagine.'

Dan's cock was tingling. His breath caught in his throat. 'Have you ever done anything really disgusting?'

'Well ... I once had a lover who wanted to lie under a glass table and have me shit on it. He went on about it so much that eventually I upped the ante, thinking it would put him off. I agreed to do it, but without the table.'

Dan's cheeks blazed with heat and colour. 'And what did he say?'

Jo laughed. 'He leapt at the chance. It turned out that the table was his way of making it acceptable to me.'

'And what was it like?

'Messy, incredible, intense, filthy, but I don't care if I never do it again.' She stretched out her legs and crossed them at the ankle. She looked languid and sensual and utterly aware of the effect she was having on him. Dan reached out a finger and ran it along her shin. She shivered like a cat who'd been stroked. 'What's your most filthy experience?'

'Let me think. Nothing that rivals yours I'm afraid, but I do have a strange one. When I was at university my roommate would come silently into the bathroom when I was in the bath and masturbate into the water. I would get an enormous erection and I found it unbelievably exciting but neither of us ever spoke about it.'

'And did you ever consider reciprocating?'

'I considered it many times but never acted on it. Does that make me bisexual?'

She shrugged. 'Don't ask me. You know how I feel about labels. How do you feel about sex with another man? Would you?'

'Not even curious really. But I can see how it would work in a submissive context. More coffee?'

Jo nodded slowly. He topped up their cups from the cafetière. 'Tell me, Jo. A woman like you . . . I bet you have lots of lovers.' He looked down into his coffee.

'A few. My assistant at work . . . Sam of course . . . and Adam – I see him once a week. And I've got a lover who lives in America now. We see each other a couple of times a year.'

'Don't you want someone more permanent? Someone to love?'

Jo picked up her cup and sipped it, deliberately avoiding his gaze. 'Until quite recently I was happy with my lot but I've come to realise I want the intimacy of a committed relationship, it's just a question of meeting someone.' She looked directly at him. 'I don't suppose you happen to know anyone kinky and single, do you?'

Dan felt his heart quicken. 'Single yes, kinky maybe, confused certainly.'

Jo laughed. 'What's your next question?'

'I know . . . how did you lose your virginity?'

'I'm not sure if it counts as losing my virginity but the first time I had an orgasm with another person was when I met an older man in the cinema. I was in the sixth form and I'd bunked off school to see an X film.'

'You must have been an absolute hussy.'

'I certainly did my best. I never did get to see the end of the film. He talked me into going for a drive and he took me to a local country park and licked me in the back of his car. I offered to reciprocate but all he'd wanted was to wank off in my face and I eagerly complied. I hung about in the cinema often after that, but never saw him again. How about you?'

'I lost mine on a family holiday to Crete when I was 17. On the beach. It was quite romantic until I realised she'd given me the crabs. But I didn't get my cock sucked until university. My first proper girlfriend loved it but she always insisted on spitting it into a handkerchief which made me feel ashamed and dirty and unreasonable. When I first met a girl who swallowed I thought I was in heaven.'

Jo drained her cup. She looked him straight in the eye. 'Well, maybe it's just me, but I don't think you should put it in your mouth unless you're prepared to swallow.'

At the end of the evening Dan offered to walk Jo home but she wouldn't hear of it. He took her hand and led her into the hall.

'Will you do something for me before you go?' Jo's voice was a tender caress.

'Anything. I'll do whatever you ask.'

'Then I'd like you to get on your knees and kiss my feet.' Her eyes were shining.

Dan slid silently to his knees. He cupped her foot in both hands and brought his mouth to the soft suede. His face rasped softly against the nylon of her stocking as he rubbed his lips against her shoe. His thickening cock was squashed and restricted inside his clothes.

'Mmm ... that feels good. I can feel your face through my stocking. You look beautiful on your knees.' Her voice sounded dreamy and languid.

He lavished her shoe with kisses. He rubbed it with his lips. The suede felt soft and velvety against his face. His crotch throbbed with heat and pleasure.

'Thank you, Dan. You can get up now.' She withdrew her foot. Dan stood up. Without speaking, he grabbed her hand and put it on his crotch. He felt her fingers slowly exploring his erection. 'I assume you'll be playing with that after I've gone.'

Dan could hear the excitement in her voice. 'What do you think?'

'Well, when you do, I want you to think of me.' She smiled softly.

'That won't be a problem, I assure you.'

'And, when you've finished, I want you to eat it.' Without waiting for an answer she opened the door and walked down the steps.

When Dan was climbing into bed his phone beeped as it received a text. He retrieved it from his trouser pocket and pressed the button to retrieve the message. 'Remember that you promised to do WHATEVER I wanted so I hope you aren't thinking of disobeying me. Talk soon, Jo.'

He laughed out loud.

Eleven

The next day Dan was getting out of the shower when the phone rang. He picked up a towel and ran, naked, into the bedroom.

'Dan Elliot.'

'Dan, it's Jo. I'm not disturbing you, I hope. I know it's early.'

He laughed. 'As a matter of fact I've just got out of the shower. I'm standing here naked and wet.'

'Really? That sounds like a line out of a porn movie. Do you want me to call you back?' Her voice was soft and full of humour.

'No, it's fine. What can I do for you?' He wrapped the towel around his waist and sat down on the bed.

'Well ... we pussyfooted around it last night but I think we'd both like to take things further.'

'Yes. That's what I want.' He closed his eyes and tried to picture her.

'And so do I. So I was thinking that it might be easier to explore things away from everyday life. Somewhere the normal rules don't apply. The school's empty for the summer holidays and it's a wonderful place to play. If you come over on Friday night and leave on Monday morning that should give us plenty of time to explore. If we don't like it, then we can pretend it was a dream, a holiday romance. What do you think?'

Dan imagined her sitting at her desk, leaning back in her chair and looking out of the window as she spoke. He pictured the sun making her golden hair gleam and her porcelain skin glowing. 'I like the idea. It gives a certain element of safety to what would otherwise be terrifying and bottomless.'

'And it ends on Monday, unless you want it to continue.'

'Is that what you want? For it to end?' There was an odd light sensation in his chest and his heart boomed.

'No, not at all,' she answered quickly. 'But it has to be your decision. I have no doubts at all but you aren't even sure if you're kinky.'

'At least I know I'll be in good hands.'

'So you trust me?' She sounded uncharacteristically uncertain.

'Of course I do, otherwise I wouldn't even be contemplating it.' He brought up his knees and curled his body around the phone. 'I only hope I don't let you down.'

'I'm sure you won't. It's a journey we make together, Dan, and I have no expectation of where it might end. Whatever happens will be right for us.'

'So what happens next?'

'I'll see you here at seven p.m. on Friday. Text me from the gate and I'll be waiting for you at the front door.'

Over the next few days Dan could hardly think of anything else. Spending all day immersed in the kinky lifestyle didn't help. He went to a fetish fair with Jim and Poppy and attended a Japanese rope bondage seminar, all under the watchful eye of the camera.

He was his usual professional self, joking and playing up for the cameras when the expert used him to demonstrate a particularly elaborate technique. As the ropes tightened around his body, in a complicated lattice pattern that bound him from his shoulders to his ankles, he experienced a rush of excitement that coloured his cheeks and make him feel light-headed.

When the other end of the rope was attached to a hook and he was hoisted into the air he felt an utterly surprising and thoroughly seductive sense of wellbeing and fulfilment.

But every second of the day he thought of Jo and the weekend to come. Each item of equipment at the fetish fair, each crop, butt-plug and ball-gag brought to mind images of her lovingly using the implements of him as he lay helpless, at her mercy and totally satisfied.

At the end of the day he was exhausted, sweaty and restless, bubbling over with arousal, longing and frustration. Masturbation only made him feel worse. After several days of unrelieved tension and desire he decided to visit Sarah but that didn't help either. It was just too familiar, too safe, too predictable. It reminded him of what he was missing and the sexual release it gave him was all too temporary.

As he walked up the school's drive on Friday evening his mind was buzzing with excitement and trepidation. The tip of his cock was sticky inside his boxers and his crotch ached with tension and arousal. As he drew close he saw her standing in the open doorway.

She was dressed in black flared trousers and a long-sleeved top. As he got closer he could see that she was wearing a pair of narrow glasses he'd never seen before and that her hair was up. As he walked the final few yards, his feet crunching over the gravel, his head swam with endorphins and he felt as though his heart was in his throat.

'Come in, Dan, and follow me.' She turned and began to walk away, leaving him to close the door.

He followed her down a long corridor. Maybe it was

his imagination but, from behind, she looked like she meant business. There was a determined set to her shoulders and something authoritative and slightly impatient in the clip, clip, clop of her stilettos against the tiled floor. He looked down at her feet and he noticed that her heels looked like gleaming metal spikes terminating in a flat base, like a pair of huge nails. His cock tingled.

She'd wound her hair up into a French pleat. He could see the fine pale hairs on the back of her neck and the smooth hollow of her nape. As he walked behind her, he couldn't take his eyes of those few inches of bare flesh and downy blonde hair. It seemed intimate and exciting and as illicit and arousing as if he'd accidentally stumbled on her naked.

They passed through a set of double doors into the main school building. Jo strode ahead as if she'd even forgotten he was there. She opened a door and held it open, waiting for him to catch up. They stepped inside. It was an old-fashioned classroom with rows of desks facing the front and a huge old teacher's desk on a raised dais. Dan instantly felt twelve years old again.

'Let me start by telling you the rules.' Jo leaned against the teacher's desk. Standing on the raised dais she was a good six inches taller than Dan. His heart was beating so fast it felt as though it was rattling his ribs. 'And listen carefully, because I have no intention of repeating myself. At any rate, it won't take long, because there's really only one rule. I'm in charge. You do whatever I tell you when I tell you and how I tell you. Do we understand each other?'

'Yes, I understand . . . sorry, Jo . . . but I'm really not sure how I should address you.' He gazed up at her.

'Under the circumstances I think "miss" might be appropriate, don't you?'

Dan felt his cock twitch. 'Yes, miss. Absolutely perfect.'

'Now sit down there and behave yourself while I get ready.'

Dan sat down behind the first desk. He watched as Jo pulled her top off over her head and folded it carefully before putting it down on the teacher's chair. She undid her trousers. Dan noticed that they fastened at the side rather than the front and, as he watched her sliding them down her legs, the detail seemed mysterious and foreign and utterly exciting.

Underneath she was wearing a long-line black bra made from silk and lace, and black high-waisted panties which were so sheer that he could see not only her pubic hair but also her appendix scar. His crotch burned.

He watched as she picked up a black garment from the back of the chair and began to put it on. Dan instantly realised that it was an academic gown and his heart leapt. She fiddled with the front of the gown, adjusting it so that it lay properly across her front, then she opened the desk.

For a moment, she was concealed behind the open lid and Dan hardly dared to breathe. The desk closed with a bang and Dan saw that she was now wearing a mortarboard and, in her hand, was a long swan-necked school cane.

'Now. I'd like you to undress please. Take everything off, fold it neatly and put it on your chair.' She somehow managed to sound both authoritative and disinterested at the same time.

Dan stood up. He bent to undo his shoes then toed them off. He took off both socks and slipped them into his shoes. He lined them up neatly beside the chair. He unbuttoned his shirt, struggling to control his trembling fingers.

Time seemed to slow down. He could hear the tick, tick, tick, of the classroom clock. He could hear his own heart beating. He folded his shirt and put it on the chair.

He unbuckled his belt and unzipped his trousers then slid them down.

He knew that she'd be able to see that he was already hard. His erection tented the front of his boxers and he didn't need to look down to know that they'd be stained dark by pre-come. He put his trousers on the top of the pile then faced Jo and removed his boxers. He gazed up at her, his cock rigid and his heart pounding.

Jo stepped off the dais and walked over to him. She looked him slowly up and down and Dan felt a stab of anxiety. More than anything he wanted to measure up to her expectations.

'You're shaved. Thinking ahead?'

'No, miss. Mistress Sadie did it.'

Jo laughed. She ran the tip of her finger slowly along the underside of his erection. His cock twitched and his blood pounded in his ears.

'Well, I like it. Keep it that way.'

'Yes, miss.' Dan felt an irrational swell of pride.

'Now. I'd like you to open your desk and put on the outfit you find in there.' She turned and walked back to the dais.

Inside the desk was a neatly folded school uniform. A girl's uniform. On top of the pile was a pair of navy-blue school knickers and a pair of white frilly ankle socks.

Dan picked up the knickers and stepped into them. He slid them up, pausing to manhandle his erection into place. They felt thick and rather too warm and restrictive and Dan felt his face colouring from humiliation and excitement. He sat down on top of his own clothes and put on his socks.

The next item on the pile was a short-sleeved white school shirt. Dan put it on. He buttoned it up to the neck and raised the collar to put on his tie. When the tie was knotted and his collar smoothed down he picked up the final item in the pile. It was a short grey pleated gymslip with a bib at the front and straps which crossed over at the back.

Dan's cock tingled. When he'd finished dressing he looked up at Jo, waiting for approval. He felt ridiculous and utterly humiliated yet, beneath it all, blazed a heat and arousal that was so profound it was almost frightening.

'Now, Danielle, I'd like you to come up here and clean my shoes with your tongue.'

'Yes, miss.' Dan stepped up onto the dais. He dropped to his knees. He cupped her left foot between both hands and began to lick. Her shoes were shiny patent leather and his tongue slid easily over the surface. Her naked foot brushed against his face as he licked. Her skin was silky soft and seemed unnaturally warm.

'I think you ought to clean the sole while you're about it.' She raised her foot off the ground. Dan bent his head down and began to lick her sole. It felt gritty and dry and tasted bitter.

His hands trembled as he held her foot in place. His cock was fully hard, trapped and uncomfortable inside his tight hot knickers.

'You like that, don't you?' Her voice was full of contempt and arousal. 'You were born to kneel at a strong woman's feet. To serve her . . . to take punishment or pleasure, whichever she chooses to bestow, and not caring which of them it turns out to be. Yes . . . we both know what you are. Don't we?'

'Yes, miss.'

'Open your mouth and suck my heel.' She leaned back against the desk and extended her foot.

Dan looked up at her. Her cheeks were flushed pink and her eyes were glistening. She gazed down at him silently, waiting. He opened his mouth. He felt the tip of her stiletto against his lower lip. It was hard and cold like the blade of a knife. Sharp and dangerous. He closed his lips and sucked it into his mouth.

He watched her face as he began to rock back and forth, allowing her heel to fuck his mouth. Dan's cock ached.

She withdrew her heel and Dan felt as if he'd been robbed. His hand slid unconsciously between his legs. He rubbed the heel of his thumb against his erection, adjusting it inside the restrictive underwear.

'Did I give you permission to play with that thing?' Jo put her hands on her hips.

'No, miss. I'm very sorry.'

'You need to be taught a lesson. Stand up immediately.'

Dan scrabbled to his feet.

'Now pull your knickers down to your knees and bend over your desk.' Jo slapped the desk with her cane. It swished through the air and landed with a thump.

He pushed his knickers down to his knees. His erection stood out in front of him. He bent over the desk, flattening his body across it and hanging his head.

He felt Jo flip up his skirt, exposing his naked rear end. Heat and excitement pumped around his bloodstream.

'I don't know if you've ever been caned before, but I think you'll enjoy the sensation.'

Dan knew that his cock and balls would be clearly visible. The tip of his erection was pressed up against the edge of the desk. Jo pressed the tip of her cane against his perineum. He gasped. She ran the cane's cold pointed tip down over his ball sac and along the underside of his stiff cock. He moaned. She ran the tip of the cane around the margin of his puckered arsehole.

She brought the cane down across his buttocks. It landed with a crack and Dan's body jerked forwards. He heard her gown rustle as she raised her arm high and brought it down. The cane swished through the air and made a loud thwacking noise as it made contact. Dan grunted. Jo delivered three strokes in a row. Dan arched his back, lifting up his head and panting.

She whipped him with the cane. It swished noisily through the air and landed with a crack. Instantly, Jo hit him again, bringing the cane down a couple of inches higher.

Dan's body was rigid and trembling. Every time Jo hit him the tip of his erection was pressed against the edge of the desk and he'd begun to thrust his hips.

Her gown swished as she raised the cane into the air and brought it down with all her weight behind it. It wooshed and cracked as it landed. Dan's body jerked and his hips pumped.

'I can see what you're doing and it won't work. I want you to take a step backwards so that your cock is nowhere near the desk.' Jo slashed his buttocks with the cane. Dan grunted. He stepped away from the desk.

She delivered a hail of stinging strokes. His belly felt liquid and tight. His nipples burned.

'Stand up.' Her voice was soft and deep.

Dan straightened up and turned to look at her. He inhaled sharply. Her robe had fallen open, displaying her underwear. His cock was fully erect, poking out under his skirt.

'Hold out your hands.'

Dan extended both hands, palms uppermost. She slashed the cane down on his left hand. It burned and stung and he had to fight the urge to pull it away. She must have read his mind because she held onto his wrist and delivered two more stinging strokes. Dan grunted. Blood pounded in his brain.

She gripped his other wrist and delivered three vicious slashes. Dan gasped in shock and pain. She dropped the cane and it landed on the wooden floor with a thud. His cock felt ready to burst.

'That was for rubbing your cock against the desk.

You don't get to come unless I want you to. Understand?'

'Yes, miss.'

Jo leaned forwards and cupped the back of his head with her right hand and used the fingertips of her left to stroke his cheek. She was smiling. She ran her thumb across his lower lip.

Dan could feel her hot breath on his face. Her skin smelled lemony and sweet. She closed her eyes and kissed him. Dan felt something clutch at the base of his belly. Her lips were soft and moist and yielding. He put his hands on her waist, under the gown and pulled her close. Her body was warm and silky. His erection pressed up against her belly, its tip wet and tingling.

'We'd better stop, or we'll be late for dinner. I've booked a table.' She released his face. 'Get dressed in your own clothes.' Jo walked back to the dais. 'But put these on underneath.' She opened the desk and tossed something at him. Dan caught it.

'What's this?' He stretched out the garment. It was a pair of little girl's knickers, decorated with rows and rows of frills. He felt his face colouring and his cock twitch. He took off his uniform and began to put them on. He pulled the tight knickers up over his hips with difficulty and arranged his tackle inside their restrictive embrace.

Jo slid off her gown and began to dress. 'Nobody else will know, but we will . . . that's the point.'

Over dinner they never mentioned what had happened in the classroom. Dan could barely take his eyes off her. Even in her plain top and trousers she seemed the most glamorous woman in the room. There was something elegant and compelling about her and he wasn't the only one to notice it. Their waiter was obsequious and fawning and barely even glanced at

Dan. And a diner at a nearby table almost tripped over on the way to the loo because he was looking at her.

Dan was conscious of the unfamiliar feel of his little girl's knickers. They dug in at the legs and the front flattened his crotch. Occasionally, he'd shift his weight in his chair and his sore behind would give him a twinge and his palms were hot where she had caned him.

They walked home from the restaurant, enjoying the warm evening. At the front entrance Jo took a huge iron key out of her handbag and unlocked the door. Instead of heading for the stairs she walked off in the direction of the corridor that led to the school.

'Follow me,' she called, without even bothering to look back.

Dan's cock stirred inside his tight panties. Jo turned on lights as she went. The school seemed enormous and silent and slightly ominous. The only sound was the echoey clack of Jo's high heels.

She led him into the classroom. She switched on the overhead light and the fluorescent tubes clicked and flickered into life. Without being told, Dan went and stood over by the same desk. His cock was aching and uncomfortable inside the grip of his knickers.

'Strip down to your knickers and wait for me here.' She turned and walked away.

Dan could hear the sound of her heels retreating down the corridor. He undressed and stood to attention in front of his desk. Standing practically naked in the huge room he felt foolish and vulnerable. It was dark outside and he could see his reflection in the blackened windows. He looked as ridiculous as he felt and yet his skin felt prickly and sensitive and his cock was tingling.

He heard her high heels approaching and Jo came back into the room followed by a man. A wave of shock crashed over him. His heart thumped.

She came over and stood in front of him, the man

following at her heels like an eager puppy. 'Dan, this is my friend, Costas.'

The man stuck out his hand and Dan shook it. Costas was tall and dark-skinned. Dan thought he was probably Mediterranean, Greek or Italian maybe. Like Jo, he was dressed head to toe in black, in tight jeans and a cap-sleeved T-shirt that clung to his impressive muscles. He was smiling slightly and his chocolate-dark eyes seemed to gleam.

A hard knot of anxiety and excitement had settled under Dan's ribs.

'Put your clothes in your desk please, and sit down in your chair.' Jo's voice left him in no doubt that she expected unquestioning and instant obedience.

He eagerly complied, lifting the lid of his desk and putting his clothes inside. He sat down. The chair was cold and clammy against his naked skin.

Jo turned and went over and opened the teacher's desk. She closed the lid and came back to him with a long chain and a padlock. Dan's eyes widened. His cock ached.

'Put your hands behind your back please.' Jo walked behind him and wrapped the end of the chain around his wrists several times. It was icy cold and the links dug into his skin. She began to wind it around his body and the chair. Heat and excitement pumped through his blood.

She wrapped the chain around his body over and over again, then passed it under the seat and over his thighs and soon he was completely encased in chain. It felt heavy and cold and tight.

Jo tugged on the chain, making sure it was tight. He could see the concentration on her face. There was a thin sheen of sweat on her upper lip and a lock of hair had fallen forwards over her forehead and trembled slightly as she tightened the chain.

Finally, she reached the end of the chain and she used the padlock to fasten it. Dan was immobile. Layer upon layer of heavy chain encircled his body like a chrysalis. His crotch was on fire.

When she'd finished, she knelt down beside him. She cupped his face and kissed him. Dan could taste the coffee and brandy they had drunk after their meal. Her hot breath hissed onto his face. She broke the kiss and stood up.

'Undress please, Costas. You can put your clothes on one of the desks.'

Costas pulled his T-shirt over his head, revealing a sculpted six-pack and an impressive set of pecs. He unzipped his jeans and pushed them and his underwear down to his knees in one movement. Dan could see that he was fully shaved. His cock was already semi-erect and seemed huge to Dan, but then he'd seldom seen another man's in that condition.

Costas straightened up and waited for orders. Dan could see his chest heaving.

'Go and stand beside my desk please.'

Costas obeyed. Jo stepped onto the dais. She retrieved a canvas travel bag from the seat and put it down on the desk. She began to undo the bag. The noise of the zip was the only sound in the building. It seemed unnaturally loud, obscene and full of promise.

Jo took a leather item from the bag. Costas obviously recognised it because he gasped. She began to fiddle with the leather item and Dan realised that it was a strap-on harness. There was a triangle of leather at the front from which protruded a black silicone cock, realistic in every detail. He could see that inside there was a smaller dildo, designed to fit inside her. A watery shiver of excitement slid along his spine.

'I'm going to fuck Costas, Dan, if you hadn't already worked that out. He loves to bend over for me and have his arse used like a cunt.' She looked at Dan as she said the final word, gauging his reaction. Inside his underwear, his cock ached.

Jo began to undress. 'On the inside of the harness there's a series of little bumps which press against my clit and, if I fuck him hard enough, they'll make me come. I think you'll find it exciting to watch.' She dropped her top onto the chair and unhooked her bra.

Her breasts were small and round, her nipples a pale rosy pink. She unzipped her trousers and pulled them down, bending to step out of them. She put them on the chair and began to slide down her knickers. When she straightened up, naked, Dan realised he had been holding his breath.

She was nude except for her high heels and she was magnificent. Porcelain-pale and perfect. Her rosy nipples were already wrinkled and hard. Her pubic hair was short and trimmed, the same light blonde as her hair.

Dan was growing hot and sweaty inside his chain bindings. He couldn't move a millimetre.

Jo stepped into the harness and pressed the small inner dildo against her crotch. He saw her eyes narrow as it slid inside her and she let out a soft sigh. She buckled the harness around her hips, pulling it tight. The fake cock stood out in front of her, curved upwards towards the ceiling.

She reached into the bag and tossed Costas a bottle of lube. He caught it and dispensed a big dollop onto his fingers. He dropped the bottle back into the bag then reached round and began to lube himself up.

Dan could hear the gel squelching. Costas sighed and his eyes narrowed and Dan realised he must have slid a finger into his own arse.

'That will do. Now come and bend over the desk.' Jo's voice managed to convey both authority and tenderness. Dan could see her chest heaving.

Costas bent over the desk. His body was flat against the top, his arms bent at the elbows. He turned his face to the side and laid his cheek against the surface. He closed his eyes.

His naked arse looked rounded and inviting. Dan could see a mottled patterning of old bruises. His belly tightened.

Jo stepped forwards and bent over Costas. She pressed the tip of her cock between his cheeks. She leaned forwards and Dan saw the tip of the dildo disappear. Costas lifted his head off the desk and balled his hands into fists.

Dan's cock was aching and squashed. He tried to wriggle to relieve it, but the chains held him fast. Jo slid forwards until the front of her harness was pressed up against Costas. She slowly circled her hips then leaned forward and gripped his shoulders.

She held onto Costas's shoulders with her eyes closed and her head back. Her nipples were crinkled and erect. He longed to be able to take one into his mouth and suck on it. He struggled against his chains.

Jo pulled on Costas's shoulders. Her hips thrust in and out, knocking him forwards and banging his thighs against the desk.

Dan could see the taut muscles in her thighs. He imagined the silicone bumps inside the harness rubbing against her clit. Costas was biting his lip. Dan's erection felt as though it was being gripped in an iron fist. He wriggled and the chains clanked.

Jo fucked Costas like a woman possessed. Her hair had come loose and fell around her face. Costas was panting and moaning. Dan could see that he was thrusting backwards on the dildo, matching her rhythm.

Dan wished it was him bent over the desk with Jo's cock in his arse. He longed to feel her hands digging into his shoulders and the urgent thrusting of her hips as she fucked him.

Jo pulled on Costas's shoulders and stabbed her hips. She let out a deep guttural grunt on every jab. Sweat ran down her body. Her breasts bounced as she fucked him. Dan was beside himself with frustration. Heat and excitement pumped around his body.

Costas's erection stood out beneath him. Every so often he would wriggle his hips, trying to rub his cock against the edge of the desk.

Jo's hips pumped. Dan could tell that she was building towards orgasm. Her throat and chest were covered in a blotchy red rash. She was moaning and sobbing.

Dan couldn't think of anything more wonderful or exciting than having her use his eager hole to make herself come. His cock was leaking pre-come and he could feel a wet patch on the front of his panties.

She was fucking Costas so hard that the desk began to rock and his body banged against it on every thrust. Her mouth was open and she was screaming and howling.

Jo began to thrust shallow and fast. Dan could see that her knuckles were white as she gripped him. Costas held onto the desk, bracing himself.

Dan tried to imagine the feel of the fat dildo in his arse and the leather harness bashing against him on each stab. The desk would feel smooth and slick underneath him and he'd have to grip the edge and brace himself to meet her thrusts. Jo was making high keening cries. Her body gleamed, her breasts danced.

Costas's erection was purple, the skin tight and shiny. Jo began to wail and Dan saw her body begin to tremble. She was coming.

Dan's crotch was on fire. He struggled in frustration and the chair wobbled and almost teetered over.

She gave one final thrust, pulling hard on Costas's shoulders and punching her hips forwards. Her body was rigid, her back arched. Her hair was wild around her face. She wailed and sobbed. Her body shook

Dan's crotch burned as he struggled against his chains. He couldn't take his eyes off her.

He saw her muscles soften as she released Costas's shoulders. She laughed and opened her eyes. She stepped back and her cock slid out of him. Costas turned his head and looked at her, an expression of loss and disappointment in his brown eyes. Jo patted his arse.

She unbuckled the harness and let it fall to the floor. She rummaged in the travel bag and found a key then held it up for Dan to see. She walked over to him and unlocked his padlock.

The chains clanked and tinkled as Jo unwound them. Finally, Dan was free. His body felt suddenly cold and his arms had gone to sleep. He brought his hands to his knees, wincing in pain.

Jo dropped the coil of chain onto the floor. 'I suppose you'd like to come now.'

'I assume that's a rhetorical question.' He looked up at her.

Jo laughed. She bent down and whispered. 'Take off those ridiculous knickers and play with it then.'

Dan stood up and slid down his pants, pausing to extricate his erection. He gripped his cock in his fist. He exhaled in relief and pleasure. He rubbed his foreskin back and forwards over the tip, spreading the pre-come.

It wouldn't take him long, he knew. His cock was pumped with blood and heat. He closed his eyes and pumped his fist.

It was bliss to handle himself after so much frustration. He could feel the delicious hot tingle spreading up from his groin and along his spine. This was no time for making it last or teasing himself. His need was urgent, visceral and intense.

He fucked his fist, gripping his erection tight. He could hear the rhythmic slapping sound of his hand on his cock. He began to groan and roar.

'You're going to come soon, aren't you?'

He could feel Jo's hot breath on his face. 'Yes, miss. I am.' He was panting and gasping. Sweat trickled down his body. His muscles were taut and trembling. His legs shook.

'Well, when you do, I want you to catch it in your hand and eat it.'

'Yes, miss.' Dan's voice was a sibilant hiss. The thought of eating his own spunk for her was all it took to tip him over the edge. He brought his hand down hard, pulling back his foreskin. He cupped his other hand over the tip of his cock. He grunted and moaned through gritted teeth. His cock pumped out spunk and the hot liquid splashed into his hand.

He gasped in relief and delight. Every twitch of his cock was accompanied by a wave of shivery exquisite pleasure. Tingles slid along his spine.

Dan opened his eyes and looked down at the cooling spunk in his hand. He looked at Jo and brought it to his lips. He licked up the salty liquid and swallowed it.

Twelve

Costas went up to his own flat and Jo took Dan upstairs for a quick shower before bed. She soaped his body, allowing her hands to slide over his slippery skin and paid loving attention to his cock. Her pussy ached.

They towelled each other off and climbed, naked, into bed. Jo lay with her head on Dan's chest. He stroked her back, making her tingle. She could hear his heart beating. She listened as his breathing slowed down into the rhythm of sleep. She closed her eyes.

When she woke up in the morning Dan was leaning on an elbow looking at her.

She smiled at him then leaned forwards and kissed him. 'Hello. Have you been staring at me long?'

He shook his head. 'Only a couple of minutes. I don't think I've ever told you how beautiful you are.' He stroked her hair.

'Thank you. So you still like me after I was so mean to you last night?' She propped herself up against the pillows.

'Yes, of course I do. Though you were very mean.'

'I know . . . you understand why I brought Costas downstairs, I hope.' She took his hand.

'I think I do. Sadie has a slave – a lover – who helps her in the dungeon. I thought it must be torture for him to watch her with other men. I couldn't imagine how he stood it. But when I asked her she told me that she made him do it to bring home to him quite how thoroughly she owned him. I imagine you had something similar in mind.' Dan was gazing at her. Without his glasses he looked vulnerable and boyish.

'Yes, that's more or less it. I wanted you to understand that obedience means doing whatever I ask, no matter how unpalatable it might be.'

'Or frustrating . . .' He smiled.

'You got to come in the end, didn't you?'

'But I had to do it myself and, more importantly, you robbed me of the pleasure of making you come.' He slid across the bed and slid his hand between her legs. Jo gasped as his warm fingers covered her crotch.

'I certainly didn't intend to deprive you of that pleasure for ever.' She opened her legs.

'Why don't I make up for lost time, then?' He threw back the covers and crawled across the mattress. He nestled down between her legs. She felt heat and moisture as Dan opened his mouth and began to lick.

Jo sighed as Dan's mouth awakened her clit. She gripped the bed's rails and began to slowly move her hips. She felt pinpricks of pleasure creeping up her nape and over her scalp.

Dan's fingertips trailed over her thighs. She shivered. They moved up her sides, slowly enlivening every pore and particle with pleasure. She gasped.

His thumbs flicked across the tips of her nipples, making her shiver. She writhed and bucked as his tongue worked its magic. Hot breath rushed out of his nose, warming her skin.

Jo was beginning to sweat. Her nipples throbbed. She reached down and pinched them, rolling the fat buds between thumb and forefinger. They prickled and stung with pleasure/pain. She arched her back.

She had begun to moan. Her body thrashed. Dan's

arms were wrapped around her writhing hips. She imagined his cock, rigid and painful now, aching for release.

She rocked her hips, rubbing her excited pussy against his face. Her clit tingled. Her hands gripped the bedrails behind her head tighter. She looked down at his face. His eyes were half closed, slitted and dancing.

The rest of his face was hidden beneath her crotch. Heat and tension was beginning to spread out from her pelvis. Her arms were locked rigid as she gripped the rail. She rocked her hips, rubbing herself against Dan's eager face, establishing a rhythm.

Excited shivers slid up and down her spine. Her crotch ached. She looked down at Dan's face. His eyelids gleamed in the light. He sucked on Jo's clit, lavishing it with his tongue. Jo's body quivered and shook. She held on tight to the railings, holding herself in place.

Dan's mouth was slippery and soft. She could feel his body heat seeping into her. Her nipples were erect and sensitive. Dan's mouth slid against her excited cunt. Tension twisted in her gut. Dan's lids flicked open his eyes and looked up at her, his eyes glistening and intense.

Her skin was sensitive and alive. Her crotch prickled with pleasure and congestion. She dug her heels into the mattress and rocked her hips.

Excitement pumped around her bloodstream. Her clit responded to every tiny flutter of his tongue and, a moment later, she felt the same excitement and pleasure in her swollen nipples. She arched her back.

Jo reached down and stroked Dan's hair. She trailed her fingertips down over his face. He shivered. Dan stepped up the pace, matching the rhythm of her pumping hips. Her clit was tense and tingling.

She felt a finger at her entrance which then slid past her muscles. He curled his finger and pressed it hard against Jo's sweet spot. A jolt of excitement shot up her spine. She felt a second finger against the tight ring of her arsehole and she knew she was going to come.

Her body was rigid and quivering. Her hips moved urgently. Dan sucked on her clit, pressing both fingers hard inside her.

She felt electrified. Little shocks of pleasure slid over her skin. She thrashed her head against the pillow, matting her hair.

Jo was grunting and moaning. The pleasure was building, ready to explode. Her body was rigid. She ground her crotch against Dan's mouth.

Jo's thrusts had grown shorter and more urgent. Dan sucked hard on her clit and massaged her G-spot. Jo could feel her muscles grip his fingers. Her body trembled and shook.

She ground her crotch against Dan's face, her strokes short and urgent. The tension burst and she let out a high keening cry as she began to come.

Waves of pleasure and release shot up her spine and slid down her legs to her feet. Her back arched. She pressed her heels down into the mattress, bringing her hips up off the bed.

It kept on coming. Shivery tingling ripples crept up her nape and over her scalp. Her toes curled, her nipples throbbed. She gasped and mewled.

She was sweaty and exhausted, her muscles ached. She relaxed back against the pillow. Dan crawled up the bed and took her in his arms. She could feel his heart beating as she lay against his chest. She stroked his belly.

'I hate to spoil the moment,' he said finally, 'but I need a piss.'

Jo laughed softly. 'Do you? That gives me an idea. Come with me.' She slid off the bed and towards the bathroom.

After a moment's hesitation, Dan followed.

She picked up her tooth glass and handed it to him. 'There you are . . . can you fill that for me?'

Dan raised an eyebrow. 'Not from here – as the old joke goes.' He walked over and took it. He gripped his cock in one hand and lowered the glass. 'I'm not sure I'll be able to go, actually . . . I'm not used to an audience. And it's still a bit hard. Which doesn't help.'

Jo watched his cock. She noticed that his pubic hair had begun to grow, speckling his skin with dark stubble. Even soft, his cock was thick and long. He held it between thumb and forefinger, pointing it into the glass. He exhaled and began to piss.

Hot piss filled the glass. Her nipples stiffened. Her crotch still felt liquid and soft from her orgasm and her clit tingled.

'Oops. Better stop.' Dan handed her the glass and stepped up to the loo. He bent to lift the seat and began to pee again. Jo admired the strong muscles in his long thighs. His body was lean and lithe and his hand, holding his cock, was slender and elegant. He gazed down at his crotch as the arc of golden liquid tinkled into the bowl.

He noticed her looking and he looked up and smiled. When he'd finished he rolled his foreskin between thumb and forefinger to shake off the drips. 'If you'll move away from the sink I can wash my hands.' He smiled at her.

'I want you to drink this first.' She held up the glass.

'All of it?' He made a face.

'A couple of mouthfuls at least.' Heat welled up in her crotch.

He took the glass. He brought it to his nose and sniffed it. 'I think I'd find it a lot more palatable if it was your piss.'

'I know. That's the point.' She leaned against the

sink. 'But don't worry. You'll be drinking mine before too long.'

'Bottoms up.' Dan brought the glass to his lips and drank it down in one. He handed her the empty glass.

'Well . . . that was above and beyond. Thank you.' She took the glass.

'I wanted to show you how serious I am about this.'

'So . . .' She reached for his hand. 'I've corrupted you. How wonderful. Now I think it's time you fucked me.' She could hear the arousal in her own voice.

'With pleasure.' He turned towards the bedroom but she pulled on his hand, holding him back.

'Why don't we do it in here? Pervery is always more exciting if you do it in unexpected surroundings, don't you think?'

Dan smiled. Jo stepped forwards and bent over the vanity unit. She did it slowly, knowing that he was drinking in every detail. The granite top was cold and smooth against her skin. Her nipples brushed against the surface and she tingled all over.

She felt Dan's warm palms against her buttocks, then his thumbs stretching apart her cheeks. She sighed as he teased the wrinkled bud with the tip of his thumb.

'That feels quite lovely . . . but I think I'd like it in the usual place, if you don't mind.'

Dan moved his hands away and, a moment later, she felt him pushing the hard wet tip of his erection along the length of her pussy. She could feel the heat of him. He pushed it against her hole and he shifted his weight and began to press it home.

It slid slowly past her muscles. Her cunt was alive, tingling, on fire. She sighed. Dan pushed his cock home. Jo could feel his balls flattening against her pussy.

For several long moments he stayed motionless inside her. She could feel his hard hot cock inside her and her muscles gripping him. Dan pulled away from her. He moved agonisingly slowly and Jo's cunt seemed to burn with excitement. She sighed.

When he'd withdrawn almost fully he stayed motionless for a moment with just the tip of his erection inside her. Jo felt empty, abandoned. She wriggled her hips.

Dan laughed softly. She felt his fingers pressing into her hips as he held her in place, resisting her. The tips of her nipples were touching the granite and they burned. She looked over her shoulder at him. Dan was looking down, his eyes focused on the spot where their bodies met.

'Tell me what it looks like.' Jo could hear the excitement in her own voice.

'It's beautiful. Your cunt's swollen and glistening. My cock's all pumped up and purple. I can't see the tip because it's inside you but I can see it stretching you open. I can feel your muscles gripping me, it's incredible.' Dan's voice was breathy and deep.

She felt him shifting his weight behind her and his fingers dug into her hips. He slid back into her, filling and stretching her. She sighed in relief and excitement. It hit home and she could feel his crotch pressing up against hers.

He shifted his weight suddenly backwards and she felt him sliding out of her then immediately forwards with such force that she slammed forwards against the sink. She gripped the taps and pressed herself back against him.

Dan began to fuck her hard and deep. She braced herself against the vanity unit and met his thrusts. Dan grunted behind her. His fingers dug into her hips. Her nipples were dragged backwards and forwards across the granite on every thrust.

She could feel his cock sliding inside her. There was an obscene wet squelching noise. Slow shivers of excitement slid up and down her spine. Jo could feel tension congesting her pelvis. Her nipples prickled.

Dan pounded her. Jo banged against the edge of the vanity unit over and over again, mashing her breasts and nipples against the stone. She held onto the taps and matched his rhythm.

Her body was taut and trembling. Pressure throbbed in her belly. Dan was grunting, deep animal sounds of exertion and hunger. He fucked her hard and deep and rough. His crotch slapped against hers. Jo's crotch was tingly and tense. Heat pumped through her bloodstream.

Her body thrust forwards on each stroke, rubbing her breasts against the granite, providing delicious friction for her nipples. He was rigid and fat inside her. Dan released her hips. He pressed his body over her back and laid his hands over hers on the taps. His mouth was right beside her ear and she could feel hot moist breath on her skin.

Jo looked down at his hands covering hers. She saw the muscles in his forearms flex as he pulled himself forward in one sudden vicious jab. Her body banged against the edge of the sink.

He slid backwards an inch and did it again, tightening his hands over hers and pulling on the taps, thrusting himself hard into her. Jo grunted. She could feel her muscles, tight around Dan's cock. Tension throbbed in her pelvis.

Dan began to establish a rhythm, sliding back an inch or two then pulling hard on the taps. She banged against the unit, her tits mashed against the stone. Her crotch ached.

'I don't think I'm going to last much longer, I'm afraid.' Dan's words hissed in her ear.

'OK. Give it to me nice and hard, I'm almost there.' Jo pushed back against him.

He kissed her neck. He began to bite her and she arched her back and lifted up her head. He tightened the muscles in his arms and she felt his fingers gripping hers. His hips pistoned.

Dan pounded her. Her body slid backwards and forwards. Her nipples were ablaze, her crotch ached. Dan's crotch slapped against hers, growing faster and faster as his strokes grew shorter. He was hot and hard inside her. Her muscles gripped him. She pulled hard on the taps and met his thrusts.

Dan's hot breath hissed against her ear. His hips hammered. Jo was gasping and sobbing. She was on fire, taut, excited and on the edge. Her crotch burned and throbbed.

She felt his muscles stiffen and his body tense. He was fucking her hard, rapid shallow strokes that knocked her forwards and rubbed her excited nipples against the stone.

Dan's body went rigid behind her. He'd begun to quiver and he was fucking her in short urgent thrusts. Jo could feel the tension in her cunt building to a pitch. Dan's hands squeezed hers as he pulled himself forwards, pressing her fingers into the taps.

The tension shattered. Heat and relief flooded through her body. Blood rushed to her head making her feel drunk and dizzy. She trembled and shook. She sobbed and moaned.

Dan gave a final deep thrust and his cock began to twitch inside her. He lay over her back, grunting and panting.

Jo was tingling all over. Her nipples pulsed with fire. Her breasts were squashed beneath her and her body stuck to the granite.

Dan relaxed and she felt his weight pressing her against the unit. He released her hands and pushed her damp hair off her face. He kissed her neck.

'Well, now . . . that was definitely worth waiting for.'

'Why don't you come into the bedroom? I've got something for you.' As Jo straightened up she caught sight of herself in the mirror. Her hair was tangled and messy and her cheeks were flushed. She took Dan's hand and led him into the bedroom. They sat down on the bed and she took a long narrow leather box out of the bedroom drawer. She pushed it across the bed to him.

Dan smiled. He opened the box. Nestling in a depression in the purple velvet lining was a thick silver necklace. At the front was a heart-shaped padlock. Lying inside the oval of the necklace were two tiny silver keys.

'It's a collar . . .' He smiled. 'Thank you.' Dan picked it up.

'You understand what it means?'

He nodded. 'I think so – because of Hellfire 2000 – it means I belong to you . . . that you're my owner, or mistress, or whatever.'

'That's right. Look at the back of the padlock. I've had it engraved.'

Dan turned it over. He read aloud. 'It says, "This dog belongs to Jo Lennox." That makes my cock feel all tingly . . . I don't know why. Shall I put it on?'

Jo took the collar from him and opened the padlock with one of the keys. She handed it back and he eagerly fitted it to his neck. 'Obviously, I'll keep the keys.' She dropped them into her bedside drawer.

They spent the day at the Cass Sculpture Foundation in Sussex. Seeing the pieces in their outdoor setting, nestling among the beauty of the park's trees and flowers, seemed to imbue them with a sensuality and life that the sterile surroundings of a gallery would never have achieved.

It was another beautiful day and they wandered around the park discovering the sculpture at random. The beautiful artworks and the heat of the day made them feel languid and sensual. After lunch Dan took her hand and led her to a secluded area of the park where he fucked her up against a tree. They were rearranging their clothes when a coach party of septuagenarian American tourists appeared from nowhere. They held hands and ran to the car, laughing.

Thirteen

When they got back to the school Jo led him to the gymnasium and told him to undress then left him alone and went back up to the flat to change.

She could just imagine the look of surprise and excitement on Dan's face when he saw what she'd chosen to wear. There was a tight black corset with scooped semi-circular cut-outs beneath each breast, leaving them bare. The supple flared leather skirt reached almost to her ankles and the shiny spike-heeled ankle boots laced up the front. Already her nipples had begun to harden and she could feel a pulse beat throbbing behind her temples.

She sat on the bed to put on a pair of sheer black self-supporting stockings. She eased the stocking up her leg, smoothing out the wrinkles at the ankle and making sure that the seam was straight.

She laced up the boots and put on the skirt. She hooked up the corset and its tight elastic embrace gripped her waist. She felt her breathing restricted as she fastened it over her ribs. Her crotch was tingling and tight. Her nipples sang with heat.

At the dressing table, she put on a fresh coat of scarlet lipstick then twisted her hair up into a French pleat and fastened it in place with a tortoiseshell comb. Her naked breasts rose and fell visibly as she breathed. She opened

195

a drawer and took out an old-fashioned school cane with a bent handle like a bishop's crook.

Jo picked up her bag of equipment and let herself out of the flat. Her sharp heels echoed against the bare floor and her steps seemed to fall into rhythm with her heartbeat. She felt like an Amazon, strong and power- ful, marching into battle. She leaned on the door of the gym and it slowly opened with a long loud creak.

Dan was standing naked in the centre of the room. His cock was already half hard. When he caught sight of her in her outfit his mouth fell open and she heard him gasp.

Jo strode over to him, the sound of her boot-heels resounding around the high-ceilinged room. She stop- ped in front of him and dropped the bag onto the floor. She held the cane between her two hands and slowly flexed it into an arc. 'I'm going to cane you.' Jo extended her cane and ran the tip along the length of his cock. Dan's body juddered and he moaned.

Blood pounded in her ears. Between her legs she felt liquid and hot. 'I'm punishing you because you belong to me and I can, but also because I want to leave marks on your body. There will be bruises . . . it might even break the skin. It's definitely going to be painful. But you'll enjoy that, and the bruises will remind you that you're my property. Do you think you can take it?' She flipped up his cock with the tip of her cane and watched it wobble. Dan clenched and unclenched his fists.

'Yes, miss. I can take it. I want you to punish me.'

Jo smiled. 'Come over here and straddle this bench.' She walked over to the side of the gym where there was a series of long low exercise benches. She watched as he lifted one leg over the nearest bench and lay flat along its length. She saw him flinch as his body made contact with the cold polished wood. With one knee on the floor on either side of the bench his buttocks were stretched apart and his arsehole was exposed.

Jo tickled the puckered hole with the tip of her cane and Dan's body jolted forwards. 'I'm going to give you twenty strokes.' She ran the end of the cane along his arse crack. 'I want you to count the strokes out loud and, if you lose count, we'll begin at one again. Do you understand?'

'Yes, miss.' Dan's voice was thick with arousal.

Jo raised her arm high into the air. There was a light fluttery sensation under her ribs. Her nipples tingled.

Dan's arse was round and smooth. She could see his balls dangling beneath him and the underside of his rigid cock. She brought the cane down hard across both his cheeks. It gave off a loud satisfying thwack as it made contact. Dan's body jerked forwards and he grunted.

'One . . .'

She could hear the pain and satisfaction in his voice. Already there was a thin angry stripe visible, cutting across both of his normally pale buttocks. Jo's crotch was tight and aching. She hit him again and the cane landed with a loud crack.

'Two . . .'

Jo delivered the strokes one after another. Dan's body jolted forwards on every crack. His arse was darkened by thin red stripes, and already bruises were beginning to form. His hands were clenched into fists. He was clearly in pain yet his cock was purple and erect and, when he called out the number of the stroke, his voice was heavy with arousal and pleasure.

Jo's arm ached. She delivered another stinging slap and the bench creaked as Dan was thrust forwards and almost lost his balance.

'Twelve . . .' He raised himself onto his elbows and his rear end was thrust obscenely upwards. Jo knew he was

197

only repositioning himself so that the force of the blows wouldn't make him lose his balance but she could almost believe that he was deliberately lifting up his arse in his eagerness for punishment.

Jo's nipples burned. She brought the cane down across his buttocks three times in quick succession. The force of it made her breasts wobble and the front of her hair fall in her face.

Jo was sweaty and slippery under her corset. She brought the cane down, putting all her strength behind it. It landed with a crack, low down across both buttocks. Dan let out a deep guttural grunt and she saw his fists clench and unclench.

'Sixteen . . .' His voice was practically a whisper.

Jo struck him again, across the outside of his right cheek. She could see dark livid patches standing out against his pale skin.

'Seventeen . . .' Dan was trembling all over.

She slashed his other buttock and he moaned. Jo was conscious of the moisture between her legs. She was tingling all over.

'Eighteen . . .' Dan's head was hanging down, his forehead practically on the bench. She brought the cane down noisily across both his cheeks.

'Nineteen . . .' Dan's voice was barely audible.

Jo delivered the final stroke, bringing the cane down in exactly the same spot. She could see his erection jiggling beneath him from the impact of the blow.

'Twenty . . .' He sounded exhausted, in pain and utterly sated. 'Thank you, miss.'

'Now I want you to turn over onto your back.' Jo's voice sounded breathless and deep.

Dan used his hands to heave himself up then he sat down, straddling the bench. He lay back along the wooden surface. He gazed up at Jo. Behind his glasses, his eyes shone. His erection stood up, its tip purple and swollen.

'Put your feet on the bench and open your legs.'

Dan put his feet up and let his legs fall open like the pages of a book. His hands gripped the edges of the bench. His gaze never wavered.

Jo brought the cane down. It swished through the air and thwacked down onto his inner thigh. Dan grunted and bit his lip. His knees came up in reflex for a second then his legs opened again.

She raised the cane and brought it down across his other thigh. Dan's body shook. Jo could see livid red slashes across the inside of each of his thighs. Her nipples were erect and tingling. Her crotch was liquid and tight.

She whipped him again, two stinging noisy slashes across each inner thigh, and through it all his cock remained rock-hard, its tip glistening and purple.

A strand of Jo's hair had come loose and fell over her forehead. Heat pumped round her body. She slashed him again and again, overlapping the strokes so that his pale skin became patterned by red stripes.

Jo was breathless and hot. Her crotch ached. She dropped the cane. She sat on the end of the bench and ran her hands over his stripes. She could feel the raised bumps under her fingertips.

She leaned forwards and rubbed her cheek against his swollen reddened skin. She kissed the scarlet weals.

Dan reached down and stroked her face with his trembling fingers, leaving a trail of blazing heat on her skin. She caught his wrist and turned her head to kiss his palm.

Jo shuffled forwards and gripped his cock. Dan sighed. She stroked it up and down in a single practised movement sliding across the glistening sticky head.

She watched Dan's flat belly rise and fall as she handled his cock. She pulled his foreskin down hard. She could see it pulling on the tiny strip of skin that joined it to his glans and Dan's body shifted and he moaned softly.

Without hair, his crotch looked somehow more impressive. His cock seemed huge and thick, displayed in all its purple glory. 'I hope you don't mind, but I've just got to suck it.'

'You can do whatever you want. It's yours.'

She bent her head and took it into her mouth. Jo could feel the blood and heat pumping under the skin. She loved the way it strained her jaw, forcing her to open her mouth wide. It felt iron-hard yet impossibly silky and smooth. She dabbled her tongue in the eye, then ran it under the ridged helmet.

She felt juicy and hot and – as she sucked him – suddenly empty. Her nipples were hard and swollen and a Niagara of tingles was tumbling down her spine. She sat up.

'I'm going to fuck you now.' She massaged his cock. 'Is that OK?'

'Yes ... fuck me. I want it.' Dan's voice was hoarse and full of urgency.

She buckled herself into her harness, sliding the inner dildo inside her and fitting a medium-sized purple dildo to the front. She picked up a bottle of lube and walked over to Dan.

'Spread your legs a bit more ... that's right.' Jo knelt down behind him. Her legs fitted inside the bent V of his. She could feel his body heat. She dropped the lube on the floor and ran her hands over his thighs and buttocks. Dan moaned.

She bent her head and began to kiss him. She trailed her mouth over his arse, kissing the marks of her cane. His body trembled. Jo slid her wet tongue down along the crack of his arse. Dan gasped.

Already, her heart had quickened and her nipples tingled. She laid a hand on each of his hips and began to lick the puckered bud of his arsehole. She lavished it with her tongue, running it around the edge then pushing the tip against his entrance and teasing his hole. Tension throbbed at the base of her belly.

Dan moaned and shook. She rimmed him, loving the sensation of his dark secret opening against her face. She poked her rigid tongue inside him. Her pussy prickled with excitement and heat.

Jo felt his muscles relaxing and softening as she licked. She pressed her face to his crack and tongued his hole. Her crotch ached.

Excitement slid down her spine. She pushed the pointed tip of her tongue against his hole and inched it inside. Dan had begun to rock his hips. Though she couldn't see it, Jo knew he was rubbing his erection against the edge of the bench.

Still licking him, she fumbled for the bottle of lube, and squirted a blob into her hand. She gave his arse a final kiss and sat up. Dan gasped in disappointment but she immediately brought up her lubed fingers and began to work it into his hole.

Excitement pumped around her bloodstream. She fingered him, spreading the gel and sliding the tip of her finger inside him. The lube squelched as she worked and Dan's hips rocked rhythmically.

Dan was gasping and moaning. She could see that his fists were clenched and his face, turned to one side with his cheek against the bench, was damp with sweat. His eyes were wide open and his mouth was formed into an obscene O.

Jo slid a lubed finger slowly inside him. She slid it past his sphincter and felt the heat of him and his muscles contract as she entered him.

She slid her finger in and out, fucking him. Dan moaned. She added a second finger and he roared. Jo reached between his legs and stroked his cock. He was

201

hard, full of heat and blood. She ran her fingers over the wet tip and his body shuddered.

Heat blazed between her legs. She felt her muscles contract around the dildo inside her harness. She squirted a blob of lube into her hand and smeared it over her purple silicone cock. She rested one hand on the edge of the bench and leaned forwards.

Dan's body was taut with expectation. He was looking over his shoulder at Jo, his face flushed. She pushed the tip of the dildo against his hole then used her body weight to slide into him.

She watched Dan's pupils dilate. He sighed as the dildo slipped inside him. She pressed her hips slowly forwards until the front of her harness was flat against his body. The pressure pushed her own dildo deeper and she moaned.

The leather harness creaked as Jo circled her hips, rotating her cock inside him and the dildo inside her. Her crotch burned as her nerve endings responded. Dan moaned and arched his back.

Jo pulled back, sliding out of him. She looked between their bodies to where her silicone dick glistened, its tip poised at his stretched hole. She pressed her hips forwards and plunged back into him. There was a soft thump as her harness slapped against his body and Jo felt her own dildo pressing against her G-spot.

Jo began to fuck him, slowly at first. She watched the dildo slide inside his stretched hole then disappear out of sight as she hit bottom only to reappear, glittering and slippery, a moment later.

Icy tingles slid up her spine and over her scalp. Her crotch was alive. She held onto Dan's hips. She picked up speed, establishing a rhythm.

She'd begun to moan. Dan was gasping and panting. The harness slapped rhythmically against his body.

Coils of heat throbbed in her belly. She could feel her

stretched muscles gripping the dildo inside her. On every in-thrust, its curved tip pressed against her G-spot, eliciting a flood of tingling excitement.

Dan had begun to pump his own hips, pushing his arse back onto her cock. She saw him slip a hand down to his crotch and he gasped in relief as he took his cock in his fist.

Jo picked up speed. She could feel her orgasm building. Her breasts jiggled as she fucked him. Her cunt gripped the dildo.

Sweat trickled into her eyes. Her hands on Dan's hips were wet and slippery. She wiped them dry on her skirt and repositioned them.

Jo pounded him, rhythmically pulling on his hips as her own jabbed forwards. She imagined the slippery fat dildo sliding in and out of his arse, stretching and opening him. She could see him working his cock, one arm hidden underneath his body and the other bent at the elbow and braced against the bench as he met her thrusts.

Jo jabbed her hips. She felt brutal, powerful, alive. She was nearly there. Her crotch tingled and throbbed, her cunt gripped the dildo.

Her strokes grew short and staccato. She pounded him. The bench creaked and shook. Dan's body was rigid and trembling. He turned to look at her over his shoulder and Jo saw that his face was streaked with sweat and his eyes were shining.

She stabbed her hips and her orgasm exploded. Her body shuddered. Pleasure flooded over her. Her muscles contracted around the dildo.

Dan watched her come. His mouth was open and his eyes blazed. He groaned and began to shake. His eyes closed and he hung his head.

Jo kept on coming, wave after wave. She was tingling and alive. Her toes curled, her back arched in pleasure.

She was inside him and she was coming and he loved it. She collapsed over his back.

They stayed like that for ages. She slid her hand along the bench and laid it over Dan's and he held it, curling his fingers around her. She brushed his hair off his face. Slowly her breathing returned to normal.

'You're still inside me . . . it's wonderful.' Dan's voice was a breathless whisper.

She kissed his shoulder. 'I don't need to ask you if you liked it, then.'

'I loved it. Ever since I saw you fuck Costas I've wanted you to do it to me. It was incredible. I felt utterly different. Passive and vulnerable and . . . I don't quite know how to say it . . . like I was yours. I'd given myself to you totally. Do you understand?'

She kissed him again. 'Of course I do. It's about power exchange . . .' She slid out her cock and Dan gasped in disappointment. She stood up and began to unbuckle the harness. 'When you fuck a man he becomes the submissive partner and the woman becomes the aggressor. It's very powerful.' She stepped out of the harness and sat down on the bench beside him. 'Was that your first time?'

He turned onto his side and looked up at her. He nodded. 'Sadie fucked me with a dildo, but it was nothing like that.'

Jo stroked his soft cock. 'I'm glad you liked it but, intense or not, I don't recall giving you permission to come.' She pointed at the bench. 'I think you'd better lick up all your mess.'

Dan sat up. 'I'm sorry . . . I didn't realise I needed permission.' He slid onto the floor.

'Well, now you do. And you'll be punished later for your lapse.'

'Yes, miss.' Dan bent over and Jo watched as he licked up his own sperm.

* * *

On their last morning together they ate breakfast on the balcony overlooking the lake. It was already a blisteringly hot day. Sunlight glinted on the green surface of the lake. Jo felt languid and relaxed. She smeared butter on a slice of toast.

'I hope you've enjoyed yourself these past few days.' She reached for the marmalade.

Dan laughed. 'That's an understatement. I'm not usually lost for words but I couldn't begin to describe how I've felt. It's been absolutely mind-blowing. I'm a changed man.'

Jo smiled. 'So you'd like us to take it further?'

Dan opened his mouth to speak but Jo brought up her hand and covered his lips. He caught her wrist and turned his hands to kiss her palm. Jo's scalp tingled.

'Don't answer yet. A lot's happened . . . you need time to think about it. I don't want you to contact me for a week. If you decide it's what you really want then I'd like you to come over on Friday evening with a weekend bag. And if it's not for you then . . .' She shrugged.

Dan's cup was halfway to his mouth. He put it down. Jo could see dark beard stubble on his jawline. The sun was glinting off his glasses and Jo couldn't see his eyes but she knew he was looking at her. 'You sound as though you don't want me to come back . . .' His voice sounded flat and hesitant.

'No, not at all. Please don't think that. It's just . . . you've got to remember I've done this before. I know it's what I want. I know you're what I want. But it's all new to you. It's overwhelming. It can completely knock you off your feet and you end up questioning everything you thought you knew about yourself.' She laid her hand over his.

'You can say that again.'

'So you need to be sure if it's what you really want . . . that I'm what you really want. You need to take some time to think about all this on your own when the excitement and the novelty of it all isn't influencing your judgement. Doesn't that makes sense?'

Dan nodded. 'Yes, of course it does. You're right I've got so much stuff running through my head at the moment . . . I don't know how to even begin to make sense of it.'

'Then some time to think will do you good.' Jo pushed her plate aside and leaned across the table. 'But I don't want you to be in any doubt. I have no reservations about it . . . or you.'

'Thanks. That helps.' He brought her hand to his lips and kissed it.

'And – don't forget – this is only the beginning.'

Dan pulled a mock-terrified face. 'You're scaring me now.'

Over the next few days, Jo could barely concentrate. She knew she'd made the right decision in giving Dan time to think. She'd invested far too much to risk losing it if he decided it wasn't for him a few weeks down the line. It was all perfectly logical, but somehow her libido didn't seem to agree.

She'd sit at her desk trying to concentrate on timetables and budgets but her mind kept returning to Dan. She was surprised and delighted by how eagerly and completely he had surrendered to her. He was a complete natural. His sessions with Sadie had obviously unlocked his inner submissive. She made a mental note to thank Sadie for doing the groundwork for her.

Several times she'd been tempted to pick up the phone and call him, but she had to be strong. She couldn't expect him to refrain from contact for a week if she couldn't even manage it herself. If only she wasn't so damned horny.

Though it wasn't normally in her nature to ration her sensual pleasures she had intended to wait until she saw Dan at the weekend so that both of them would be equally horny and eager for release. But she hadn't even managed to last out the day.

Costas had spent hours on his knees bringing her to one orgasm after another with his talented mouth, but it never seemed quite enough. She whipped and rogered him until he was sore and she was exhausted but still she wasn't satisfied.

On Wednesday night Jo drove to Adam's house. Adam lived in a fashionable square in Notting Hill, a few streets away from where Jo had grown up. In those days, the area had been run-down and neglected. She hardly recognised the neatly painted elegant homes as the same peeling tatty and overcrowded houses she remembered from childhood. But the Georgian façades and railings and communal gardens were the same and, whenever she visited Adam, she always experienced a warm familiar glow in her chest, as if she were coming home.

She parked the car and walked up his path, carrying her overnight bag. She climbed the six steps up to his front door. The house where she had grown up had had the same black and white checkerboard tiles, she remembered, smiling. She rang the bell.

After a few moments she could see Adam's dark shape through the stained glass of the door, walking down the hall. When he opened the door, Jo saw that he was wearing only a towelling dressing gown and his hair was wet and untidy.

'Hello, darling. I've just got out of the shower. You're early.'

'I'd have thought you'd be pleased ... after all, it must be at least a week since I last allowed you to come.' She kissed him. He smelled of shampoo and shaving foam. Jo stepped into the hall and Adam shut the door behind her.

'Nine days . . . not that I'm counting. But if you've come over early to end my frustration then I'm not just pleased, I'm delighted.'

Jo undid the belt of his dressing gown and pulled it open. His cock was already thickening and growing hard. She smiled. 'So I see. Shall we go upstairs?'

She walked behind Adam. She flipped up the back of his dressing gown, uncovering his arse. His buttocks were covered in yellowing bruises. He looked over his shoulder at her and smiled.

When they reached the top Jo walked along the landing. She opened the bedroom door and walked over to the bed. She pulled her sundress off over her head and tossed it aside. Underneath she was naked. Her chest was heaving and her crotch was already hot and wet.

Adam closed the door behind him and shrugged off his robe. 'You seem very keen . . .' He walked over to the bed and knelt at her feet. Jo sat down. She spread her legs and lay back on the bed. Still in her high heels, she lifted her feet to the edge of the bed, displaying her moist crotch.

Adam whistled. 'I'll never tire of that sight. How may I serve you, madame?'

Jo raised herself up on her elbows and looked down at him. His eyes were shining and intense. 'Make me come . . . and make sure you do a good job, because I'm in a vicious mood.'

'It'll be my pleasure.' Adam spread her lips with his fingertips and Jo gasped. She lay back on the bed. He ran a finger between her lips and over her clit and it slid easily in the slippery juices. She sighed.

She was trembling by now and her heightened senses made her aware of every sensation. The duvet beneath her felt crisp and cool. She could hear her own heart beating.

'Don't move,' he whispered. 'Close your eyes.'

Jo silently obeyed him. She lay there, patient and blind. He blew on her wet crotch and she shivered. She could sense him kneeling there, still and silent, and she knew he was looking at her body: her hard dark nipples, the rise and fall of her breasts, the soft curves of her hips, her rounded belly. But, most of all, she knew he was looking at her cunt, spread open by his strong fingers like an offering.

'Stay there.' His voice was soft, heavy with desire. She was conscious of how wet she was. She could feel it dripping down the cleft in her bottom, wetting the duvet, and the knowledge that he was watching it happen made her raise her pussy towards him.

'Lick me,' she begged.

She heard him laughing softly. She felt his hot mouth on her and his breath gently touching her wet skin. He kissed her cunt tenderly, running the flat of his tongue around the margin of her clit.

He spread her lips with strong fingers and covered her with his hot wet mouth. His tongue darted over her sensitive flesh. She opened her legs wider and reached down to stroke his hair.

'I want to make you come,' he whispered, raising his head momentarily from between her tensed legs. He blew gently on her pussy, cooling the wet folds and making her tingle and shudder.

He covered her clit with his mouth and sucked. He licked and nibbled. He pushed his tongue deep inside her. She laced her fingers through his damp hair and rocked her hips.

She moaned and grunted. She tightened her grip on his hair and began to move her pelvis to a rhythm of her own. She could feel his beard stubble prickling her sensitive flesh. He wrapped one hand round her hip and pulled her onto his mouth.

She ground herself against him. She was panting and moaning. She gasped as she felt two fingers sliding into her. Exquisite sensations coursed through her excited body. Every nerve ending was transmitting pleasure and excitement. A wave of contractions began in her belly, filling her with heat and pleasure. She pumped her hips.

She was tingling all over. Her cunt gripped his fingers. It tightened under his mouth, and she shuddered with pleasure as she reached her peak. He held her tight, pulling her onto his face. He worked his fingers inside her as she shuddered, rocked and throbbed to orgasm.

Jo let her feet fall to the floor and flopped back against the duvet. Adam climbed onto the bed, making the mattress creak as he half crawled, half slithered to lie down beside her.

'I don't think I've ever known you to come so fast.'

'I was very horny . . .'

He planted a kiss on her cheek. He brushed back the wet strands of hair from her face and smiled down at her while she got her breath back. Slowly his gentle amused smile became more knowing and slightly wicked. Quickly and elegantly he rose up to his knees and straddled her, his erection jutting out invitingly from its blond curly nest.

He looked magnificent above her, his muscular body glistening and tense with desire. She knew what he wanted and she opened her mouth to take him. He mounted her and his thick rigid cock slid past her lips until he was buried up to the root.

Quickly he began to move inside her, establishing a rhythm which she easily followed. She explored his helmet with her tongue, probing his slit and tasting salty pre-come. She wrapped her arms round him, grasped his buttocks and pulled him towards her.

He began to slowly rock his hips. Jo held onto him and matched his rhythm. Her crotch still felt tingly and wet.

His pubes bashed against her nose. His tight ball sac slapped against her chin. He moaned softly and reached down to cup her head with his hands.

Jo's head bobbed. His slippery hot cock slid in her mouth. Her jaw ached. He was fucking her face now, pumping his hips and pulling her face onto him. His arse muscles were hard and tight under her hands. Her clit ached.

She could feel his excitement building as he picked up speed. He'd begun to groan and pant. His hips pistoned. His cock pounded her.

He was hot and hard and slippery in her mouth. Jo relaxed her face muscles and surrendered to his fucking. His strong hands pulled her onto his cock.

He was moving faster now, fucking her mouth with every stroke. His cock was rigid and engorged, his balls small and tight. His strokes grew short and urgent. Under her hands, his buttocks tensed and he began to throb in her mouth. She grasped him more tightly, opened her mouth wider and relaxed her throat expectantly.

After a couple of short hard thrusts his cock began contracting, spilling hot salty seed on her tongue. His body was rigid and trembling. He was gasping and panting. His sperm surged down her throat, its rich musky odour filling her nostrils.

Gradually the contractions began to slow and his dick began to soften between her lips. His tensed buttocks and thighs relaxed and he lay down beside her and took her in his arms.

'I must say, Jo –' his voice was breathless and soft '– you seem exceptionally horny today. What's got you so worked up?'

* * *

Dan buried himself in work, spending long hours at the production office when he wasn't actually filming, but it didn't help. All he could think about was Jo and the things they'd shared. He was so wound up and excited that he felt like a teenager again, semi-hard most of the time and powerless to control it.

He considered relieving his frustrations with Sarah but, tempting though it was, he knew it would feel like cheating. Jo hadn't exactly forbidden him to have sex with anyone else but he was pretty certain that she expected him not to. She wanted him to live with his frustration and hunger and to understand that she alone was capable of relieving it.

But he hadn't bargained on how helpless and distracted it would make him feel. He couldn't concentrate, his mind wandered and he was so horny that he had to keep nipping into the toilet.

He'd stand in the locked cubicle with one hand pressed up against the wall and his other curled around his disobedient cock as a slideshow of images of Jo at her most commanding ran through his mind. He did it so often that Sarah grew concerned that he had tummy trouble. He wasn't sure why he couldn't tell her the truth – after all, she knew him better than anyone and they'd been lovers for years – but somehow he just didn't think she'd understand.

But he needed to talk about it with someone. Thoughts and fantasies ran around and around in his mind, getting nowhere. He was usually extremely logical and organised but he simply had no frame of reference to help him make sense of his conflicting feelings. He'd never found a decision so agonising. There was no doubt that what Jo offered excited him, but it was so new and so overwhelming that he lacked any objectivity or clarity.

On Wednesday evening he sat at his desk in the office long after Sarah and the admin team had gone home.

He was still no closer to a decision than he had been when he'd walked away from the school on Monday morning. He needed some impartial informed advice. He picked up the phone and dialled Sadie's number. She answered almost immediately.

'Hello, Sadie. It's Dan. I hope I'm not disturbing you.'

'Not at all. Is there something wrong? You don't sound quite yourself.'

'You could say that . . . the fact is . . . I could really do with a chat. I've got myself into a situation and . . . well, I need to talk to someone with experience to help me sort things out.'

'Well, if I can help. I must say it all sounds very mysterious and intriguing. Tell you what . . . why don't you come over? I was just about to cook and there's plenty for two.'

'Sadie, you don't know what this means to me. You're an angel. If I leave now I can be with you in twenty minutes.'

Sadie fed Dan a Thai curry as authentic as anything he'd eaten in Bangkok, except that it was made with Quorn. She'd poured him some white wine and made sure his glass was topped up. Dan was beginning to relax for the first time in days.

'So what's up? I'm assuming that, since you've come to me, it's a sexual problem.' Sadie pushed her plate away and picked up her glass.

'Sex is involved, certainly, but it's the type of sex that made me think you might be able to help me. It's your area of expertise.'

'Kink?'

Dan nodded. 'I . . . I've met someone.'

'And she's kinky?'

'She's very possibly the kinkiest woman alive.' Dan took a long swallow of wine.

'Well, now ... she must be some woman. What's the problem?'

Dan told Sadie everything. As he spoke he felt the heaviness and confusion that had been weighing him down slowly begin to lift.

When he'd finished speaking Sadie reached for the bottle and she refilled both of their glasses. 'And do you intend to go back?'

'I'm still not sure. I can't seem to think of anything else ...'

'And yet?'

Dan shook his head, chasing away the confusion. 'I don't know, really. I suppose what worries me most is not knowing where it might lead. When you and I had our session together it was exciting and wonderful but what made it so special with Jo was ... I don't know ... the intimacy of it, I suppose. It was like there were no barriers between us. It was pure naked intimacy.'

'That sounds pretty wonderful to me ...'

'It was. But that's both the allure and the problem. It was captivating, intoxicating, breathtaking ... yet, at the same time, it was utterly terrifying.'

'All intimacy is frightening. Didn't your mother ever tell you that?' Sadie sipped her wine silently for a moment, staring at him. 'I must say, Dan, I never pegged you as commitment-phobic. I'm not telling you what to do, but all I can say is that if you turn down what Jo has to offer you must be insane.'

Fourteen

On Friday evening when Dan rang the school's doorbell his cock was already half hard and his heart was pounding. Jo opened the door wearing a short flared velvet skirt which barely covered her arse and a corseted bodice made from the same material. She wore seamed stockings and a pair of impossibly high stilettos in black suede. Her breasts seemed to spill over the top of her bodice and the shoes made her legs seem endless.

She didn't speak, but the longing he saw in her eyes told him all that he needed to know. She closed the door behind him and walked away, expecting him to follow. As they climbed the stairs, Dan couldn't keep his eyes off her arse. The hem of her skirt flicked up as she walked revealing a glimpse of sheer lacy knickers. His cock tingled.

Jo led him straight into her bedroom. 'Strip.'

Dan undressed with trembling fingers. By the time he'd got down to his boxers he was fully erect. He slid them down and stood up straight, waiting for orders.

He could see Jo's chest rise and fall as she breathed. A flush of arousal stained her throat. 'Come into the bathroom.' Her voice had an unmistakable edge of authority.

Icy shivers slid down his spine. His crotch ached.

In the bathroom Dan immediately spotted several items of unfamiliar equipment laid out on the vanity unit. There was a coil of clear plastic tubing, a measuring jug, a tube of KY jelly and something made of thick plastic which he couldn't recognise. 'What's that?'

'I'm going to give you an enema. It's nothing to worry about,' she added, when she saw the look of alarm on his face. 'You might even enjoy it.'

'How does it work? I've never had one before.' Dan fingered the tubing and his cock tingled.

'We lube this and put it into you.' She held up a tapered nozzle at the end of the tube. 'This bit is a sort of bag.' She held it up. 'It has a handle which we hang over here.' She indicated a hook on the wall. 'I mix up the enema in the jug – just warm water and soap – and then pour it into the bag. There's a little valve to hold the water back until we're ready. We turn the tap and it starts to flow. Simple.'

The hairs on the back of Dan's neck were standing on end. 'And does it hurt?' He could hear the alarm in his own voice.

Jo laughed. 'No, not at all. It just feels a bit strange but most people quite like it.'

'OK then. Where do you want me?'

'Why don't you sit on the edge of the bath for a minute while I get it ready?'

Dan sat down and watched as Jo put on a pair of medical gloves. She squirted some liquid soap into the jug. She ran the hot tap and held her hand in the stream until she judged it was the right temperature then filled the jug. She hung up the bag and poured in the mixture. As she picked up the tube of KY and began to lube up the nozzle a wave of heat crashed over Dan making him feel instantly light-headed. His cock was rigid.

When the nozzle was lubed to her satisfaction she held it up for Dan to see and raised an eyebrow in mock wickedness. Dan got down on all fours and Jo knelt behind him. He gasped as Jo's lubed latex-covered finger touched his hole. The jelly was cold against his skin and, as Jo worked it in, he felt his legs begin to tremble. Her finger pushed slowly inside him and he sighed.

'I'm going to insert the nozzle now.' Jo removed her finger and pressed the end of the tube against his hole. He felt the hard plastic begin to slide past his muscles, bringing his nerve endings to life and making them tingle. His cock dangled beneath him, hot and hard.

Jo reached between his legs and gave his erection a squeeze. He gasped. 'No need to ask if you're enjoying it so far. I'm going to start the enema, OK?'

'Yes.' The word hissed with urgency.

He heard Jo standing up and fiddling with the enema bag. Blood pounded in his ears. He barely dared to breathe. At first nothing seemed to happen, then he began to feel a fullness as the enema slowly filled him.

Jo knelt down beside him. Her eyes seemed to glow and her lips were on the edge of a smile. He felt his belly distending as the water flowed into him. His crotch smouldered, his arse was tingling.

The enema felt strange and incredible and unbelievably exciting. He gazed at Jo's beautiful face. Her cheeks were pink and her pupils were huge. He lifted a hand to her cheek and pulled her gently towards him for a kiss. Dan's cock gave an involuntary twitch.

'I think it's finished.' Jo got to her feet. 'Yes. Let me pull out the tube.' Dan sighed as she pulled out the nozzle. 'Now you have to get rid of it.' Jo walked over to the toilet and lifted up the cover. She patted the seat.

'I think I can manage this bit on my own.' Dan stood up slowly, clamping down with his muscles to retain the enema.

Jo laughed. 'Doing it in front of me is part of it. It's taboo and dirty and alien, that's its power. We're shattering boundaries here. That's what it's all about.' She patted the seat again.

Dan sat down and allowed the enema to drain out of him. His face burned with shame yet excitement flooded through him like a drug rush. Jo knelt beside him holding his hand. When it was over, she left him alone to have a shower.

Dan went into the bedroom with a towel around his waist. Jo was fiddling with an outfit she had laid out on the bed. She looked up at him and smiled. 'I think it ought to fit you. But I wasn't sure about your shoe size.'

'I'm a twelve.' The outfit on the bed seemed to be a replica of what Jo was wearing. Icy fingers trailed over his scalp.

'Then we're in luck.' Jo went over to the wardrobe and retrieved a pair of shoes. 'They're not quite the same as mine, but they'll do.' She held them up. 'Now let's get you dressed.' She pulled off Dan's towel.

Dan looked down at the clothes. 'I think you might have to help me. Everything looks very complicated.'

She picked up a garment that looked like a pair of thong panties. 'When a man puts on women's clothes he has to hide his family jewels, so we use this. As you can see, it's made of strong elastic and it's got a little pocket inside.' She demonstrated. 'You put everything into the pouch and then pull it underneath and hook the end of the pocket to the back of the waistband. It's what drag artists use. It's called a gaff.'

'I see. Ingenious.' He took it from her. 'Is it painful?'

'I'm told it's restrictive but not unpleasant. Shall we find out?'

Dan bent down and stepped into it. He pulled it up his legs and over his hips. As he slipped his genitals into the pouch he saw that the top of the pocket was gathered by elastic to hold everything in place. He fumbled with the crotch of the panties for the end of the pouch.

218

'Let me do that.' Jo knelt down beside him and found the end of the pouch. She fastened the hook to the back of his waistband and Dan felt his tackle being pulled back between his legs and held in place by the strong elastic. 'And now you're nice and flat –' Jo stroked the front of his knickers '– this goes over the top.' Jo handed him a filmy garment made of black lace. 'It's the same as mine.' She flipped up the front of her skirt and Dan saw that she was wearing a pair of panties with four suspender clasps hanging from the band at the top.

He put his own panties on over the gaff. He stroked his crotch. It felt flat and feminine and unfamiliar. His cock stirred but was gripped tightly by the gaff. Jo handed him a pair of sheer black stockings.

Dan sat down on the bed. 'Let me see . . . I've watched women put these on . . .' He rolled the stocking down and put it on over his toe. The stocking felt silky and delicate against his skin. He pulled it up slowly, making sure there were no wrinkles, as he had seen women do.

He tried to attach it to the suspender clasp but his fingers felt big and clumsy. Jo showed him how. He put on the other stocking and Jo knelt down and put on his shoes.

He looked down at his legs. The stockings gleamed in the light and his calves looked shapely and elegant. He felt an irrational rush of pride. His scalp prickled. 'I should have shaved my legs.'

Jo laughed. 'Stand up and we'll put your skirt on.'

Dan stood up unsteadily on his high heels. He tottered and shuffled as he tried to step into his skirt. Jo zipped it up at the back.

'Now, before we put on the bodice we've got to give you a better chest. These are called Bosom Friends.' Jo picked up something from the bed and held them out, one in each hand. They were fake silicone breasts. They had dark thick nipples and Dan noticed that they even had the little pinprick bumps around the margin of the areolae.

'How do they stay on?' Dan took one of the breasts and turned it over in his hand.

'There's glue on the back. Just peel off the tape.'

Dan did as instructed. He positioned the fake breast carefully and pressed it against his skin. Jo repeated the process on the other side. He cupped a hand over each of his breasts. 'I don't feel like myself any more.' He tweaked his latex nipples. Inside the gaff, his cock twitched.

Jo picked up the bodice. 'It hooks up the front. There are laces at the back, but we probably won't need to touch those unless it needs adjusting.' She wrapped it around his body and began doing up the hooks, tugging hard on the material to get the two edges to meet.

'I think it's too small.' He could feel the bodice pulling in his waist and constricting his breathing. His half-hard cock felt pleasurably constricted inside the gaff.

'That's the point of a corset. It'll fit . . . trust me.'

'Do you think I'd be standing here in high heels and knickers if I didn't trust you?'

Jo laughed. 'I suppose not.' She hooked up the last few inches of the corset. 'How does that feel?' She stepped back to look at him.

'Strange . . . but I think I like it. It's as if someone's giving me a tight bear hug.' Dan ran his hands over the corset. His body felt unfamiliar and different. A wave of shivery tingles slid down his spine.

'Now all we need is the wig and a touch of make-up.' Jo went over to the dressing table where there was a long dark wig on a stand.

Dan walked carefully across the room on his high heels. When he arrived at Jo's side he was breathless and delighted.

'You look as though you've done that before.' Jo patted the stool in front of the mirror and Dan sat down.

'Not really, but I made a film at Charlie Brown's – you know, famous drag club in Atlanta – and one of the "girls" there told me how to walk in heels. I've never actually done it before today but it seems to work.'

Dan watched in the mirror as Jo fitted his wig. It felt itchy and tight and he could tell that it would get warm and uncomfortable after a short while, but he loved it. It seemed to soften and feminise his features, disguising his angular jaw and covering his manly brow.

Jo carefully removed his glasses. 'I'm going to put on some foundation, otherwise your beard stubble will show, then we'll put on some blusher and do your eyes and lips. It shouldn't take long.' She picked up a compact and began to apply make-up base with a sponge applicator.

The sponge was slightly rough and utterly alien. The make-up felt moist and thick against his skin. He could see Jo's face, inches from his, frowning slightly as she worked. Pinpricks of excitement slid up Dan's nape and over his scalp.

Jo covered his whole face with make-up, pressing the sponge into the hollows of his eyes and the creases round his nostrils. In the mirror he looked ghostly pale and somehow featureless. She put the compact down and picked up another smaller one and a big soft brush. 'This is blusher.' She dabbed the brush into the compact and dusted it across the apples of his cheeks.

Dan strained his eyes to look in the mirror. The blusher seemed to bring his pale face to life, giving it shape and warmth. Heat and tension throbbed at the base of his belly.

'If you close your eyes I'll do your eye shadow and liner. I think a nice mauve ought to bring out the blue of your eyes.'

Dan closed his eyes. He could feel her applying the

shadow with a small brush. He could feel her warm breath against his face. He heard her putting the eye shadow and brush down on the dressing table. Then he felt her finger pull at the corner of his eye, stretching and elongating his eyelid. She ran something solid along the base of his lashes. 'What's that?'

'It's the eyeliner pencil. It won't take long.' She repeated the process with the other eye. 'You won't need mascara because you've got such lovely thick dark lashes. I'm quite jealous actually. Blondes like me just can't get away with it. I'll just put some lipstick on and then you can look at yourself.'

He hardly dared to breathe as she applied his lipstick. He sat with his eyes closed and his hands on his stocking-clad knees.

'There. You're ready ... and you're beautiful!' Jo sounded surprised and delighted.

Dan opened his eyes. He put on his glasses and looked at his reflection. The masculine, manly Dan had been replaced by a soft feminised gentle version of himself. 'I look like a tartier version of my sister. I'm rather gorgeous, aren't I?' He smiled at Jo.

'You are. You remind me of ... what's her name? She was in *The English Patient* ... you must know who I mean.' She stroked his long hair.

'Not Juliette Binoche?'

Jo laughed. 'Even I'm not that talented with a make-up brush ... no, the other one.'

'Kristin Scott Thomas. Yes, I can see it now.' Dan gazed at his own reflection.

'I don't know ... put a man in a dress and he turns into a total narcissist. If you can tear yourself away from the mirror I think it's time for dinner.' She held out her hand to him.

Jo led him through the living room and down the hall. She opened the front door. Dan paused.

'You're not making me go out in public dressed like this?' His heart pounded.

'Don't worry, we're only going upstairs to Costas's flat.' She pulled on his hand and he followed. 'But you'd better get used to the idea of going out in a dress, because the day will come . . .'

Costas had cooked a simple but delicious meal, a beef stew followed by almond tart. Dan discovered that Costas was warm and witty and widely travelled. He chatted away, never once mentioning Dan's unusual attire.

But, in spite of Costas's apparent lack of interest, Dan spent most of the meal semi-hard with his cock trapped inside the rigid grip of his restrictive underwear. The strong elastic felt like a strong hand wrapped around his erection, as tantalising as it was frustrating.

Back in Jo's flat she made him take off his bodice, skirt and underwear and peel off his fake breasts then bend over the sofa. Jo left the room and came back naked, carrying her strap-on leather harness, a fat dildo already in place, and a bottle of Astroglide. She began to put on the harness and Dan noticed that she had fitted two smaller dildos on the inside for her own pleasure.

He watched as she placed the crotch of the harness between her legs and positioned the first of the silicone cocks on the inside. She slid it into place with a sigh. Then she reached behind to manipulate the second dildo into place against her arsehole. Freed from its elastic prison at last, Dan's cock was already fully erect. Icy fingers slid up and down his spine.

Jo pulled up the strap designed to fit between her buttocks and struggled with the fiddly leather behind her back then wrapped both ends of the belt around her waist and began to buckle them at the front.

Dan knew that the knobbly bump inside the harness rubbed pleasurably against her clit when she moved.

The purple silicone cock stood out from the triangle of leather, curved and obscene.

Jo bent down and picked up the bottle of Astroglide. 'Lube this thing up then do the same to yourself.' She handed him the bottle.

Dan flipped the cap and squirted a blob into his hand. He smeared the gel over the silicone cock. He was tingling all over and the darkened tip of his erection was peeping out from its foreskin cowl. He squeezed another blob of lube onto his fingers. The gel came out with an obscene squelching noise.

Dan reached behind him and began to lube his own arsehole. His eyes narrowed and his breathing quickened as he rubbed in the cold gel.

'Let me see you doing that, bend over.'

He turned round and bent at the waist. He braced himself with his free hand against the sofa. His fingers worked his hole with the lube, circling the puckered opening. He tried to imagine Jo looking at his rigid cock dangling beneath him.

He pressed a slippery fingertip up against his hole and pushed it gently inside. He let out a deep moan. He fucked himself slowly with one finger for several moments then slid in a second. He rocked his hips. He could feel his hole stretching and opening as he fucked himself.

'Get on your hands and knees.'

He obeyed instantly, removing his fingers and dropping to the carpet. He leaned on his elbows and raised his arse obscenely into the air. Jo knelt behind him and positioned the dildo. With one slow deep thrust of her hips she slid it home.

Dan moaned. Jo grabbed his hips and began to fuck him rhythmically. Already his crotch was tingling and tight, building towards climax. Jo fucked him in short vicious stabs.

Dan's long fake hair fell in his face. He could hear Jo's breath hissing out like steam. Heat bubbled inside him. She reamed his arse, plunging in her fake cock over and over again. He imagined her watching as it slid in and out, covered in shiny lube. She lifted one leg and put her foot outside his knee to provide better leverage.

Jo was moaning and muttering under her breath like someone speaking in tongues. He moved his hips in rhythm with her thrusting, pushing back against her cock. His fingers clawed the carpet.

Under his stockings his legs felt prickly and uncomfortable. Jo's cock plunged into him, thrusting him forwards. After one particularly violent thrust her cock dislodged and she had to reposition it. It slid in easily, almost as if he was swallowing it. He sighed in satisfaction as it filled him.

Jo's hands, holding onto his hips, were sweaty and slippery and she kept losing her grip. Dan's heart pounded.

He was shaking all over. He could feel melted make-up running down his face. His body pumped backwards and forwards, meeting her thrusts. His cock was rigid and painful, longing for release. He knew better than to ask for permission to touch himself and it was taking every ounce of self-control to obey her orders.

Jo was making noises; a combination of groans, inarticulate mumbling and noisy laboured breathing. He knew she was going to come. She stepped up the pace, plunging her cock into him over and over again. She leaned forwards, bending over his back. She put her arms under his body and grabbed him by the shoulders. She pulled with her hands, fucking him deep and hard.

Her body above his was wet and slick. Jo's thrusting grew frenzied and fast. She plunged into him over and over again, pulling violently on his shoulders.

She was making a high keening cry in rhythm with her jabbing hips. Dan bucked beneath her, responding to his inner need. His chest heaved as he struggled for breath.

Jo cries grew shorter and more staccato as she neared orgasm. The constriction in Dan's crotch was building to a pitch. Jo gave one final cruel jab of her hips and rotated her cock inside him. She was coming.

Dan's cock was on fire. He longed to grip it in his fist. A couple of quick pumps of his wrist would be all he needed to tip him over the edge. His body was rigid and trembling. Blood boomed in his ears.

Jo trembled all over. Her muscles were taut and straining. She was sobbing and moaning.

When it was over she slid out her cock and rolled over onto the floor. Dan reached over to the sofa for a cushion and placed it under her head. She looked down at his crotch. His cock was rigid, pointing at the ceiling as eager and infallible as her strap-on dildo. She reached out a hand and gave it a playful tap, making it swing.

'I suppose you want to come now.'

'I wouldn't say no . . .'

Jo bent her head and took his cock in her mouth. Dan gasped. Her mouth was hot and wet and soft. She wrapped her hand around the base and began to bob her head. Her eyes were half closed and she seemed totally lost in the moment. Tension throbbed in his gut.

He relaxed back against the edge of the sofa and closed his eyes. His cock felt tight and pumped with blood. Jo ran the tip of her tongue around the underside of his helmet and he gasped.

He began to slowly pump his hips, establishing a rhythm which Jo matched. Her face bumped up against his pubic bone on each thrust and he felt her hot breath on his skin.

His arse was still tingling and slippery. Every so often it seemed to throb in rhythm with Jo's moving mouth.

He reached down and cupped the back of her head with his hand. He rocked his hips, pulling her onto his cock.

His balls ached. He was tingling all over. He kicked off his shoes and dug his heels into the carpet.

Jo's long hair covered his lap. She sucked hard on his cock and a jolt of electric pleasure shot up his spine. His hips pistoned. Every so often she made little excited grunting noises as she sucked. Her head bobbed.

Dan's thighs began to quiver. He arched his back. He moaned out loud. The dam burst. His cock throbbed as he shot into her mouth and he could feel Jo swallowing. She kept her mouth clamped around his pumping cock.

Pleasure throbbed through him. He was trembling all over. His hand was pressed against the back of Jo's head as he came in her mouth. She swallowed it all down eagerly, sucking it out of him.

They stayed like that long after it had finished. Jo lapped up every trace of come as his cock softened in her mouth and his muscles slowly relaxed.

'Thanks for letting me come at last.' He stroked her hair. 'It was certainly worth waiting for.'

Jo looked up at him and laughed. 'I think you need a shower, your make-up's ruined.' She reached up and pulled off his wig. Dan scratched his scalp. 'Come on, let's hit the shower.'

In the bathroom Jo turned on the shower and stepped into the cubicle. Dan climbed in beside her. He washed his face under the running water.

'That's better. Now ... kneel down.' Jo laid a hand on his shoulder and pushed him down.

Dan slid to his knees and looked up at her. The water made her body gleam. Her nipples were erect, dark and prominent. Water droplets clung to her blonde pubes like beads. She reached down with both hands and spread her lips. Dan sighed as the dark interior of her pussy came into view, glittering, rosy and moist.

'Wait . . .' Jo's voice sounded urgent and excited. All Dan's attention was focused on her exposed cunt. She seemed to be holding her breath. 'Here it comes . . .'

Dan gasped as a stream of hot piss hit him in the chest. He could smell the familiar urine tang. As it splashed onto his body it felt warm and surprisingly soothing. He looked up at Jo's face. She made a tiny nod of her head and he instantly understood. He opened his mouth and lowered his face and swallowed down several mouthfuls. It tasted salty, but not unpleasant.

He felt tingly and alive. His cock was rigid. The stream began to weaken and Dan leaned forwards and fastened his mouth directly over her cunt. He lapped and sucked at her clit as the hot urine dribbled into his mouth.

The following Monday, Dan and the crew went to Hellfire 2000's monthly gathering. This time the venue was Christina the transsexual's house. While Dave was setting up the lights, Dan and the club members drank coffee in the kitchen. Christina bustled about, handing out home-made biscuits, the perfect hostess. She'd even put on a frilly pinny for the occasion.

Dan wondered why transsexuals and TVs always seemed to opt for such stereotypes of femininity; few women who'd been born that way bothered to wear aprons these days.

But maybe, he reflected as he watched her taking a fresh batch of cookies out of the oven, he could understand it a little now that he'd tried it himself with Jo. When he put on a dress he wanted to be the best woman he could be – for Jo.

'Is that a collar you're wearing?' Jim reached out a finger and touched Dan's silver chain. 'Don't tell me someone's nabbed you at last. Maybe it's engraved, let me look . . .'

Dan reached up and covered the engraved padlock with his hand. 'It's nothing. Just jewellery. I saw it in a shop and liked the look of it.'

Madame Cyn leaned across the table. 'Come off it, Dan. A straight-laced public schoolboy like you doesn't suddenly start wearing a dog collar. You're not Johnny Rotten.'

'Someone's obviously given it to you. Whose little doggy are you, Dan?' Nick raised both his hands in front of him in imitation of a begging dog.

'Oh, leave the poor boy alone.' Christina put a plate of biscuits down on the table. 'If he doesn't want to tell us then that's his right.' She sat down beside Dan. 'Though I reckon we've all got a pretty good idea who it is . . .'

'What do you mean?' Dan tried to sound dignified.

'It's Jo, isn't it? Come on, you can tell us.' Christina knelt down in front of Dan. She carefully turned over his padlock and read the inscription. 'It says, "This dog belongs to Jo Lennox." Well, now . . . aren't you a lucky dog?'

Fifteen

The next weekend Jo dressed them up in identical leather retro dresses with nipped-in waists and shoulder pads. Underneath they both wore waspie corsets, long-line bras and silk French knickers. Jo had applied heavy red lipstick and pinned back the front of her hair in a style which reminded Dan of his grandmother's wartime wedding photos. Dan wore a wig in the same style and Jo did his make-up to match hers.

'What do you think?' Jo stood beside Dan, looking in the full-length mirror.

Dan was tingling all over. His cock twitched inside his gaff. 'If there were three of us we could be a kinky version of the Andrews Sisters. Are you going to tell me where we're going, now?'

'To a play party at a friend's house. It's public yet private – a safe way to explore public surrender.'

'I'm looking forward to it . . .' Dan frowned. 'Do you think anyone from Hellfire 2000 is likely to be there?'

Jo fiddled with his wig. 'Possibly. Cold feet? I thought you'd already "come out" to them.'

'I have . . . no . . . not cold feet. I'm proud to be your sub. It just makes me feel . . . I don't know . . . vulnerable.'

Jo kissed him carefully, so as not to spoil their lipstick. 'You feel vulnerable because there's nowhere for you to hide. You've taken off your mask. It's a good thing, believe me. It means anything can happen and – when it does – you're open to it ... experiencing everything life has to offer. Doesn't that sound inviting?'

Dan smiled. 'What are we waiting for?'

The party was in a tree-lined avenue in Ealing. Jo stopped the car outside a large mock-Tudor detached house. On the doorstep Jo took a slender leather dog lead out of her handbag and attached it to Dan's collar. Icy fingers trailed up his nape and over his scalp. She tugged on the leash, pulling his face towards hers. She kissed him softly on the lips.

'Ready?' Jo smiled up at him.

Dan nodded. She rang the bell. After a few moments it was answered by a petite blonde woman in a body-hugging rubber suit and a Catwoman mask. The zip on her bodysuit was undone almost to her waist and Dan couldn't help noticing her spectacular gravity-defying breasts.

'Jo. Glad you could come.' The two women kissed.

'Dan, this is Sally. Sally, this is Dan Elliot.'

'My ... isn't he tall?' Sally gazed up at him. She extended her gloved hand and Dan shook it. 'Come on in.'

As Dan sat beside Jo on the sofa he could feel the gentle tug of his lead. He looked around. It was an ordinary suburban living room, decorated in modern minimalist style in shades of chocolate and cream. It was tasteful and understated and might even have seemed bland if it wasn't for the motley collection of occupants.

Everyone had dressed up for the occasion in rubber or leather. Some people wore only lingerie and several were nude or nearly nude. Sally was sitting in an armchair by the window with three naked collared male slaves kneeling at her feet. All of them bore the marks of recent whippings and Dan felt a slow cold shiver slide up his spine.

Jo tugged on his lead and he turned to look at her. 'Are you looking at Sally's boys?'

'Yes.' Dan looked over at the slaves and noticed that they weren't completely naked. Each of them was wearing plastic cage like devices over their genitals. 'I was looking at the bruises on their arses and imagining what it must feel like to have everyone know that someone else has the right to beat you.' Dan was conscious of his cock expanding inside his restrictive underwear.

'And how does it make them feel, do you suppose?'

'That's the funny thing. I think it must be a huge turn-on but at the same time it's got to be enormously shameful – only the shame's part of the pleasure.'

Jo had begun to smile. 'An interesting theory. Why don't we put it to the test?' Without waiting for an answer she got up and began to walk over to Sally. Dan leapt to his feet and followed at the end of his taut lead. 'Dan was admiring your boys' stripes, Sal, and you know what subs are like . . . I think he'd like me to show you his.'

Dan's cheeks burned with embarrassment and exhilaration.

Sally laughed. 'They're all exhibitionists under the skin, aren't they? Come on, Dan. Let us have a look at Jo's handiwork.'

'Lift up your skirt please, Dan. Up to your waist.'

Dan could hear the challenge and tenderness in Jo's voice. His scalp prickled. He pulled up his skirt, bunching it up around his waist, displaying himself.

The room was silent. He felt dozens of eyes on his exposed body. He knew that, even through his stockings, they would be able to see the latticework of red slashes and dark bruises on the front and back of his thighs. His crotch ached.

'Pull down your knickers so that we can get a proper look.' Jo let go of his lead.

He slid his French knickers down to his ankles. Though his gaff covered his crotch, he had never felt more naked. He could hardly breathe.

'Now turn round and bend over.'

Dan instantly obeyed, bending over and resting his hands on his shins. He'd never felt so alive. He was absolutely ashamed yet at the same time his heart burst with pride and satisfaction. He was Jo's slave. She had marked his body and everyone knew it. Endorphins exploded around his body. His legs trembled.

Jo ordered him to pull up his knickers. They went through to the buffet in the kitchen and loaded their plates with food.

'What are those things Sally's subs were wearing?'

'They're called CB2000s – they're a kind of chastity device.' Jo smiled. 'You look horrified. Don't you like the idea?'

'I like the theory. The idea that you're in charge of my body so completely that you can deny me access to my own cock is very appealing. And you're already in control of whether or not I can come anyway. But actually locking it away . . . it seems a bit cruel.'

Jo tugged on his lead and led him through the crowd. 'But you like it when I'm cruel . . . There's someone over there trying to attract your attention.' Jo pointed across the room.

Dan looked up and saw Master Nick and Madame Cyn waving at him. Dan moved to approach them but his leash held him back. He shrugged in apology and waited for Jo to lead him across the room.

'Don't you look lovely, Dan? I hardly recognised you.' Cyn looked him up and down.

'Thanks.' Dan couldn't help feeling pleased by the

compliment even though his cheeks were burning with embarrassment. 'I'm rather growing to like it, actually.'

Nick laughed. 'You've reminded me of something the body piercer said to me when I got my Prince Albert: "One more of us, one less of them" . . . you're one of us now, Dan.'

After they'd eaten they went upstairs to a room Sally referred to as "the dungeon" even though it was situated in the loft. The room was painted black and dimly lit. There was a huge metal rack on one wall from which hung a frightening array of whips and other implements of torture. Dan's heart raced.

In the middle of the room stood a whipping bench. Beside it there was a suspension rig, with a leather hammock affair and other hanging straps for legs and feet.

A naked woman was lying in the hammock, her wrists suspended above her head and her legs spread by two leather straps under her knees. She was being fisted by a shaven-headed man in motorcycle boots and a leather kilt. The front of his kilt was tented by his erection and his greased arm shone in the light. She lay there with her eyes closed as if in a trance. As they walked behind the hammock Dan realised that the man was fisting her in the arse.

Dan's armpits prickled with sweat. The gaff held his stiffening erection in its elastic grip.

At the opposite end of the room there was a man in stockings, suspenders, high heels and nothing else tied to a St Andrew's cross. Beside him, a woman dressed in a long leather skirt with a thigh-revealing slit up the front and corset stood holding a multi-tailed whip. She was whisking it in circles, barely brushing his skin. Nevertheless, his body was rigid with tension and excitement and he had the beginnings of an erection.

Dan imagined himself in the man's place, his body trembling and his cock erect as he waited for the lash.

The woman had long red hair that reached almost to her waist. She wore the heavy black make-up of the Goth and bore a complicated tattoo on her upper arm and shoulder. As she raised her arm to wield the whip Dan noticed that there was a big dildo sticking out through the slit at the front of her skirt. Purple and as thick as her wrist, it pointed upwards in an exaggerated arc in parody of an erection.

'I'm glad yours isn't as big as that,' he whispered to Jo.

She laughed softly. 'I've got more than one, you know . . .'

The woman brought the flogger down across the man's buttocks. His body jerked against the cross and he let out a deep appreciative groan. She brought the whip down over and over again across his buttocks. The tails landed with a sort of soft whoosh rather than the sharp crack of a whip, but the man's response told Dan they were no less painful.

Dan could barely breathe. His trapped erection pumped with heat and blood. Confined inside his underwear, the sensation was tantalising and exciting in equal measure. Jo tugged on his lead and they moved on.

The room was filled with the sound of moaning, heavy breathing and creaking leather. A naked girl had been buckled to the whipping bench and a woman in a Morticia Addams dress and a long black wig was thrashing her with what looked like a tawse.

The onlookers were mostly silent, whispering close to each other's ears when they wanted to speak, as if they didn't want to break the spell. There was a man in leather chaps and an upper-body harness watching the whipping. Kneeling in front of him was a female slave clad only in a leather G-string eagerly sucking his erect cock.

Leather slapped against flesh. On the whipping bench it was a deeper thud as the tawse made contact with the girl's naked arse. Dan could see broad scarlet stripes forming on her pale skin and he could almost feel the stinging kiss of the tawse. The girl rocked her hips and he saw her shaven pussy peeking out beneath the globes of her bottom.

The woman on the sling had begun to scream. Dan turned to look and saw that her partner was fingering her clit with his free hand. She was clearly coming, her body thrashing uselessly as the sling creaked and swung. When she finally stopped wailing the man slid out his hand and parted his kilt to reveal his erection. He grabbed her thighs and swung the hammock towards him, embedding his cock in her. Dan couldn't see which hole he had put it in but he hoped it was her arse.

The slave on the cross was standing with his head bowed as he received his whipping. He seemed to be lost in his own world; subspace Dan knew it was called, a territory of pain, surrender and ecstasy. His buttocks were crimson with patches of dark bruising already beginning to appear.

Dan turned to speak to Jo but she put her hands on his waist and pulled his body hard against hers. She began to kiss him, her mouth hot and wet and hungry. He could feel her breasts pressing against his body. He could feel her heart beating against his.

At the end of the evening they drove home in silence, both of them knowing what was going to happen the moment they were behind closed doors. Back at her flat she led Dan along the corridor and opened a door he had never noticed before. It led to a steep stone staircase. Their high heels echoed as they climbed and the air smelled strange; damp and old with a faint edge of decay.

At the top of the stairs was a locked oak door. Jo retrieved an enormous bunch of keys from a hook on the wall and unlocked the door. She lifted the latch and it opened with a melodramatic creak. Behind the door was a small stone lobby and another door. The lobby was about six feet square with a single window which was barely more than a slit. The floor and walls were crudely carved from stone blocks.

Jo fiddled with the bunch of keys. She opened the door and Dan followed her inside. The room was circular and, in the centre, stood an enormous stone plinth with a carved wooden box resting on it.

The rest of the room was completely plain, carved from rough stone blocks. High up in the wall, at least eight feet from the ground, there were small rectangular windows which let in light.

'I had no idea this was here. It's fantastic.' Dan's voice echoed.

'Isn't it? It's called a muniment room. In Tudor times they kept their valuables in here.' She went over and closed the door. 'I tend to use it for a rather different purpose, however.' She walked back over to Dan and lifted the lid of the wooden box. 'This is a quirt.' She laid a plaited leather whip on the stone plinth.

It was about eighteen inches long with two flat six-inch tails protruding from its tip. Blood rushed to his head. 'It looks . . . serious.' He reached out a finger and touched the handle.

'It's my favourite type of whip. This particular one is a twelve-plait kangaroo quirt with lead shot in the shaft to give it weight. These two tongues –' she pointed at the tails '– are the business end. It's not quite as stinging as a single-tail whip, but has less thud than a tawse or a paddle. I'm certain you'll enjoy it.' Jo picked up the wooden box and put it down on the floor. 'Pull down your knickers and bend over this.'

Dan stepped up to the plinth. He pulled his French knickers down to his ankles and leaned across the stone.

It was cold and rough against his skin. He laid the front of his body flat across the plinth and turned his face to the side, pressing his cheek against the stone. The musty scent of decay filled his nostrils.

The sound of his excited breathing echoed around the bare room. His cock was already half hard, trapped and uncomfortable inside his gaff. Jo lifted the back of his skirt, uncovering his naked arse.

He waited. He could hear her heels clip-clopping against the stone floor. An insistent beat of arousal thumped in his groin. He closed his eyes. He felt the soft tips of the quirt trailing over his naked arse. He shivered.

'You look quite beautiful like that. Sort of vulnerable . . . lying there all naked and expectant . . . utterly at my mercy. Somehow it fills me with tenderness and it almost seems too cruel to beat you.' The quirt tails teased the crack of his arse. 'Almost . . . but not quite.'

Dan heard a short breathy sound like someone exhaling hard. It was immediately followed by a stinging moment of agony as the quirt made contact with his buttocks. His body jerked forwards, banging the front of his legs against the plinth.

The quirt delivered a focused sting which burned for a second and instantly dissolved into delicious pleasure. Jo gave him half a dozen strokes in quick succession. Dan's body slammed forwards against the cold hard stone over and over again. Beneath his female clothes he'd begun to sweat and his wig felt itchy and uncomfortable. He pulled it off and dropped it onto the plinth. His arse was on fire.

Jo made a little guttural grunt each time she brought the whip down. He imagined that she, too, had grown hot and uncomfortable. He pictured her chest gleaming with sweat as she raised the quirt.

Jo brought the whip down across the top of his thighs and he cried out. Somehow the flesh there was more sensitive. She laid her free hand on the small of his back, holding him down, and thrashed his thighs with the quirt.

He held onto the edge of the stone, bracing himself. He felt overloaded with sensory input, sharp stinging pain, heat and tingling pleasure. He couldn't separate the individual components. All he knew was that his body was alive with intense wonderful sensation.

His cock was fully hard in its elastic confinement, straining against the strong material. The smell of his own sweat mingled with the musty aroma of the stone. He gripped the edge of the plinth, his back arched and his bottom raised for the quirt.

She whipped him hard. Dan knew that his pale skin would be embroidered with cruel raised red slashes. There might even be patches of purple bruises by now. He imagined Jo admiring her work as she wielded the whip, deciding that the pattern would look better if she lashed him in a particular spot.

A stroke landed across the centre of both buttocks. The sting took Dan's breath away, and almost immediately he felt an electric jolt of incredible pleasure in the same spot. A wave of heat and exhilaration crashed over him. His cock ached.

Jo whipped him savagely with the quirt. Her arm must ache by now and the exertion had probably made her sweat. Dan imagined the front of her hair coming loose and falling over her face as she lashed his arse.

His body was rigid and trembling. His abused skin tingled and blazed. He dug his fingers into the lip of the stone plinth, bracing himself in expectation of delicious pain.

She slashed him hard across the top of both thighs. It burned for an agonising moment and, almost before he had time to register the pain, it became pure profound pleasure. Shivery tingles slid up his spine.

He felt Jo's hand on his arse. She ran the tips of her fingers over his skin, touching and gently stroking his weals. Dan arched his back and let out a long, satisfied sigh. She unhooked the back of his gaff then reached beneath him to free his erection from the elastic pouch.

He gasped as her warm fingers made contact with his rigid cock. She stroked up and down its length then pulled his foreskin down hard. He shuddered.

'You shouldn't have stopped whipping me . . . it was incredible.' Dan's voice was a hoarse whisper.

'There will be plenty of time for that later. Let's get you out of your clothes. Quickly.' Jo released his cock and Dan felt cheated.

Dan straightened up slowly. He felt dizzy and light-headed so he leaned on the edge of the plinth for support. Jo unzipped his dress at the back and he pushed it down over his arms and let it drop to the floor. She unhooked his long-line bra and he pulled it off. He peeled off his fake breasts. He unhooked his stockings from his suspenders then undid his waspie corset at the front and dropped it on the floor. He kicked off his shoes and took off his stockings.

His cock stood out in front of him, dark and pumped with blood. Jo looked down at his cock then back up to his face. She smiled.

'Follow me.' She opened the door.

She led him out of the flat and through the hall into the school. She took him into the boys' toilet and told him to wash off his make-up. He bent over the low sink, using the harsh school soap to wash his mascara-streaked face.

When he was clean, Jo led him through a maze of corridors. She walked ahead of him, striding along like a soldier on parade, her high heels clip-clopping noisily against the tiled floor.

She stopped outside one of the doors and waited for Dan to catch up with her. As he reached her he saw that it bore a sign printed with the words 'Medical Room'. Dan's heart seemed to leap into his throat. His cock twitched. Jo pushed open the door and they stepped inside. Dan noticed that the light was already on.

Jo led him across the room, which seemed to be a small office, towards another door which, the sign announced, was the examination room. As Jo led him into the room he realised that it was already occupied. Blood rushed to his head. His crotch ached.

The examination room was tiny, with only room for a high leather-topped examination couch covered with a sheet of paper and a trolley of equipment. At the foot of the couch was a single chair. Standing beside the trolley was a young man in a pair of combat shorts and a slashed sleeveless punky T-shirt bearing a picture of Jo Strummer from The Clash. His arms, legs and his shaven head were all covered in complex tribal tattoos. He was wearing latex gloves and he was fiddling with the instruments on the trolley.

'Hi, Jo. Everything's ready.' He turned to smile at Jo and Dan noticed that he had a disc as big as a ten pence piece through each ear lobe and a metal bar through his nasal septum. A cold shiver of excitement and anxiety slid along Dan's spine.

'Climb up onto the couch please, Dan,' Jo instructed.

Dan mounted the couch and lay down. He felt vulnerable and uncertain and bursting with excitement. His cock stood upright, pointing at the ceiling.

'I've arranged for Egg to pierce your nipples.' Jo stepped over to the couch and laid a hand on his thigh. Dan could feel her body heat sinking into him.

'Do I get an anaesthetic?' He could hear the alarm in his own voice. Jo slowly shook her head. Dan noticed that she was smiling.

241

'No, mate. It's all in the breathing. If you follow my instructions you'll be all right.' Egg swabbed Dan's chest with alcohol. It felt cold and slightly stingy. Dan felt his nipples begin to harden.

'That shouldn't present him with any problem. He rather likes following orders, as a matter of fact.' Jo stroked his thigh.

Egg chuckled. 'You don't say . . .' He picked up a medical instrument, like a pair of scissors with a small loop at the tip of the blades. 'This is a clamp. I clamp your nipple then put the needle through the hole . . . simple.' He pinched Dan's right nipple between thumb and forefinger then applied the clamp.

Dan gasped. The cold metal bit into his skin, making it burn and tingle. His cock seemed to grow an inch.

'People often tell me the clamp hurts worse than the piercing.' Egg repeated the process on the other side. 'I put the needle through first . . .' He held it up for Dan to see. 'Then I put the jewellery through.' He picked up a heavy gold ring. 'This is what Jo's chosen for you. I think it should look good. Are you ready?'

Dan nodded. Blood pounded in his ears. His heart thumped.

'Breathe in slowly . . . a nice long deep breath.' Egg positioned a thick hollow needle against Dan's nipple through the hole in the clamp.

Dan took a long slow breath.

'Now breathe out . . .'

Dan complied. He closed his eyes.

'Now, a nice slow deep breath in . . . that's it.' Egg slid the needle through Dan's nipple. There was a second of biting pain and heat followed by a rush of relief and endorphins that made Dan feel dizzy. Egg fiddled with his nipple, pushing the ring through and twisting the ball closure closed.

Dan continued to breathe deeply. He could feel Jo's

warm soft hand on his thigh. He gasped as her fingers slid across to his erection and began to stroke it.

'OK ... same thing for the other one. Some people say it hurts worse than the first one because you know what to expect but it's over in a second. Are you ready?'

Dan nodded. He could feel crinkly paper and warm leather under his body. Jo's hand slid lazily up and down his cock. His pelvis was tight and tingling. His newly pierced nipple burned.

He took a deep breath as Egg picked up the clamp. He felt the cold sharp tip of the needle pressing against his flesh.

'Breathe out ... nice and slowly ... that's it ... now in again.' He pushed the needle through. Dan exhaled noisily. His nipple throbbed with heat and excitement. Egg released the clamp and fitted the ring. 'There, it's done. Why don't you take a look?'

Dan opened his eyes and looked down at his newly pierced chest. 'It looks fantastic. Thank you.' He moved to touch one of the gold rings but Egg caught his hand and pulled it away.

'Mustn't touch for a while, I'm afraid. Got to give them time to heal. I'm leaving you an aftercare leaflet.' Egg put an A5 leaflet down on the trolley. He began to pack up his equipment.

'Thanks, Egg. When you're ready I'll show you out.'

The piercer put his instruments and needles away in an old-fashioned leather doctor's bag. He closed it with a snap. 'Good to meet you, mate. I hope you enjoy the piercings.'

'I'll be back shortly. I'd like you to stay there. Put your hands behind your head and don't move a muscle.' Jo escorted Egg out of the room.

Dan waited for Jo with his hands behind his head, as ordered. He hardly dared to breathe. It was stuffy and hot in the small room. The leather couch had grown clammy beneath his body and the paper sheet covering it was creased and uncomfortable.

His nipples burned. He lifted his head to look at them. They were red and swollen still but they looked fantastic. Dan couldn't wait for them to heal so that Jo could pull and twist them. His cock pointed up towards the ceiling, aching and purple.

After what seemed an eternity he heard the door to the office open and Jo walking towards the examination room. He could hear her clothes rustling and her breathing. He wondered why he hadn't heard her heels on the tiles in the corridor.

The door opened and Jo stepped inside wearing a white nurse's uniform. She had white stockings and flat lace-up shoes. Her hair had been put up in a bun and she even had a starched cap pinned to her head. Dan noticed that she was carrying a tray. She put the tray down on the trolley beside him.

Dan looked down at the tray. There was a pair of latex gloves, a clear plastic speculum, a tube of KY jelly, a small plastic sample bottle and a roll of thin gauze bandage and a pair of scissors. He looked back up at Jo. 'What are you going to do to me?' His heart was thumping.

'Nothing to worry about, Mr Elliot. Doctor's just asked me to obtain a sample.' Jo picked up the bandage and the scissors. She unrolled a length and cut it off. She went down to the bottom of the bench. She took hold of his leg. She bent it at the knee and laid it on its side then tied one end of the strip of bandage around Dan's ankle. 'Now scoot down the bed a bit so that your bottom's near the edge.'

Dan complied. She tied the other end of the bandage tightly to the leg of the couch. She cut off another length of bandage and did the same to his other leg. Soon he was tethered to the bench at all four corners, helpless and rigid with excitement.

Jo pulled on the latex gloves and dispensed a blob of lube onto her fingers. She rolled the trolley down to the bottom of the bench. She picked up the speculum and sat down. 'I'm just going to examine you then we'll get on with the procedure.'

She smeared lube over the jaws of the speculum. She spread his buttocks with her fingers then positioned the instrument against his hole. She pushed it forwards and Dan felt it entering him. It felt cold and hard and uncomfortable but her silicone cock was bigger and harder to take. He took a few deep breaths and it entered him easily.

'Now we open it up ...' Jo began to open the speculum and Dan gasped. It was a strange and slightly alarming sensation as he felt the walls of his anus spreading apart. His body was rigid. His cock twitched. Jo folded down an angle-poise lamp from the wall and shone it between his legs. She bent down to look. 'I can see right inside you ...' She laughed quietly, as if she was delighted.

Dan felt her close the speculum and withdraw it. She switched off the light and pushed it out of the way.

'Now we just need to take our sample.'

She slid a lubed finger into his hole. Dan gasped. His muscles softened and his nerve endings prickled into life. She curled her finger. Dan's body jolted as she located his prostate.

She laughed softly. 'I see I've found the right place.' The tip of her finger stroked his prostate in small circles.

He looked down at Jo. She was leaning forwards, her eyes focused on his crotch. Dan could see that her cheeks were glowing and her chest heaved as she breathed. His cock stood to attention between them, announcing his arousal and his helplessness.

Dan could feel her teasing his sweet spot. Every so often she'd push hard and he'd feel a sudden urge to pee, then she'd move her finger and it would pass. The prostate itself seemed incredibly sensitive, but the feeling was too localised, too focused to even have a chance of getting him off.

It was a strange sensation; half pleasure, half discomfort. He could feel his muscles clamping down on her finger. He wished she'd slide in another couple of digits or, better still, fuck him with her strap-on. But, more than anything, he wanted her to touch his cock.

It stood to attention, its tip glistening. He wriggled his hips, hoping she would get the message. Jo looked up at him and smiled. She slowly shook her head.

He tried to turn all his attention to Jo's finger inside him. If he focused in on the pleasure, tuned into it, maybe it would be enough to bring him off. He concentrated on the sensation of her latex-covered finger opening his sphincter. His nerve endings tingled and buzzed with pleasure.

He focused on the pressure on his sweet spot. He could feel tightness and congestion and heat building, like a tiny bundle of excitement. It was powerful and intensely pleasurable yet it was narrow and confined only to his prostate. He turned all his awareness to the glowing point of heat, willing it to grow and spread.

His pierced nipples ached. The leather beneath him felt damp and clammy. His cock throbbed.

'How are you doing?' Jo looked up at him.

'It's strange . . . wonderful, yet maddening. What are you trying to do?'

'It's called prostate milking. The idea is to get you to ejaculate without the sensation of orgasm.' She reached up with her free hand and flicked his erection.

Dan gasped. 'So you're intentionally trying to deny me pleasure?'

Jo nodded slowly. The tip of her finger rubbed his prostate.

Dan could feel the tension building but it was localised and tiny. He closed his eyes and focused on the pleasure. He pictured it as a bright ball of white light and he imagined it expanding and growing, filling his gut. He could see sparks breaking away from the sphere and getting into his bloodstream, bringing every part of his body to fiery life. It crackled and fizzed as it flowed into his balls then his cock.

He was rigid with tension, his fists clenched. Sweat ran down his face. He screwed up his eyes, focusing inwards. Nothing. There was a tiny shimmering point of tension deep inside him but that was all. He opened his eyes and moaned in frustration. He struggled against his bonds.

Jo's finger worked his prostate. The sensation seemed to be intensifying, growing tighter and more intense, but he still couldn't call it exactly pleasurable. He felt the muscles in his pelvis growing tight and hard.

Dan saw her pick up the sample bottle from the tray. He watched her face as she fingered him. She was smiling slightly and Dan could just see the glistening tip of her tongue. Her eyes glinted in the light.

He felt an odd inner tremor. Jo pressed her fingertip hard into his sweet spot and he watched, fascinated, as his cock began to dribble sperm. She used the bottle to catch the semen.

Dan felt none of the exhilaration and release of a normal orgasm. His cock didn't throb and jerk, it just dribbled sperm in a steady stream as Jo jabbed her fingertip into his prostate. When the flow stopped, she used the bottle to scrape up the drips. She withdrew her finger and capped the bottle. She dropped it onto the trolley and pulled off her gloves.

Jo got up and lifted her skirt. She climbed up onto the couch and straddled him then reached between them and positioned the head of his cock. She unbuttoned the top few buttons of her uniform and Dan noticed that she was braless. Her naked breasts swung free, her nipples already hard and dark.

Slowly she lowered herself, deliberately making it last. Dan felt his erection nudging at her moist folds, coaxing them to open. Slippery skin slid against slippery skin. He began to slide inside, waking up his aroused nerve endings with sparks of fire. His body shuddered.

He could feel his cock slide past her muscles, millimetre by intoxicating millimetre, setting off a cascade of delicious tingles. Jo looked down at Dan. Her body glistened with sweat and her nipples were dark and crinkled. She was smiling as she gazed down at him, her eyes blazing with lust and tenderness.

Dan could feel her muscles gripping him, sucking him in. It was bliss. He loved the heat of it and the way her muscles gripped him. Pinpricks of pleasure burned his nipples. His scalp tingled.

Jo sat down on Dan. Her skirt was spread out over his legs. Her thighs were hot and slick against his skin and he could feel the itchy prickle of her stockings. She tilted her hips back and then forwards, rubbing her clit against him. 'That feels good.'

Dan brought his hips up to meet her. 'It feels fantastic.'

Jo leaned forwards and untied his hands. 'Can you pinch my nipples for me? If you do it really hard I'll come like a train in no time.'

Dan squeezed her breasts. He ran his thumbs across the tips of her swollen nipples. 'I can do that.' He began to pinch them, pressing them hard between his thumb and forefingers. Jo sighed and arched her back. Electric sparks slid along his spine.

She began to ride his cock, rocking her hips backwards and forwards rather than bouncing up and down. His whole crotch blazed.

Dan felt fiery hot and ready to burst. Jo was panting and breathless. Her eyes shone. Jo's hips rocked. His belly throbbed with tension and excitement as he climbed towards orgasm. He moaned.

Dan's fingers teased her nipples. He'd dig his fingertips in and make her gasp with pain then lightly run his nail across the sensitised tips, making her sigh. Icy sparkles of pleasure rushed straight to his crotch.

He brought up his hips to meet her, matching her rhythm. Dan was on the edge. His crotch tingled and throbbed. He dug in his fingertips and twisted her nipples, pulling and stretching them. She gasped and arched her back.

Jo's torso was glistening with sweat. Her throat and chest were stained with blotches of red. She had begun to moan. She rocked her hips slowly backwards and forwards, grinding her clit against his crotch. Dan was tingling all over. Excitement and heat pumped around his bloodstream.

Jo leaned forwards and gripped the edges of the couch either side of Dan's chest. Her belly was pressed up against his and her breasts dangled down. Jo's face was now directly above Dan's and her green eyes were glinting and intense. He could feel her hot breath on her face and smell the heady womanly aroma rising from her heated skin.

Jo's hair had escaped its combs and fell around her shoulders, heavy and damp. She pulled on her hands, grinding herself against him. Hot sparkles of delicious pleasure burned his crotch.

Dan's eyes never left her face as he worked her nipples. He responded to her excitement, pinching harder when she moaned and backing off if she whimpered and pulled away. His body was a mass of pleasure. His heart thumped. He trembled and shook.

Jo was gasping and sobbing. She arched and rounded her back, grinding her taut clit against him. Dan's fingertips dug into her nipples and she grunted. Jo's sweat-moistened belly slid against his. Tension and excitement vibrated inside him. His cock ached.

Dan had begun to moan. Jo's cheeks were stained scarlet. She pulled hard on the edge of the couch for leverage. She gave a final savage thrust of her hips and she began to wail.

'Yes ... I can feel you coming ... your cunt's gripping my cock ... it's incredible.' He released Jo's nipples and slid his hands under her skirt and gripped her buttocks. He could feel Jo's fiery breath on his face.

He pulled hard on his hands and began to pump his hips in short urgent strokes. He was grunting as he breathed, making short guttural sounds in rhythm with his moving hips.

He pulled hard on her buttocks and shortened his strokes. His crotch was exploding with release and sensation. Tingling jolts of pleasure burst along his spine like fireworks.

He let out a long low sound, halfway between a grunt and a sigh and he stopped moving. He was coming. His cock pumped out hot sperm inside her. His fingers dug into her buttocks. It went on and on, delicious jolts and shivers shot around his body. His scalp tingled, her toes curled.

Their faces were inches apart and Dan gazed up at her, his eyes wide and unblinking. He released her buttocks and slowly ran his hands up her back. He brushed hair away from her face and Dan saw that his hands were trembling.

'I don't remember giving you permission to come.' Jo sat up.

'I ... I forgot. Sorry.'

Jo climbed off the couch. She straightened her uniform and buttoned it up, covering her breasts. 'I see you have a problem with your memory, Mr Elliot.' Jo straightened her nurse's cap. 'But don't worry. There's a new experimental medicine for men who need help with their memory and I've been lucky enough to procure a single dose for you.' She picked up the sample bottle from the trolley and unscrewed the cap. 'Drink up.'

Dan sat up and took the bottle. He looked straight at Jo as he upended it and drank the cold thick liquid down in a single gulp.

251

Sixteen

Six months later Dan booked a preview cinema to show his finished film to Hellfire 2000. As the lights came up there was a round of applause and cries of 'Speech, speech'. Dan held onto Jo's hand, drinking it all in.

Sarah leaned across and touched his arm. 'I'll go and get the champagne.'

'Thank you all for making it possible.' Dan couldn't help smiling. 'You've helped me produce a fantastic film and –' he looked at Jo '– in more ways than one you've also helped me to change my life. I never thought I'd say it, but I'd like to thank you all for corrupting me.'

Madame Cyn got to her feet. 'Say it once, say it loud, we're kinky and we're proud.' The room erupted into applause and laughter. Cyn sat down beside him. 'It's like that scene in the movie *Freaks* – do you know what I mean? "We accept you as one of us . . ." We've come a long way together, haven't we? And, in your wildest dreams, I bet it never crossed your mind that you'd be joining us, did it?'

'Not at all. Jo and I have a lot to thank you all for.'

Sarah passed around champagne. Cyn grabbed two glasses and handed one to Dan. 'Unfortunately, not all of us are so lucky in love.' She took a sip of her champagne. 'But I live in hope.'

'What sort of man are you looking for, Cyn?' Jo asked.

'That's the problem I think. I'm strictly dominant but the problem is, my type of woman only seems to attract wimps. What I'm really looking for is a man with real power. I've always liked ... oh, I don't know ... soldiers and firemen ... men in traditionally masculine jobs.'

'Can't resist the uniform, eh?' Dan smiled.

'I think that's part of it, yes. I love muscles ... sweat ... power. And I love the thought of him surrendering all that power to submit to me ...' Her eyes looked far away and wistful. She shrugged. 'But I know it's just a pipe dream.'

'Well –' Dan leaned close and lowered his voice '– he might not meet your criteria, but I happen to know that someone here has been nursing a secret passion for you for a very long time. It's obvious to anyone ... except you, it appears.'

'No! Who?'

Dan pointed across the room. 'Nicholas. I don't know whether he's a fireman or not.'

'He isn't.' Cyn couldn't take her eyes off Nick. 'He's an accountant as a matter of fact.'

Dan laughed. 'An accountant?'

'What's so funny?' Jo thumped his arm.

'I don't know ... somehow I just don't expect kinky people to have such normal jobs.'

'Normal jobs like film making or running a school, you mean?' Jo laughed.

'OK, OK ... you always said I should try not to label people.' He turned back to Cyn. 'What do you do for a living, Cyn?' Dan tried to imagine her dressed for the office in a business suit with her wild hair tamed and caught back in a matronly bun.

She fixed him with a steely glare. 'I have my own florist shop. Jade and Peter run an organic vegetable business and Christina is a personal development trainer. Take away our costumes and our props and we're Mr and Mrs Average. Now, if you'll excuse me, I think I'll just go and have a word with Nick.' She got up.

Trolleys full of food were wheeled in and white-jacketed staff served trays of finger food. Dan took Jo's hand and led her to the back of the cinema. He flipped down two seats and they sat down.

'I've got a present for you. I never thanked you properly for my collar . . .' He fingered the silver chain that encircled his throat. 'So I got you this . . .' He reached under his seat and handed her a small wrapped gift.

Jo undid the ribbon and tore at the paper. Inside was a small picture frame. She began to laugh. 'It's a dog licence . . .' She read aloud. 'It says, "Ms Jo Lennox is the registered owner of the dog known as Dan Elliot." Thank you.' She kissed him.

'I'm glad you like it. Will you hang it in your office, do you think? Along with your degree certificates?'

'I think not.' She leaned close and lowered her voice. 'Do you think anyone would miss us if we skipped off early?' She smiled.

'I doubt it. Why? What have you got in mind?' Dan kissed her.

'Well . . . I was thinking that my doggy might be in need of a spot of obedience training.' She stroked his collar.

nexus

The leading publisher of fetish and adult fiction

TELL US WHAT YOU THINK!

Readers' ideas and opinions matter to us so please take a few minutes to fill in the questionnaire below.

1. Sex: Are you male ☐ female ☐ a couple ☐?

2. Age: Under 21 ☐ 21–30 ☐ 31–40 ☐ 41–50 ☐ 51–60 ☐ over 60 ☐

3. Where do you buy your Nexus books from?
☐ A chain book shop. If so, which one(s)?

_____

☐ An independent book shop. If so, which one(s)?

_____

☐ A used book shop/charity shop
☐ Online book store. If so, which one(s)?

_____

4. How did you find out about Nexus books?
☐ Browsing in a book shop
☐ A review in a magazine
☐ Online
☐ Recommendation
☐ Other _____

5. In terms of settings, which do you prefer? (Tick as many as you like.)
☐ Down to earth and as realistic as possible
☐ Historical settings. If so, which period do you prefer?

_____

☐ Fantasy settings – barbarian worlds
☐ Completely escapist/surreal fantasy
☐ Institutional or secret academy

- ☐ Futuristic/sci fi
- ☐ Escapist but still believable
- ☐ Any settings you dislike?

_____

- ☐ Where would you like to see an adult novel set?

6. In terms of storylines, would you prefer:

- ☐ Simple stories that concentrate on adult interests?
- ☐ More plot and character-driven stories with less explicit adult activity?
- ☐ We value your ideas, so give us your opinion of this book:

_____

_____

_____

7. In terms of your adult interests, what do you like to read about? (Tick as many as you like.)

- ☐ Traditional corporal punishment (CP)
- ☐ Modern corporal punishment
- ☐ Spanking
- ☐ Restraint/bondage
- ☐ Rope bondage
- ☐ Latex/rubber
- ☐ Leather
- ☐ Female domination and male submission
- ☐ Female domination and female submission
- ☐ Male domination and female submission
- ☐ Willing captivity
- ☐ Uniforms
- ☐ Lingerie/underwear/hosiery/footwear (boots and high heels)
- ☐ Sex rituals
- ☐ Vanilla sex
- ☐ Swinging
- ☐ Cross-dressing/TV
- ☐ Enforced feminisation

☐ Others – tell us what you don't see enough of in adult fiction:

_____

_____

_____

8. Would you prefer books with a more specialised approach to your interests, i.e. a novel specifically about uniforms? If so, which subject(s) would you like to read a Nexus novel about?

_____

_____

_____

9. Would you like to read true stories in Nexus books? For instance, the true story of a submissive woman, or a male slave? Tell us which true revelations you would most like to read about:

_____

_____

_____

10. What do you like best about Nexus books?

_____

_____

11. What do you like least about Nexus books?

_____

_____

12. Which are your favourite titles?

_____

_____

13. Who are your favourite authors?

_____

_____

14. Which covers do you prefer? Those featuring:
(Tick as many as you like.)

☐ Fetish outfits
☐ More nudity
☐ Two models
☐ Unusual models or settings
☐ Classic erotic photography
☐ More contemporary images and poses
☐ A blank/non-erotic cover
☐ What would your ideal cover look like?

_____

15. Describe your ideal Nexus novel in the space provided:

_____

_____

_____

_____

16. Which celebrity would feature in one of your Nexus-style fantasies?
We'll post the best suggestions on our website – anonymously!

_____

THANKS FOR YOUR TIME

Now simply write the title of this book in the space below and cut out the
questionnaire pages. Post to: Nexus, Marketing Dept., Thames Wharf Studios,
Rainville Rd, London W6 9HA

Book title: _____

NEXUS NEW BOOKS

To be published in September 2007

LONGING FOR TOYS
Virginia Crowley

Robert and James are upstanding members of the community. They are young professionals with bigoted, conservative upper-middle-class girlfriends. When Michele – a gorgeous stripper at the notorious club Hot Summer's – sees Robert's shiny red new roadster, she is overcome by a desire to possess it. Manipulating his friends and neighbours with offerings of ever more sordid sexual delights, she engineers Robert's descent into a tangled world of erotic temptation. As his character degrades from that of an altruistic medical researcher into a drooling plaything around the manicured fingers of his keeper, Robert's fiancée and best friend try to help him; unfortunately, their involvement also subjects them to the irresistible lure of pretty toys.

£6.99   ISBN 978 0 352 34138 9

BEING A GIRL
Chloë Thurlow

When Milly is late for a vital interview on a sweltering day, casting agent Jean-Luc Cartier pours her some water and holds the glass to her lips. When the water soaks her blouse he instructs her to take it off. Milly is embarrassed but curious. As Milly strips off her clothes, not only her shapely body but also her deepest nature is slowly uncovered.

Jean-Luc puts her over his knee. He spanks her bottom and her virgin orgasm awakens her to the mysteries of discipline. Milly at eighteen is at the beginning of an erotic journey from convent school to a black-magic coven in the heart of Cambridge academia, to the secret world of fetishism and bondage on the dark side of the movie camera.

£6.99   ISBN 978 0 352 34139 6

If you would like more information about Nexus titles, please visit our website at www.nexus-books.com, or send a large stamped addressed envelope to:

Nexus, Thames Wharf Studios,
Rainville Road, London W6 9HA

NEXUS BOOKLIST

Information is correct at time of printing. To avoid disappointment, check availability before ordering. Go to www.nexus-books.com.

All books are priced at £6.99 unless another price is given.

NEXUS

☐ ABANDONED ALICE	Adriana Arden	ISBN 978 0 352 33969 0
☐ ALICE IN CHAINS	Adriana Arden	ISBN 978 0 352 33908 9
☐ AQUA DOMINATION	William Doughty	ISBN 978 0 352 34020 7
☐ THE ART OF CORRECTION	Tara Black	ISBN 978 0 352 33895 2
☐ THE ART OF SURRENDER	Madeline Bastinado	ISBN 978 0 352 34013 9
☐ BEASTLY BEHAVIOUR	Aishling Morgan	ISBN 978 0 352 34095 5
☐ BEHIND THE CURTAIN	Primula Bond	ISBN 978 0 352 34111 2
☐ BEING A GIRL	Chloë Thurlow	ISBN 978 0 352 34139 6
☐ BELINDA BARES UP	Yolanda Celbridge	ISBN 978 0 352 33926 3
☐ BENCH-MARKS	Tara Black	ISBN 978 0 352 33797 9
☐ BIDDING TO SIN	Rosita Varón	ISBN 978 0 352 34063 4
☐ BINDING PROMISES	G.C. Scott	ISBN 978 0 352 34014 6
☐ THE BOOK OF PUNISHMENT	Cat Scarlett	ISBN 978 0 352 33975 1
☐ BRUSH STROKES	Penny Birch	ISBN 978 0 352 34072 6
☐ BUTTER WOULDN'T MELT	Penny Birch	ISBN 978 0 352 34120 4
☐ CALLED TO THE WILD	Angel Blake	ISBN 978 0 352 34067 2
☐ CAPTIVES OF CHEYNER CLOSE	Adriana Arden	ISBN 978 0 352 34028 3
☐ CARNAL POSSESSION	Yvonne Strickland	ISBN 978 0 352 34062 7
☐ CITY MAID	Amelia Evangeline	ISBN 978 0 352 34096 2
☐ COLLEGE GIRLS	Cat Scarlett	ISBN 978 0 352 33942 3
☐ CONCEIT AND CONSEQUENCE	Aishling Morgan	ISBN 978 0 352 33965 2
☐ CORRECTIVE THERAPY	Jacqueline Masterson	ISBN 978 0 352 33917 1
☐ CORRUPTION	Virginia Crowley	ISBN 978 0 352 34073 3
☐ CRUEL SHADOW	Aishling Morgan	ISBN 978 0 352 33886 0

NEXUS CLASSIC